This book is dedicated to

My sons, Justen, Jordan and Joshua, who have never given up on me and always encouraged everything I have done. You have been my greatest accomplishment.

My sister, "Tarma Shena" Richardson, who encourages me to be myself and for myself to be more. I appreciate all that you do.

And to my mom, who gave me a love for reading, a desire to write and a thirst for knowledge, that has given me a lifetime of enjoyment.

The characters and events depicted in this story are fictional. Any resemblance to actual persons, living or dead, is purely coincidental.

Preface

There are many livestock guardian dogs who are loved and respected partners on farms and ranches, all across the US. Their job, much as it has been for hundreds or even thousands of years, is to protect livestock from predators. They are considered a form of non-lethal predator management, because they will allow a predator to flee and learn, negating livestock and wildlife conflicts. Although, like any protector, they will fight if they must.

There are also places in the US, where these dogs are considered less worthwhile than the stock they protect. They are left to defend livestock, with little to no human contact or influence. Many are expected to survive by their own devices, much like the wild animals they combat. With an admitted fail rate of up to 50%, for these dogs, it is success or death, often at human hands. These dogs often live, breed and die with no human contact. Many end up shot or abandoned by the very people who use them. This story is for those dogs.

Chapter 1 - All is Lost

Somewhere in the distance a rooster crowed.
She recognized the sound, but not the maker.
Such noises had ceased to exist in the place
she called home. She stood, walked slowly to
the door of the barn and gazed out across the
field. The air was still and quiet. A misty haze
hung all across the field making it impossible to
see much of anything. She sat and looked
anyway.
She could smell the wet grass, the scent of
damp manure and the residual smell of a skunk
off in the distance borne on the morning air.
She sighed in her head. It was going to be
another hot day.

Suddenly, she was hit from behind with enough
force to push her shoulders and face into the
dew-soaked soil. Her assailant ran over her and
continued out of the barn. She leaped back to
her feet with a growl and chased her brother
down the field, snapping and snarling as she
closed in on him. He continued running until he
tripped in the tall grass. She pounced on him
from behind, biting at his ears as he rolled
upside-down, laughing the whole time. She
growled into the fur on his neck, "It's not funny,
Fur!"
He laughed still. "You never heard me coming!"

She growled and bit his nose. He yipped slightly but still giggled with a foolish puppy grin. She pounced again but he struggled up and the chase turned into a rolling, tumbling, wrestling match in the cool morning air. They raced back to the barn and flopped down in the dirt. The sun was creeping over the horizon and soon it would be too warm to play or romp or do anything at all.

"Roger" said a voice.

They looked up to see their mother coming around from the back of the barn. They both rose and scurried away from the coming of Roger. Mom moved with them. The two pups slunk under the small equipment shed where they were born. It smelled of gas and old oil, but it was home. Their mother moved past them and dropped down into the tall grass on the far side of the goat corral.

The pups waited with nervous anticipation. The appearance of Roger could mean food, but they would have to wait. It was difficult to lay quiet with the hunger ever present in their bellies as of late. Even the rats mom used to catch had mostly moved on these days. The last coon had been over a week ago as there was little to draw them in. They found themselves unable to stay as quiet as mom would have liked. They knew it but they couldn't help it.

Roger appeared beside the barn with the small milk pail in hand. On a good day, the milk was all for them, but some days, the milk went to the house and visitors bore it away in small bottles. One never knew until the milking was done. Wee tried to be patient. She really did. The air was just right, and she could smell the goats and the milk and with the emptiness of her stomach she couldn't resist squirming out for a peek. Roger, she knew, was just behind the wall to the right of the barn door. If she did it right, he would have his back turned and never see her. She crept a bit closer trying to catch a glimpse, the sweet smell of the milk drawing her in.

"Wee! No!"

She heard her mother's voice, but she could not turn away. She wanted to listen, but her hunger was stronger than her mother's warning. She continued closer, staying to the far side of the doorway until she could see Roger. He was putting away one goat in exchange for another. The bucket hung on a hook out of reach. She backed out of sight as Roger turned towards her dragging the goat out of the stall.

There used to be so many goats and sheep and a horse. In just her short life, so much had changed. The sheep had gone one day in a large truck, rounded up and forced inside along with the family Wee once knew. The horse had left on a different truck and most of the goats a short time later. Shortly after, the rats began to leave too. With mom giving less and Roger only giving intermittently, the days had grown long and hungry.

She moved forward as Roger had gone back to milking. Her stomach grumbled and she moved into the doorway. She glanced back and her mother was on her feet, still on the far side of the corral, willing her to return. She slipped silently into the barn.

The goat was giving Roger a hard time, dancing away and stamping her feet. Roger struggled to hold the goat still while keeping the pail safe. Once he would have emptied the milk into a large jug before beginning the next goat but these days, it was all so hurried. Milk had slopped over the back of Roger's hand as he cursed and muttered under his breath at the uncooperative doe. Wee crept forward, unable to resist the scent. As the farmer reached out and moved the bucket back in place under the fidgeting goat, Wee licked the back of his milk-soaked hand from the other side. Roger's hand jerked in surprise, hitting the underside of the goat who jumped forward knocking the bucket sideways across the floor. The man shoved the goat aside with a roar "YOU STUPID MUTT!"

Wee was already fleeing the situation, but Roger moved to the opening faster than she had ever seen him move. He grabbed up a rake from the wall and moved towards her using the rake and his bulk to block the aisle. Panic overtook her and she ran back and forth whimpering and trying to find a way past. Outside, her mother began to bark in a high pitched, nervous tone from right outside the barn. When the volley of barking began, Roger shifted his eyes for just one fraction of a second and Wee barreled between the man and the waving rake and fled in terror out the door and down towards the shed with the running farmer close behind. She squeezed back under the shed squealing the whole time. Unable to see him advance, she expected the worst at any moment.

She managed to get under the broken front board and drove her brother against the back of the hollow, still terror stricken and frantic. A string of curses and angry words about what would happen to her followed her retreat, then flying dirt and rocks, as Roger kicked dirt into the small sanctuary in frustration. They lay still for a long time after it was silent. Finally, their mother's nose appeared at the opening. "It's safe." Partially pushed by her brother, she crawled out looking left and right for Roger despite her mother's assurance he was gone.

When she cleared the shed, she sat in front of her mom, head down, looking regretful. Her mother sighed. "Don't you ever, ever…"

"I know, momma", Wee interrupted. "I know, I know, I know. I'm sorry." Her small voice trailed off into a whine.

Her mother sighed again. "If he was that angry, it probably wasn't for us anyway."

She led them to the barn where both pups smelled the milk-soaked soil. Wee tried a lick but all that stuck to her tongue was wet dirt. She continued smelling but that only made her hunger worse. "Come on," said her mother. "Maybe I can find something."

They followed obediently, with Wee still looking this way and that in case Roger should appear out of nowhere, as he would in her dreams for days to come. As they strolled through the pasture, in the now hot sun, her mother kept her nose to the ground. Eventually, she came across an old bone that one of the dogs had left behind in better times. It could, however, be just what she needed to keep the pups busy. She showed it to them and after a few disappointed sniffs, they lay down together, each gnawing one end. She continued on searching along logs and old branches. A tiny movement caught her eye, and she darted, grabbing the small mouse and ending its life with that one snap of her jaws. She resisted the urge to eat it herself

and instead made a soft noise that brought both pups running. She put one paw on top of the small rodent as the pups barreled in. "You must share, ok?" Both pups nodded eagerly.
It disappeared in mere seconds and mom continued on with both pups in tow again.

As they moved, Wee tried to mimic her mother's movements. She kept her head down and smelled deep into the grass. That small tidbit had both helped them focus and spurred their desire to find more.
She watched as her mother's sniffing became more intense and she bounded forward sure that mom had found something. Not wanting to miss out, her brother came close behind.
"Stop!" Mom barked sharply. Wee came to a sudden halt and her brother ran right over her... again. She wanted to bite him, but the look on her mother's face said now was not the time. She looked where her mother's attention was focused and saw the small movement. Another mouse! She bounced forward, trying to pounce but the small rodent slipped between her paws and vanished into the tall grass. Stupid mouse, Wee thought, trying not to look at her mother. She kept her nose to the ground, slowly moving away to avoid her mother's reproachful gaze. She kept at it, heading down towards the shadier end of the field. Something moved and Wee pounced. She sniffed between her paws -

nothing. She saw it move and pounced again. Still nothing. She sighed. This was so hard. She kept sniffing, unwilling to give up after her pathetic attempt at catching the mouse had cost them that tidbit of nourishment. In a spot of dirt among the grass, she saw it. She willed herself to be quiet. She moved slowly forward until she was as close as she dared without spooking her quarry. She leaped over the grass, pouncing with her paws together. She held position for a second and could feel it struggling beneath one paw. She drove her nose under her foot, grabbing up the frog with a satisfying crunch. She tossed it up and caught it out of the air by one hind leg. Holding her head high, she trotted across to her mother, beaming with pride and still holding her prize.

Her brother came racing in, trying to grab her little reward and she grabbed it up and swallowed it in one bite. "I did it, Momma. I did it."

"You did well," her mom replied. "But you didn't share it with your brother."

"He tried to grab it, Momma. It was mine and he tried to grab it," Wee whined plaintively.

Her mother, not wanting to dampen her enthusiasm, concurred. "Maybe next time, he'll remember his manners and then you'll share."

Her brother accepted the rebuke, and they moved on with Mom in the lead. Wee looked back. It was getting hotter and with at least something in her stomach, she began to think of the cool dirt under the shed. She was further from the barn than she had ever been. "Where are we going, Momma?" she asked quietly. "Somewhere," her mom replied. "Somewhere with frogs." She paused. "But you have to promise to do whatever I tell you."

The prospect of more frogs was alluring, but still, Wee sensed her mother's feelings of uneasiness. At the far end of the field, they stopped along the fence. After a moment of hesitation, their mother seemed to make a final decision. She walked down the fence line a few yards to a slight dip and crawled under the fence. The pups followed quietly. They both sensed her dislike of the situation, but they continued on.
They padded through a wooded area, and out onto the embankment of a small stream. Their mother sniffed the air in several directions and proceeded slowly down the short bank. The pups followed with the same cautious steps.

They all lapped at the water and then Wee looked around. She had never seen anything like this. They had troughs and hoses, but this was so different. Her momma walked into the edge of the water and headed west against the lazy flow of the stream. In spring it could be a raging torrent, but in the heat of summer, it barely moved. They continued along a short distance to where a cluster of alders hung over the water on both sides, creating a cool retreat from the heat of the day. The water felt so good on hot feet and Wee thought that this must be the best place on earth. "Momma! This place is amazing. Why haven't we come here before?" Wee asked her, while trying to voice her excitement and yet not be too loud. Momma was still uneasy.

"We used to." Her mother replied. "We always did in the summer before…" Her voice got even quieter. "Before the others left. You were too young at first and then, we were alone."

Wee thought of the times her mother had returned to the barn wet. Times when the dirt by the barn clung to her fur until she was dry.

"You've gone without us, haven't you Momma?" There was no accusation in the question. Just an acceptance of new knowledge. "Yes. I have… sometimes. It reminds me of... other days."

"When we had a pack, Momma?" The expression on her mother's face turned forlorn and Wee was sorry she had asked. She pushed her head against her mother's side. "We'll be your pack, Momma." she whispered.

Her mother lowered her head. "Why don't you go look for frogs with Fur," she said softly. Wee looked through the tunnel of small trees and saw her brother pouncing in the shallows.

Frogs! That's right. They were supposed to be hunting frogs. She trotted along the water's edge where not just one, but two frogs hopped into the water. She pounced after them, missing them both. She remembered her earlier success and slowed her pace. Her brother was a bit further, pouncing over and over. Wee rolled her eyes. He never planned anything.

They spent the afternoon hunting frogs in the water and along the bank. Sometimes they failed miserably, but even Fur had successes as his excitement waned and he began to actually put effort into the stalking. Wee even caught a small fish. In the end, as the afternoon turned into early evening, they all slept on the cool bank under the trees and Wee drifted off thinking life would never be better than today. Their mother's voice woke them in the fading daylight. "Wake up! Now!" Her voice was quiet but there was a sharpness to it, Wee had never heard.
She looked up and caught a whiff of something. It was a strange and wild smell that made her heart pound, and her hair stand up all funny. She glanced at her brother and knew he was feeling the same way. "Go." her mother whispered. "Go back to the barn.
Find the space under the fence and go as fast as you can. Take Fur with you."

Wee wanted to ask questions but the urgency
in her mother's voice left no time. They ran
down through the shallow water making far too
much noise. Then up the bank and out into the
open. At the top, their mother stopped. "Go!
Now! Don't turn back."

They ran as fast as their legs could take them,
but when she heard her mother's deep growl,
Wee did look back. In the fading light, the
creature with the pale-yellow eyes and sharp,
bared teeth was the stuff of nightmares. It
glanced in her direction, making eye contact
with its intended quarry and Wee saw her
mother rush it with a loud growl and snapping
jaws. Then her brother's soft whimper jarred her
out of her trance and as the fight played out
behind them, Wee ran harder and faster than
she had ever run and surprisingly, her brother
kept the pace, close on her heels until they ran
headlong into the fence.

For a moment Wee panicked as if they'd run
into an invisible wall, but then she realized they
had come far further and faster than she would
have imagined possible. She ran down the
fence, trying to keep her wits about her and
found the hollowed-out spot where their mother
had led them out. She ducked under with her
brother right behind and they never stopped
running until they reached the shed and slipped

underneath. Then they lay in the dark listening but could hear nothing over their own heavy panting.

Time passed. Their breathing quieted and their racing heartbeats slowed. Wee thought she heard a noise, but there was silence. Then she heard soft footfalls on hard packed dirt. Her pulse began to pick up and she didn't dare to move. She glanced at her brother and knew he had heard it too as he was pressing himself along the back wall, trying to be as small as possible. Then a familiar nose sniffed under the broken board and the scent of their mother drifted into the space under the shed. Wee sighed visibly with relief and edged her way forward and looked up into her mother's face. "You did well." her mother said. "Thank you for taking your brother home."

Wee crawled out of the burrow just a little proud of herself. She moved close to her mother. Her mother smelled of blood and weariness and… that thing. "What was that, Momma?" Wee asked.
"A coyote." Momma said. "Filthy, dirty, mangy, sheep killers." The distaste in her voice was clearly evident.
Wee sniffed her mother's bleeding ear. "He hurt you, Momma," she said softly.
"Not as much as I hurt him."

Fur appeared by her side. "Did you get him good, Momma?" he asked with wide eyes.

"I did," she replied, but she sounded unhappy.

"What's wrong, Momma?" Wee asked.

Her mother was quiet for a moment. Wee waited, looking expectantly. Finally, her mother spoke. Her voice was quiet but stern and full of anger.

"When the pack was here, the sheep used to graze in that field. They drank from that stream. We all lay under those trees in the heat of the day. They would never have dared to step foot in that field, not even a dozen strong. But they are beginning to realize. The pack's scent is waning, and they know that they are gone." She continued on.

"Today we were lucky. There was just one. It will be a while before he hunts again." A small bit of pride crept briefly into her voice, "But we must be more careful. They are moving in and there is no pack anymore." At those words the pride in her voice was replaced by sorrow.

"What will we do?" Wee whispered.

"For now, we will sleep. Come on now. Let's get some rest."

They went into the relative safety of the barn and bedded down in the soft dirt mixed with manure and old straw in the empty horse stall. During the night, Wee's dreams were filled with a furry yellow eyed man with a milk pail.

Chapter 2 - The Space Under The Fence

The days that followed were much like any other. Momma did not mention the creek and the pups did not ask. The biggest change was that there was milk every morning now. Strangers still drove up to the house. Some even walked down to the barn with Roger, but the milk was all for them. Still, Wee always waited, like her mother did, until Roger was long gone to enter the barn.

She awoke one morning from the grass, where she had fallen asleep in the cool night air. Roger was already milking. It was early for him now. Not long ago, he had been there before sunrise, but since most of the animals had left, Roger usually came much later. She looked around for Fur, but he was nowhere in sight. She moved carefully around the goat corral, staying away from the barn, and crossed silently to the equipment shed to look for her brother. To her surprise, there was a board and large rocks across the hole. She sniffed around the shed. Fur was not there.

As she circled back around the shed scanning for her mother and brother, Roger's voice interrupted her confused thoughts.

"Come 'ere pup." Roger was standing just outside the barn. She didn't know what he'd

said, but he was staring at her. She stared back at him with her head lowered, not moving.
"Come 'ere Girl."
Wee didn't move. She just stood and stared at Roger. He stared back for a moment and then returned to the barn. She moved around between the equipment shed and the goat house and came to stand where she could see into the barn. She didn't approach. Roger made a small whistling noise, like he had once made to the sheep and poured milk from the pail into the dish in the barn.

Wee sniffed the air. It smelled of dry dirt, old manure, goat's milk and Roger. She didn't like Roger's smell. It was anxious and unnerving. His thoughts were muddled and his behavior cautious. He poured the milk slowly, all the while looking towards Wee as he poured.
"Come on, pup," he said in his gravelly voice. "Come on".
Wee didn't like this. She didn't like it one bit. It made the hair stand up on her back. She whined quietly. She felt hunted and alone and vulnerable. Making a decision, she moved away, around the goat's corral and into the grass again. Roger cursed and muttered. Wee lay in the grass, tense and ready to flee, and watched every move he made.

Finally, Roger moved away from the barn, but he didn't go back to the house or very far at all. He puttered around, occasionally muttering to himself. Every so often, he would look her way. The feeling of being in danger never passed and for a long time, Wee did not move.

"Wee."

Her mother's voice was soft and distant but Wee heard it. She stood and gazed out over the field. She glanced at Roger who was suddenly alert and waiting.

"Wee. Come here now."

Her mother's voice was still soft, but she sensed, more than heard, where the voice was coming from. She faded into the tall grass and out of Roger's sight. He muttered angry words as she disappeared.

When she reached her mother, Fur was beside her. They sniffed and greeted quietly. She then greeted her mother. "I wish Roger would just go away," Wee muttered softly.

"It doesn't matter now," Momma told her.

"But I'm hungry," Wee said sullenly.

"You've been much hungrier," Momma reminded her softly.

"I didn't go, Momma. I didn't." She sat down next to Fur.

"I know," Momma told her. "That was very smart. I never should have gone so far from you, but I didn't want Roger to see us."

"But why?"

Momma looked at her, her eyes turning dark and solemn. "Roger isn't safe anymore."
They were grave words of warning, but still Wee persisted.
"Roger is never safe. We still go drink the milk."
"But now, you must not," Momma said. Her voice was soft, but stern.
"But why, Momma?" Wee's voice was barely a whisper, though she wasn't sure why she felt the need.
"Roger is dangerous now. He has become like the coyote. He hunts you. He hunts Fur." Momma's voice was as quiet as her own.
Wee shivered involuntarily, but Fur spoke.
"Will you bite him, Momma?"
"We must not. Dogs who bite man have worse fates than hunger," Momma said. "I have seen it once. Though, it was years ago. We must hide and we must run, if necessary, but biting is not wise."
Fur seemed disappointed but said nothing else.
"Come," Momma said. "We will hunt mice and frogs when it gets dark. We will leave the milk for the rats."
They moved through the grass and into the shade of trees on the far edge of the field.
There they stayed until night fell, listening to the sound of the goats and the occasional noise of Roger as he checked the barn. In the dark, they lucked out, finding a possum waddling off

towards the farmyard. Missing the milk had not turned out to be so bad.

The sound of a truck woke them the next morning. They heard Roger come out to greet the people in the truck. He was greeted in return by the voices of four men. Wee looked up at her mother who was standing quietly listening. "Should we go see, Momma," Wee asked cautiously.

"No," Momma whispered. "We should not go see."

Her mother's eyes looked haunted, frightened. It was not a look Wee could ever remember seeing.

They listened as the truck drove down to the barn and they heard Roger open the gate and let the men in. Soon there were the sounds of goats in distress and the sounds of men muttering and cursing. Wee looked toward the barn and then at her mother. Her mother's ears were perked forward, her body tense. She looked towards the barn and then at Wee and Fur. She moved forward. The goat's bleats and calls were too much for her to ignore. It was her job, her duty. She trotted through the grass in the direction of the barn. Wee and Fur could do naught but follow, with dread in their steps and in their hearts.

Momma stopped when she could see the goats. The men had some already loaded on the truck and were herding the rest into corners and dragging them from the corral. Every fiber of her being wanted to end the chaos, but Fur's soft whine kept her from rushing in.

"Must they take everything from me?" She mumbled softly.

Wee felt the sadness spread over her mother and it spread through her as well. Poor Momma. She was always sad.

Suddenly, anger welled up inside her and before she could think of the potential consequences, she stepped forward and barked at the men in the goat fence.

Immediately, she regretted doing so. All movement in the pen stopped and every man turned and looked at them. Wee was frightened. They all looked dangerous. They were all like coyotes. She stepped back slowly.

"You didn't catch them damn pups," one burly man stated.

Roger's gruff voice replied, "I tried. It's like they damn knew it. I fed them milk in that barn every day for two weeks, but yesterday, they wouldn't even touch it. Never saw them all afternoon or this morning, 'til now."

"Forget them," another man said. "Let's finish up with the goats and then we'll go get them pups. If we can wrangle sheep and goats, we sure as hell ought to be able to catch a couple of stupid dogs."

Wee, Fur and Momma, all headed back towards the trees, while the men resumed catching and loading the goats. They didn't understand human words, but somehow, they knew it wasn't over. When they reached the shaded area of the field their mother was restless, pacing, making small noises. She didn't know how she knew, but she was sure just the same. Finally, she faced the pups.
"Listen to me…"
"I'm sorry." Wee said. I didn't mean to. I don't know why..."
Her mother cut her off.
"It doesn't matter. They would have come anyway. We didn't go in the barn. Roger wanted us to come into the barn. We didn't go. They would come for us, whether you barked or not."
Fur looked miserable and sad.
"What do we do, Momma?"
"We wait and when they come, we will hide, and we will run. It is all we can do. Don't let them catch you."
Wee was more frightened than she had ever been, but she was worried about Fur and Momma, even more than she worried about herself. Fur was so silly and sometimes dumb, but she loved him. And somewhere inside, she felt a deep fear for Momma. She tried to figure it

out. Momma was the most capable. She could fight a coyote all by herself. Yet the fear persisted.

She shook her head to clear her thoughts and realized all noise at the barn had stopped except the occasional quieter bleats of the goats on the truck. She looked at Momma. She was standing very still, listening. "Follow me," Momma whispered. "They will look for us now."

When they heard the first movements of grass dragging across human clothes, Momma led them silently out of the trees and out into the tall grass as well. The trees made good shade, but the lower branches had all been eaten by the goats. The overgrown grass which hadn't had sheep to keep it down, was their best hiding place. The men spread out across the field trying to cover as much area as possible. Momma kept them on the move, deftly moving between them, with shoulders slouched and head down. Every once in a while, one of the men would see movement and yell or whistle to get the other men's attention. When they looked, the man would point, and they'd all move in the direction where he pointed. It was hot. The pups began to feel the effects and even Momma was panting.

The men were hot as well, making more noise and cursing and sputtering. Finally, one of them spoke. "Look, it's been an hour and a half. We can't do this all day and the goats ain't gonna be in the shade much longer. I'm not losing twenty goats for a damn dog."

The burly man spoke too. "It's that damn bitch. She's the one keeping the pups on the move. If we could get her out of the way, those damn pups will hunker down."

The first man shook his head. "What do you want to do, Roger? It's your money and my time."

Roger took off his hat and wiped the sweat from his eyes. He pulled that hat back onto his head and spat. "Take her out. She wouldn't go on the truck last time and she sure as hell ain't going this time. She wants to die here; she can die here."

The burly man looked satisfied and walked back up to the truck. He stepped up on the sideboard and grabbed the rifle from the rear window, checked that it was loaded, switched off the safety and headed back. When he reached the place where he'd been before, they all began to move again.

The dogs had been taking advantage of the men's conversation to stop and rest for a few moments, but as the men moved this time, they made no effort to be quiet. They strode purposefully, wanting only for the burly man to have his chance. They were running out of time. It was soon or never. Momma moved the pups, finding it less easy to stay undercover as the grass became trampled from moving dogs and men's boots. As they fleetingly passed from one stretch of grass to another, the man took his chance. A sharp boom, like thunder, echoed through the field. The dirt in front of Momma scattered, taking grass and roots with it. They hunkered down, frozen for half a second and then Momma, crouching low to the ground, darted into the tall grass with the pups close behind. She wove through the thickest weeds along the edge of the fence and dropped down on the grass panting heavily. "Look," she whispered. If something were to happen to me, I want you to stay together."

Wee put her nose against the end of her mother's. She felt more grown up than she could have explained. She looked into her mother's eyes, and she knew. She knew in a flash what was going to happen. "No, Momma. No!" She spoke in a whisper, but her voice was firm and steady. "They want to catch us. They want to catch us, but they want to kill you. I know it."

She paused and looked down the fence toward the field on the other side. "Momma, Go! Now! And don't turn back. We will hide as best we can."

Her mother's frightened eyes met hers and Wee could tell that Momma knew too. "Go, Momma," she said again quietly. "Go! They're coming."

As the sounds drew closer, the mother came quickly to her feet and raced down the fence line like a flash, keeping to the thick grass, but making no move to be stealthy. As she leaped into the air and over the fence, the sharp crack of the thunder noise sounded again. Wee saw her mother's leap go slightly off kilter, but she touched ground on the other side and in seconds, she was gone down the hillside and out of sight.

The men stood for a second and then converged onto the spot where the older female had made her leap. They hoped maybe the pups had been close behind. They kicked around in the grass to be sure they didn't miss them.

"Now is our chance," Wee told Fur. Let's move." She headed up the field going towards the barn, keeping as hidden as possible while the men checked along the fence line. Fur followed behind, looking tired, frightened and very close to worn out. "Listen, "Wee said quietly. If we can just hold them off a tiny bit longer. They are tired too. I can smell it."

One of the men shouted, "Hey, they're up there." As a couple of the younger men started to run towards the pups, Wee made a decision. "Run that way," she told Fur, pointing with her nose towards the fence where the trees grew. "I'll try to lead them away."

Fur hesitated, but he was too tired to be stubborn. He headed as fast as he dared through the grass, along the fence and down towards the trees.

Wee stood up and raced up the field and into the barnyard. The young men took the bait, but the older men, Roger included, stood in the field, too tired to run, and looked for the movement of the other pup.

While Wee did her best to keep the young men busy, weaving around buildings and under equipment, staying just ahead of them, the men in the field saw Fur enter the trees and drop to the dirt, panting and tired. They began to move forward, trying not to spook him. Fur watched them. He was so hot, and his mouth was dry, and his breath came in ragged gasps between panting. He didn't know if he could even get up again. He tried and after a brief struggle, he got to his feet and moved further into the trees at the corner. The men moved in slowly and methodically.

Fur whined softly. He couldn't do it. He just couldn't. He had tried to do what Wee asked. But he was tired. His throat burned; his legs were weak. He half crawled towards the heaviest trees in the very corner of the field wedging himself under the branches of dense fir trees. He could hear the men's approach, and he whined in fear creeping even further. Almost against the fence, Fur fell into a small hole. He squeezed himself further in and realized it kept going. The opening was small and partially collapsed but he squirmed as hard as he could and squeezed through the tangled roots and rocks into the larger opening beyond. He pressed himself against the far wall in the cool dirt. It was a den. He knew that. Whether it was an old one of his mother's or one of coyotes long ago, he had no idea, but it was, for right now, the sweetest place on earth.

He heard the voices above coming closer until one of the men crawling around in the firs, trying to feel for him, discovered the hole. Fur could hear the man curse and mutter. An arm came down the hole, groping and feeling this way and that. Fur stayed against the back out of reach, panting and frightened. The fingers felt as far as they could in every direction and finally retracted with more muttering from above. Fur lay his head down in the cool darkness to catch his breath. He'd done what Wee asked after all. He'd found a place to hide. Just as he began to relax, a long stick slid down through the dirt and jabbed him in the side. He yelped in surprise and darted to one side. He could see a man's arms just above the small opening. The stick came down through the roof, between the roots, jabbing at him repeatedly. The pain came again and again as he tried to dodge in the small space. He refused to leave though. He had found his hiding place, and he wasn't going out into the waiting hands of the angry man. After a few moments and amidst more muttering and cursing, he heard the sounds of men begin to fade. He did not move. He stayed in his little haven and waited for Wee to tell him it was ok.

Wee, up by the barn, had grown tired. She knew it would not be long before some mistake would allow the men to catch her. It was time she found her own hiding place. She couldn't see Fur, but there had been no yelps or squeals to signify him getting caught, so that was good. Now, she just needed to get away herself. She moved around the men's truck once more and slipped under it when they tried to come around from either side. They both got down to look and she took advantage of the few seconds it would take them to stand up and move around the trailer, to scoot out the other side and race back towards the field.

They were faster than she'd hoped and Wee knew she had to find a way to escape, or they would catch her and if they caught her, she shuddered inside, she didn't know what they would do.

She raced down the field as she heard Fur's muffled yelps, but she could not stop. She had to keep going. She stumbled, rolled, and kept moving. She heard Fur yelp again and again, but all she could do was keep running. She ran straight until the fence at the far end of the field brought her to an abrupt halt. She turned towards the approaching men, saw Roger move to close in the gap, she turned in small circles, making uncontrollable, whimpering sounds. Turning this way, that way, against the fence and then she crouched in the grass shivering as they closed the small circle they'd created. The other men began yelling encouragement as they came out of the trees and moved to help. At the last moment as they leaned forward, she darted between Roger's legs.

The space under the fence. The space under the fence. Where? Where? Wee was beyond any real coherent thought. The only thing that ran clearly in her head was to escape. She recognized the hollow and dove through it in a panic, squeaking and crying as she went.

One of the young men leaped forward, landing flat on his stomach, thrusting his hand through the space in the fencing and grabbing Wee by one hind leg. Her whimpers turned into screams of terror, and she thrashed and pulled. The man began back dragging her towards the fence so he could get ahold of her other leg. One of the men stepped forward to assist him, leaning down across the fence to get a grip on the flailing pup. He grabbed her scruff and said in a hoarse voice, "Not so fast, you stupid mutt." He pulled her up off her front feet, terror stricken and screaming the entire time. There was no sane thought in her mind, just the screaming and struggling of captured prey.

From the grass outside the fence, a blur of movement launched itself at the men holding Wee captive. It was teeth and fangs and pinned ears. Wee only felt the release of the grip. She ran as though the hounds of hell were on her heels. She ran down the bank, through the water and up the other side and she just kept running. She barely heard the thunder noise or felt the water or smelled the coyote scent. She just ran until she collapsed into a sort of unconsciousness and lay still in the grass, unmoving and unaware.

Chapter 3 - Peace on Earth

When Wee finally awoke, for a moment, it seemed like any other night. She rolled upright and lay there in the cool air, listening. It was quiet, almost too quiet and she was horribly thirsty. The realization of her thirst brought the day's events flooding into her mind and she began to shiver as the fear swept through her all over again. She stayed like that for a few long minutes as she adjusted mentally to the silence and the darkness that meant it was over. Thirst drove her to her feet, but she had no idea where she was. She moved off, swaying and staggering through the tall grass, with all the grace of a man leaving a tavern, in the early morning hours.

Whether by instinct or luck, she soon found herself looking down onto the bank of the stream. She fell going down the bank and tumbled, sprawling into the cool water with a splash. Wee made no attempt to get up and simply began to lap the cool water in a somewhat frenzied fashion. She drank until her belly felt heavy and distended before bringing herself to her feet and still drinking a bit more. She wandered part of the way up the other side, before collapsing in the grass once again and drifting off into a troubled slumber of unremembered dreams.

When she awakened again, it was the early gray light of dawn. The sun had not yet risen, and the air was still cool. This time, she made it up the bank and out to more familiar territory. Where could she go? Certainly, she could not go home. Roger might be waiting. She paced along the grass in indecision.

Wee was brought out of her thoughts by the smell of blood. She sniffed the air and began to follow the scent. She could smell it upon the blades of grass, but she sniffed only briefly and kept going. It did not take long for her to find the source. Her mother lay in the grass, flat and unmoving. Blood was dried in a trickling trail down the side of one hind leg. As Wee moved around to her mother's face, she stopped for a moment. Her mother's head was almost unrecognizable. Blood coated her face and the top of her head; it was thick and wet and still trickling down her face.

Wee stared at her mother in horror. Gathering her courage, she poked gently at her mother's nose. "Momma?" Her voice came out in a high-pitched whine. She pushed slightly harder, "Momma!"

There was no response.

Wee whimpered over and over before she finally curled up next to her mother and took what solace she could find. She did not leave her mother's side all through the morning, into the heat of the day or even when the sun began to set. She just lay against her mother's side, feeling the erratic beating of her heart and the slow, ragged breathing. She was lost in her grief with no idea what to do.

As evening fell, Wee was no closer to knowing how to handle the situation. She pushed at her mother's shoulder but still she got no response. Finally, she began to wash the blood from her mother's face. It was something she could do at least. She ran her tongue across her ear and up over the top of her head, moving with more surety as she went. Thousands of years of instinct guided the young pup as she moved more vigorously through the hair and more gently on the open wounds. It took some time, and her tongue was sore and tired, but as the last rays of the sun blinked out of sight over the horizon, she sniffed and sat back on her haunches and looked at Momma. She was cleaner by far, but the ability to now discern the actual wounds made Wee slightly more miserable. Her beautiful Momma wasn't so pretty anymore. The thunder had taken her right eye and left a long furless streak of red across the top of her head and removed most of her left ear. In places, before the blood seeped and began to cover it, she could see glimpses of white bone.

Wee whined and poked her mother again. Perhaps now she would awaken. After three or four tries, she gave up and sat down still crying softly. She stared at her mother's face and waited, as if willing her to move.

When she could no longer see many of the details of her mother's face, she noticed her mouth was dry and her tongue ached and eventually, she wound her way back to the stream. She drank much more slowly this time, pulling in the water and letting its coolness soothe her mouth.

The distant cry of a coyote brought Wee out of her stupor. She picked her head up fearfully and listened to the answering cries. She heard movement behind her and wheeled around only to be hit head on by a fast-moving animal in the dark. She snarled and spit in a terrified, high-pitched tone before realizing she knew the figure, now lying in the water looking dazed and frightened himself. "Fur, you idiot!" she gasped. Then the feeling of not being so alone overwhelmed her and she breathed a sigh of relief. "You're okay," she said quietly.

Fur looked at her sullenly. "You didn't come find me. I was thirsty and it was dusty, and I waited, but you didn't come."

She lowered her head. "It's Momma," she said. "Momma is hurt, and I couldn't leave her."

"Then where is she?" Fur said it more as an accusation than a question.

"I just went to get a drink."

"But not to find me."

She looked at his pouting face and thought to herself that he had all the maturity of a two-month-old. Still, she was happy to have his companionship. "Just come on," she said quietly.

"I…" He dragged out the sound of it. "Am still thirsty."

Wee humphed. "Then stop arguing and start drinking or I'll go back to Momma without you."

He glared back at her. "Like you already did?"

Wee was fast losing control of her temper.

"Yes!" She sputtered. "Only this time you'll be out with the coyotes." They locked eyes for a moment but then Fur lowered his head and began to drink.

It seemed like an eternity before he was finished and her anxiety grew with each passing lap of his tongue, but she waited, partially because she knew of her own thirst when she awoke and partially because she didn't want to waste more time arguing.

Finally, he raised his head and said, "There. Now I'm done."

Wee stifled a comment despite being sure he'd probably drank more water than he wanted just to spite her. She turned without another word and headed up in the direction she had come. Fur followed behind with a slow methodical gait and Wee didn't know if he was tired or just trying to be as annoying as possible. Either way, she was annoyed.

When they reached the spot where Momma lay, Fur forgot about his indignation at being forgotten. He smelled Momma all over and then began to whine and poke and prod, repeatedly while whimpering and calling to his mother after each poke. Finally, Wee stepped in to calm him down before he brought their position to someone or something's attention.
"Stop, Fur. Just stop. It doesn't work." She kept her voice low and calm. "She's hurt bad."
"What do we do?" Fur asked her, looking as sad and unsure as Wee had felt when she was alone.
"I don't know. We just wait."

Fur whimpered and laid down against his mother's side, curling up like a small pup. Wee laid beside him, but upright, listening for any sound in the night. There she remained until the first light of day. A few times she heard strange noises or the yipping of coyotes, but nothing ever came close. It was still cool and Wee began to drift off, taking advantage of the short time of protection between dawn and daylight.

She was startled out of her little nap by the high-pitched yip from Fur.

Wee leaped up afraid some danger was upon them, but Fur was just staring at their mother silently. Wee stared too but there was nothing new except a few trickles of fresh blood.

Finally, she looked at Fur. "What are you doing?"

He just remained staring.

"Fur!" she said again.

He didn't change his gaze. "She moved."

Wee stared for a moment. She sighed. "She's not moving. She's hurt and she's not moving, and I don't know if she'll ever move."

Fur did not change his focus. "She moved. I was sleeping and she moved, and I felt it."

Wee stared again but saw nothing. Had he dreamed it, she wondered. It didn't matter. She wasn't moving now. She sat on the grass and waited. What else could they do? Eventually, Fur gave up too and came and sat beside her. They tried not to stare at Momma but kept staring anyway. It was getting hot, but neither pup moved.

Finally, Wee said softly. "Fur."

"Yeah," he answered.

"I would not have left you there. I would have come for you. But I found Momma and I couldn't leave her either."

"I know," Fur said. I didn't know, but I see now, and I know. I'm sorry I got mad."

Wee nuzzled his face. Then she walked over to Momma and pressed her nose against her muzzle. To her surprise, Momma's lip crinkled just a tiny bit. She stepped back in surprise. "Momma!"

There was no answer, but she found Fur suddenly right beside her. She looked at him. "She moved."

Fur looked at her, trying to keep this small bit of triumph off his face. "I told you," was all he said.

Suddenly Wee looked up. "Stay here. Watch Momma!"

"Where are you going?" Fur asked, sounding a bit startled.

"Maybe Momma needs something to eat. I'm gonna go catch her something. Maybe a frog or even a fish," Wee said excitedly. "But you've got to stay and watch Momma, in case she moves."

Fur sat and looked serious. "I will watch her," he said, puffing up his chest a little.

"Thank you!" Wee told him and then sprinted off to the water with a mission.

At the water, she passed up a couple of frogs in hopes of finding a tasty fish, but when she saw one briefly, it was easily lost among the reeds and feeling impatient, she grabbed the next frog she could catch and headed back up the bank with it dangling from her mouth.

When she got to Fur, his back was to her, and he was still staring. She walked up beside him and dropped the frog next to her mother's nose. She didn't ask if Momma had moved. Her head was angled slightly different, not much, but enough for Wee not to have to ask. She pushed the frog closer to her mother's face, trying not to be too excited.

"Here, Momma. I brought you something."
She picked up the frog again, dropped it closer.
"Here Momma, eat!"
She picked it up again, dropped it. The frog fell against her Momma's nose.

Wee watched as a weak tongue moved out from between Momma's lips. It licked the frog. Once, twice, and then nothing.

Wee was happy and yet unhappy at the same time. Momma had moved, but she couldn't eat the frog like that. She picked it up again and set it more carefully against her mother's muzzle where the tongue had come out. She pushed it against her. "Come on, Momma."
Her mother didn't move.

As the day wore on, they waited, sometimes sitting, sometimes laying down, but always watching. The frog began to dry out in the sun. Finally, Fur spoke in a small voice. "Wee, I could eat a frog," he said softly, as if somewhat ashamed of his hunger.

Wee looked up and realized that she was hungry too. "We should go now, before the dark comes. We have to be here for Momma then. And we'll bring her back a new frog!"
Fur was relieved he hadn't said something dumb.
"Ok," he told her. "We'll hurry and come right back. We'll each catch Momma a frog."
Wee felt some true happiness for the first time since their world had changed and she moved off toward the stream with Fur in tow.

When they arrived, she was surprised to see Fur set about looking with a business-like demeanor. He didn't splash or frolic but set to the task like a true hunter. She felt proud of him, and she began to do the same. They forgot the passage of time, each working to sate their own hunger. As the sun began to touch the horizon, it was Fur who came to Wee and announced that it was time to catch Momma's frog. For the second time that day, Wee felt pride in his sudden maturity. She waited until they had each caught their kill and said, "Fur, now why don't you lead us back to Momma."
He didn't hesitate, but Wee didn't miss the look in his eyes either, as he passed her and headed up the embankment towards their mother.

When they arrived back, they were shocked to find that Momma had moved. Not just a tongue or a lip but had moved a couple of feet in the grass. They raced to her and Wee was dismayed at the blood running down her face again. They both dropped their prizes and poked and said Momma at least a dozen times before they finally calmed enough to accept that she would not respond. They put the frogs by her nose and watched for a while. At last, tired and with food in their stomachs, they lay down. And as the shadows stretched out across the field, Wee was grateful that this night, she would not be alone. Fur laid beside her feeling much the same and before long, both pups were sound asleep.

They were awakened by the startling sounds of their mother's dry rasping noises. "Wee.." she croaked.
"Momma! We brought you frogs, Momma."
"Wee…" her mother tried again.
Both pups stood waiting in anxious anticipation.
"What do you need, Momma?" Fur asked.
"We'll get it for you."
"Water…" Momma managed to sputter.
"Water." She fell silent once more.
Wee and Fur glanced around as if there might be a dish in the field somewhere. Wee tried to think. They couldn't bring her the stream, but Momma wanted water. She fidgeted and

thought. She looked at Fur, but he just stared at her as if waiting for instructions. She paced and thought but couldn't find a solution. Finally, she laid down looking forlorn and frustrated. They had to get Momma to the water, but how?

She was startled out of her thoughts by her mother's movements. As Wee watched, her mother turned her front end partially upright and stretching out her front legs she pulled herself a few inches in the direction of the stream, before falling on her side again. She was not going the way they were used to, but by a direct route without a worn path. Fur jumped to his feet with understanding and ran in front of their mother. He began to bounce up and down, yipping "Come on, Momma, come on. You can do it." Wee's first reaction was to tell Fur to be silent before someone heard him, but as she moved in his direction, Momma tried again. Whether out of desperation or due to Fur's encouragement, she rose again, only partially upright and dragged herself forward. Wee moved beside her brother and began to encourage her mother as well.

For what seemed like forever, they alternated between encouragement and quiet waiting when their mother would fall over and sleep. A few times, she even attempted to gain her footing but could not. At those times the pups would lead the way, coaxing and talking and egging her on. At other times, when they could get no response, they would lie and wait for her to move again.

In the afternoon sun, they finally reached a much steeper bank along the edge of the stream. There the dog collapsed and did not move. Both pups began to whine and plead with her to go just a bit further. A few minutes later, with a last bit of effort, she dragged herself over the lip, letting gravity aid her and half slid, half pulled herself to the water's edge. Wee stood with trembling legs, feeling shaky and emotionally exhausted, but at long last, Momma was there. Her mother lay with her head between her legs and the bottom of her muzzle in the water. She was bleeding again, but somehow success made it seem worthwhile.
The pups waited patiently, seeming to feel the magnitude of their short journey. At long last, Momma lifted her head and began to drink. They were tentative laps, desperate thirst and utter exhaustion warring with one another, but to the pups, it felt like a great achievement.

When she had drunk all that she was able, she rolled over on her side and did not move for several hours. Eventually, the pups hunkered down by her back, and although Wee tried to tell herself, she would keep watch, evening would find them all sleeping together.

Late that night, Wee awoke to the sound of lapping water. Momma was awake again. She padded over to the edge of the stream and laid down and just watched her mother drink. To Wee, it was still like a miracle. When she finished, Wee spoke.

"Tomorrow, I will..." She hesitated and looked at Fur who was still curled up by the bank.

"Tomorrow, we will get you something to eat." Her mother gave a slight nod and Wee crept close, not getting to her feet. "I'm sorry," she whispered. "If I'd been faster, you'd be ok." Momma moved herself slightly closer to Wee and laid her head over Wee's back. Neither one spoke. Wee just pressed herself as close to her mother's chest as she could, and they both slept again until daylight.

Chapter 4

On The Run

Over the next several days, Wee and Fur did little more than stay beside their mother. They caught frogs and occasionally fish and a few mice, but mostly they waited and slept and waited some more. Momma became a little stronger every day. Her wounds no longer bled much, and her movements were less shaky. She could drink without her head wobbling and could chew much better. She was, however, very thin and still weak. Wee knew her momma needed more than just a few frogs, but they did not dare to go towards the house and at night, when the coyotes sang, they dared not move at all. She could only hope her mother could get well enough to leave the stream. Momma gradually managed to be capable of standing, but barely. Even a few short steps to relieve herself took effort and she would doze afterwards. Wee and Fur caught every small critter they could, but it never seemed enough.

One night as they lay quietly by the bank, a possum slowly made its way down the opposite bank to the stream. Wee, seeing its advance, immediately said in a quiet voice, "Fur. Do not move."

Fur went to ask why but as he followed Wee's gaze, he saw the answer.

"Can you kill it, Momma?" Wee whispered. Her mother looked at the expanse of shallow water between her and her proposed quarry, and the steepness of the bank. She sighed. "I don't know."

Wee felt the weight of what that meant, but Fur stood slowly. "I can kill it," he said.

Wee looked at him there in the growing dark. The look of determination, the way he stood, was not like Fur at all. She had thought to dissuade him, but instead, she just nodded. Fur nodded too and padded silently further up the bank and disappeared among the alders. It was so quiet that even Wee was startled when Fur leaped from the bushes on the far side landing right next to the possum. It let out a hiss as Fur's jaws grabbed the creature's neck tightly and began to shake it back and forth. It began to slip from his grasp, and he shoved the flailing body against the ground to get better purchase. He squeezed it tightly, afraid to try and pick it up again. He just held on with all the might in his jaws and held them shut as tightly as he could. The flailing began to cease and still he held. Even after the animal stopped moving and his breath was coming in short gasps, Fur still did not release his grip. As the possum stopped moving and Fur did not let go, Wee finally crossed to him and smelled the thing. "I think it's dead."

Fur remained holding it in a death grip. Slowly, after a moment his jaws slipped from its neck and he looked at Wee.

The look in his eyes was fierce, both frightening and awesome at the same time. Where was her dumb pup brother? Wee thought to herself. This certainly was not him. He stood staring at her, his head still lowered, his breathing heavy. He growled low in his throat. "But it was for Momma," Wee said almost plaintively. "To help her get strong."

Those words took all the fire from Fur's eyes. He was suddenly her brother again. "Can I take it to her?" he asked after a pause.

"Of course, you can," Wee answered. "You should be very proud."

Fur picked up the limp animal and half dragged it down the beach, through the stream and dropped it at his mother's feet. Wee followed behind him glad for her mother to have some kind of meal.

Momma looked up at Fur and smiled. "Thank you", she said softly. "You did a great job."

Fur beamed at his mother's praise. "Wee and I make a good team. I may not always think quick like her, but I'm good and strong."

Wee smiled to herself. It was the truth. She was not as big or strong, but she was a fast thinker.

Together, they had been getting things done. One day, they would be quite something. Fur was finding his place in their small pack.

The pups watched as Momma slowly worked at the body of the possum. She was having a hard time tearing it open and the pups were having a hard time not joining. It seemed like an eternity before Momma managed to eat a good portion. When she stopped eating, she looked at the pups. She was tired from the effort but still she fought to fix them with a stern stare. "The rest is for you, if you promise to share it."
The pups nodded in simple agreement. Momma nodded too." Ok, then take it," she said.
They raced toward the food, eager for something in their stomachs that was more than a mouthful. When they reached it, Momma gave them as stern a stare as she could manage. Just eating had worn her out. Her weariness was as good as her once reproachful gaze, for it reminded the pups how weak she still was.
"Don't worry." Wee told her mother. "We'll share. You get some rest."
Fur picked up the remains of the body. Half of the remainder wouldn't be a lot, but more than they had eaten at a single meal in many days. He braced his feet against it and pulled and tore at it, until he got a piece separated. He looked at the piece on the ground.

51

"You should have the bigger piece," Wee told him. "Without you, we wouldn't be eating at all." Fur said nothing, but his eyes said he was grateful. He took his share and lay down among the weeds on the bank. Without hesitation, Wee claimed the rest and ate it where it lay. She drifted off to sleep feeling hopeful they would all be okay and a sense of wonderment at her brother's behavior.

Wee awakened just before dawn, to the sound of rustling grass and soft footfalls. She lay still and listened. A glance at Fur and Momma told her it was not good. Momma was upright, tense and looking worried. Fur was crouched in the grass, on the bank unmoving.
Wee moved ever so slowly towards her mother, crouching low and trying to make no sound. The sounds spread out up over the edge of the bank and she knew they were in trouble. Whether drawn by the scent of the possum's demise or they had simply lost their fear of the events prior, the coyotes had moved in while they slept.
Momma began to move quietly back along the bank, not standing, but not dragging herself either. Her movements were shaky but determined. She eased herself back under the alders that overhung the water, though there was really no way to hide from them. They would smell what they could not see. She would

be easy prey without the ability to even run and certainly unable to fight. Wee tried to hold her composure, but she was just a terrified puppy all over again. She looked at Fur and he seemed no better. There was nothing to do but run, yet she knew Momma could not and she could not quite bring herself to leave her, after all this time. She slunk in beside her mother and Fur followed her in.

It's just not fair, she thought to herself, trying not to cry aloud. Why don't they just go away? She felt helpless and frightened.

A lone figure looked over the embankment. It was a young male. He was missing an ear and his face was still not healed. Beside Wee, Momma growled low in her throat. The coyote hesitated. It was not so long ago, he had faced the she-devil of a dog. He sniffed the air cautiously and for a moment, Wee was hopeful. This time though, he was not alone. He made a short, high-pitched yip and in moments, there were others beside him. Both pups backed up in wild-eyed terror. Momma was growling, but already, she sounded weaker with the effort. The coyotes knew it and as one, they began to descend on the small group huddled under the brush at the water's edge.

"When I say go." Momma's voice was agonizingly quiet. "You run. Run for the gap in the fence and hide."

Wee wanted to tell her mother no. She wanted to say they wouldn't leave, but the terror wouldn't let her say anything at all. She just lay pinned to the ground behind her mother and moved her dry tongue across her lips but no sound came out.

The coyotes began to move across the water and Wee whimpered but still could not move. She dared not look at Fur or her mother or do anything but cower there with her heart pounding in her small chest.

"Now! Go!" Momma said suddenly, as she raised herself quickly to her feet, almost falling, but managing to stay upright somehow. She wobbled and teetered but she stayed all the same. "Just go!" She sputtered through her teeth.

The coyotes were mere feet away when Fur suddenly made a break for it. He darted out the back of the branches and bolted up the bank. Wee turned and ran after him, crying and sobbing, knowing the sound would carry, but unable to stop it.

As they cleared the top of the bank towards what had been their home, a loud clear bang rang through the crisp morning air. Fur stopped short, dropping into the grass and Wee, not expecting his reaction, went somersaulting over him and came to rest on her back before him. Neither one made any attempt to move. The

thunder came again and Wee rolled upright, but
still they stayed where they were.

Suddenly, the coyotes came up over the bank
as well, leaped over the pups in the grass and
kept going. Another shot cut through the air and
Wee watched one coyote hesitate a moment
and then collapse into the grass, struggle
weakly and fall again, unmoving.
Then Wee heard the voices of men talking and
she began to understand. "Come on Fur," She
whispered. "We have to get out of here."
"What about Momma?" Fur whispered back.
"I don't know, Fur," she whimpered. "I don't
know."
"You're the big thinker," he said. "So think."
Wee couldn't think. She could barely breathe,
but for Fur's sake, she had to come up with
something. That was her job. "Okay." She told
him, though she really didn't have a plan.
"Follow me."
She moved further from the sound of voices but
stayed close to the bank, though still in the tall
grass. She made her way to the path where
they had come with Momma the first time. She
glanced back at Fur but he had followed without
question. This too was new, but she didn't have
the presence of mind to ponder it. At the head
of the path, she listened.

The voices came from by the stream, but where Momma was. "I thought for sure they had something, but I don't see anything."
"Me either but they've killed sheep on two farms and I'm pretty sure this is where they've been hiding out, judging by the way the grass is packed down."
"Yeah, something has definitely been sleeping here for a while."
Wee didn't understand the noises of the humans, but she at least could tell they weren't moving closer, so she made her way slowly down the bank and under the brush along the sides. Fur followed silently behind, listening to the voices as well. He shivered momentarily. Humans, coyotes… they were much the same, he thought. But according to Momma, one you could bite and one you couldn't. Maybe because coyotes don't carry booming sticks that can take your eyes and make holes in your body, no matter how far away you are. You had to make sure humans didn't see you.

That made sense to him, and he followed Wee along the shadowed dark trunks in the gray light of day.
Wee made her way until she could see the legs of the men. She listened to the chatter of their angry voices.
"Ever since the farm here closed up, them coyotes have had free reign over this field,

giving them a way to get down into the rest of the valley and back up into the hills yonder, without anyone saying nay."

"By the looks of things, they aren't even going home anymore. They're sleeping right here." The man angrily scuffed the grass with his boot as he spoke. She didn't know what he said but he seemed angry about the flattened grass. Which would mean he was angry about them. She moved back just a little and that's when she saw Momma. She wanted to run to her, but the men were between them and Momma was pressed up against the trunks of the alders just like she and Fur, which made it seem like that must be a good idea. Momma's head was down, and her eyes were closed, but still she had made it out of sight, unless you were laying on the ground, of course.

"Well, they won't be bedding down here today, and we'll come back and check it tomorrow. At least keep them on their toes."

"The loss of a couple of their own ought to rattle them too. Leave the bodies, it'll keep them out of here for a while."

"Yep. Let's get back before it gets any dang hotter."

The men stood looking a few moments more and then made their way up the bank and out of sight.

"What now?" Fur asked, when the sound of their steps had receded into the distance.

"Shhhh," Wee told him. "I want to make sure they are gone."

On the other side, Momma opened her eye and looked across the expanse between them. Wee crept across the gap with Fur tight behind her and they lay next to their mother for some time. Wee finally broke the silence when the questions in her head could not be silent any longer. "What are we gonna do now, Momma?" Wee asked. "The man was mad the grass was flat and we made it flat. If they come back, they might find us and then they'll get us too." Momma lifted her head. "We have to go. We have to leave here."

"But where, Momma? Where will we go? The men are after us, the coyotes are after us. Where can we go?" Wee's voice was plaintive, but she couldn't help it. She did not feel capable of being big anymore. She just felt sad and scared and tired.

Her mother sighed. "Tonight, we'll go back to Roger's."

Wee looked up at her mother as if she'd gone mad. "We can't go there, Momma. We can't."

"Listen," Momma said softly. "Roger is dangerous, but if he doesn't know we're there, he won't look. He can't smell us like the coyotes and he doesn't go searching like the men here. We'll hide by day and only come out at night."

Fur stood up. "She's right, Wee. All this time, Roger has never come to look. He could have found Momma, but he didn't."

Wee glared at Fur. "Stop it," she told him. I'm supposed to be the thinker."

Fur stuck out his tongue. "Fine! What do you think we should do?" His voice held a slight patronizing tone.

Wee laid her head on her paws. She tried to think, but she just felt worn out. None of her thoughts would come together and she couldn't find any solution to their problem.

Finally, she sighed. "I guess, for NOW, we go to Roger's."

Fur smirked but said nothing.

They spent the rest of the daylight hours under the alders, out of sight. They all dozed off occasionally, but it was an uneasy rest. They would waken at every sound or rustle in the grass. When the sun began to set beyond the horizon, they simply lay quietly waiting for dark.

As the last rays of light faded, Fur walked to the water's edge and began to drink. The others followed. When they finished, Wee looked up the bank and then looked at Momma. "Can you make it?" She whispered.

"I'll make it," Momma reassured her.

Wee smiled. It was the first time Momma had said she could, in what seemed a very long time.

"Let's go to the path," Wee said. "It's not as steep there."

Fur chuckled softly. "Now you're thinking."

She gave him an exasperated look but could not be angry. They had a plan, and really it wasn't the worst plan. It would have to do for now.

At the path, Momma stopped and stared up the embankment. She was still shaky and lying still all afternoon had allowed her muscles to stiffen. Wee started to worry. What if Momma couldn't make it? She fought to maintain control of her emotions and think.

She sighed out loud. "Okay Fur. Here's what we're gonna do. "You get behind Momma."

Fur nodded. He had been worried too, but if Wee was going to think of a way, he was going to do his part. He walked around her and stood in line behind his mother.

"No. Closer," Wee said. "Really close. You're gonna make sure she doesn't slide back."

Now Fur understood and he put his head up tight to Momma's tail.

"Perfect!"

Wee walked up alongside Momma and gently pressed against her side.

"You ready, Momma?" she asked quietly.

Momma lowered her head and nodded.

"Now, Go!" Wee shouted.

Momma began to move faster than they expected and for a few moments she was out ahead of both pups. Wee raced to get into position and steady her mother just as Momma began to lose momentum.

She wobbled slightly and then pressed against Wee's shoulder to keep herself going. Her back legs began to slide, and she fought to get her injured hind leg to function the way it should. Suddenly, Momma began to move forward, almost losing her balance again, as the upward thrust took her by surprise. Fur had caught up to them and in a desperate attempt to keep Momma going, he had tucked his head and shoulders under her, lifting her hind end up off the ground and propelled her forward like a wheelbarrow. She managed to get her front legs moving out before her and continued up the short uphill path. Just as their momentum began to slow again, Momma made it up over the edge and fell forward into the long grass. Fur stood at the top edge, head down, breathing heavily.

Wee looked at Momma worriedly. "Momma?" Momma rolled upright, panting but looking no worse for the fall.

Wee looked at Fur and for some reason, she began to giggle. Fur lifted his head up to meet her gaze. She bounded over to him. "You did it, Fur! Oh boy, did you do it."

She giggled again and this time Fur smiled a big puppy grin.

"Told you I was the strong one."

Wee dragged her paw down over his head.

"You sure are."

The success and relief had done much to make the pups feel better about the day's events, but after a few minutes they returned their attention to their mother.

Fur spoke first. "When you're ready, Momma, we'll get you there."

She smiled at them both. "I think for the next part, I can walk."

Fur bounced in front of her and laughed. "Okay, Momma, but if you need me, I'll be ready."

Wee imagined her brother pushing Momma across the field and she laughed with him. It felt good to finally be moving on from that place by the water and all the stress that had brought and kept them there. And in a weird way, despite the perils ahead, it felt good to be going home.

Chapter 5
Home Again

Under the cover of darkness, the small family moved under the fence and into the trees where Fur had discovered the old den. The going had been slow, and Momma had rested often. Upon arrival, they chose a spot that would be out of sight by day and Momma lay down, exhausted by the trip and Wee and Fur were, once again, left to make their own decisions.

After lying there watching their mother sleep for a time, and dozing some themselves, Wee got to her feet and began to move among the shadows of the trees in the pale light of the moon.
"Where are you going?" Fur asked her quietly.
Wee turned back. "I want to find a drink. She answered him as quietly as he had asked.
"Then I'm coming too." Fur rose and began to follow.
"Are you thirsty too?" She asked.
"I kinda am. And if we run into any trouble, two is better than one."
Wee was glad he had decided to go. She liked having this new version of her brother. It made her feel safer and less vulnerable. They passed out of the trees and began heading up to the goat pen. They wandered the fence and crawled under the gate. A quick search

revealed there were no buckets and no dishes. They were gone, just like the goats. They went back out and moved closer to the barn, going around by the shed and making no noise that might alert Roger to their presence. The house was totally dark, but they took no chances.

The bucket by the old well was also gone and the trough by the old sheep shed. Finally, they made their way to the barn itself and there they both hesitated, looking left and right as though Roger might appear at any moment. He did not and after a moment they slipped inside.
They searched every stall in the barn and finally came across an old bucket in one corner of a goat's stall. The water was old and smelled stale, but having found little else, they both drank in turns until their thirst subsided.
Wee nosed at the goat pellets among the hay, they were dry and tasteless.
"Now what?" Fur asked.
"I don't know. There's nothing here". She looked around and suddenly felt kind of sad.
It all seemed so quiet and empty.
"Let's go back," she told Fur suddenly. "I don't really like it here."

They headed for the barn door but stopped short when a stout figure appeared in the doorway. Wee heard Fur's low growl beside her and the creature made angry noises in return.

The raccoon was as surprised by the pups as they were by him. He made threatening noises and puffed himself up, readying for the fight. The pups knew this was not like the possum and there was no chance this musky creature would be dinner. Wee shifted towards one side of the aisle slowly moving towards the opening. Fur stayed close to her shoulder as she pressed closer to the stall walls. The coon moved away slightly, still posturing and making guttural sounds in his throat. Wee persisted in moving slowly in an attempt to go around the angry coon and force him to move from the doorway. When they got about four feet from the barn door, the coon would move no further and the pups did not quite dare to go by.

Wee was uneasy. The animal was no coyote, but he was certainly capable of causing damage. She whined a low whine in frustration. Escape was so near, yet not quite there. Maybe, if they made a run for it, she thought to herself. But she had no idea if this thing could catch them. Suddenly, Fur lunged forward with a loud growl scaring not just the coon, but Wee as well. The coon panicked and tried to climb the side of the doorway, knocking down a rake with a broken handle and a few odd tools. As they clattered to the floor, the pups bolted out and into the grass as fast as they could go, leaving he coon to take the blame if Roger heard the noise.

They lay in the tall grass, panting and stared at the house. No lights came on and there was no movement in the windows. They looked at each other and Wee could see the look of smug pride on her brother's face. She smiled at him, and he stood up, still obviously proud of himself. "Come on," he said. "Let's go check on Momma."

On the way back to the trees, the pups were surprised to stumble upon Momma laying in the grass. She lay upright and silent.

The pups expected a reprimand and to have to explain about the events in the barn, but when they began to speak, Momma simply said, "Shhhh…."

They turned and stood beside her. She was staring up at the house intently.

Wee stared too. "What is it, Momma? Is it Roger?"

Momma didn't answer. She just lay watching. Finally, she spoke. "It's not Roger, but it should be."

"Come," she said and rose carefully to her feet. Heading not towards the trees, but towards the house.

"But…" Wee started, but her mother was already moving off through the grass. Fur looked at Wee, obviously just as puzzled, but then turned and headed after his mother, leaving Wee no choice but to follow them.

She strode slowly all the way to the yard, and although Wee could already tell Momma was getting tired, the old dog did not stop. She continued right up to the back of the house where a pile of stuff lay in the backyard.
The pile consisted of odd dishes, broken furniture, old clothing and some random pantry items. Momma sniffed around the pile. A furry brown rodent popped its head out from under an old chair with a missing leg. Rats! Wee saw it dart back into its hole in the darkness, but her mother paid it no mind. She turned and continued along the house to the driveway, her nose to the ground, with slow measured steps. Fur looked at his mother and then at Wee as if Momma had gone crazy. They were at the house! Had their mother forgotten what lurked within that house.
Wee was torn. She watched her mother's faltering steps and knew if the door opened, Momma would be unable to run away, but she didn't like Momma being alone either. She started to follow after her but stopped short when Momma turned off the driveway and went up onto the steps of the house. On the steps! Dogs weren't allowed in the yard, never mind the steps! Maybe she had gone crazy. Wee looked at Fur, but he was staring at his mother

with the same shocked look Wee's own face had held just seconds before.

The pups watched, transfixed in horror, barely able to breathe, as Momma smelled along the landing, the door itself and finally eased herself slowly down the steps and back towards the puppies who still stood open mouthed on the lawn. She moved past them, her strength obviously nearing the breaking point, and softly flopped herself down on the grass to rest. The pups continued to stare at her as if she had tempted death once more and somehow survived. Finally, she lifted her head and looked at them. For that moment, Wee thought it was the most peaceful gaze she had ever seen upon her mother's face. It made something flutter in her chest and brought an unknown warmth she couldn't identify. Momma's words interrupted her confused emotional state.
"Roger is gone."
It took a minute for the words to sink in.
What do you mean, Momma?" Fur asked her.
"He's gone," She repeated simply.
"G-gone where?" Wee sputtered.
"I don't know." Momma's voice sounding almost giddy. "But he hasn't been here for days."
She stared at the pups, watching her words sink in.
The pups stared back and then at each other.
"Roger is gone!" Wee repeated.

"Yes." Momma said simply.

In the moonlight, the lightness in her voice was brighter than the light reflected in her one eye. Wee and Fur both felt it. They looked at each other and then back at Momma and then at each other again.

The weight lifted off their shoulders was immense.

"The place is ours!" Fur said excitedly.

What are we going to do now?" Wee asked, sounding just as excited.

Momma chuckled. "I'm going to rest. You can catch some rats... if you're skilled enough," she added, raising her eyebrows.

"Oh, we have the skills," Fur said haughtily, egged on by his mother's words and her joy.

"You take a nap and we'll get dinner," Fur looked at Wee, that happily obnoxious look still on his face.

She giggled at his antics. "Let's get to it," she said, mimicking his own tone.

Momma laid her head down in the grass, still smiling, and closed her eyes.

The pups hunted rats in the trash pile for more than an hour. They ate some and kept others for Momma. They could have had more success, but their laughter and play kept getting in the way of their focus. They kept trying to be serious then suddenly they'd giggle over each other's movements or stalking and it would start all over again. It was joy, without fear. When the first pale light of dawn came over the distant hills, Momma stood and ate her share of the meal and then led the pups, not to the trees on the far side of the field, but to the barn where they belonged.

Chapter 6
Living the Dream

Wee spent a restless first night in the barn, her dreams troubled by visions of Roger in the barn doorway. In the morning light, they were simply that - dreams. When she finally awoke fully, it was the gray light of dawn and neither Fur, nor her mother were there.

She rose and stretched before wandering out. She couldn't see her family, but she could hear Fur. He sounded as he usually did when he was proud of himself for something. She followed the sound of his bragging through the grass until she came upon them along the edge of the trees.

Between Fur and her mother lay a piece of something. Something that smelled musky and delicious at the same time.

"Bout time, Sleepyhead," Fur said with an obnoxious kind of drawl.

(Yep. He was proud of something.)

"One of us has to get beauty rest," Wee told him.

"In that case," Fur replied, still in his I'm all that tone, "You should go back to bed."

Momma interrupted before Wee could answer. "Have some breakfast. We saved you a piece." Fur snorted, trying to subdue his own laughter. "You weren't here, so I saved you the butt."

He giggled at the angry look on Wee's face. She wasn't really angry. She simply was giving Fur what he wanted.

"Thank you, Momma," Wee said sweetly, intentionally leaving Fur out of the exchange. "It smells delicious."

She picked up the piece of possum by the tail and laid down with it a few feet away.

"But I found it," Fur grumbled defiantly. "I found it and I killed it."

Wee let the meat fall from her mouth. "It's really not so hard to kill a butt." She snickered softly.

"It wasn't a butt," Fur retorted. "It was a whole possum."

"Well, I didn't see a whole possum. Just a butt." Wee tried not to smile and began to chew again, to help keep a straight face.

"Next time, I won't save you nothing", he spat.

Wee acted nonchalantly. "Well, that's even easier to kill than a butt."

Momma stood up and began to stroll across the field. Fur got to his feet. "Where you going, Momma?"

She glanced back at him. "I'm going to find a drink."

Wee realized she was thirsty and swallowed the rest of her meal which she'd only been savoring to annoy Fur. She stood and trotted after her mother. After half a dozen steps, she looked back at Fur who still stood in place, seemingly.

indecisive. "Come on, Butt Slayer," She yelled. When he locked eyes with her, she turned and began to run.

She almost made the crest of the hill when Fur crashed into her from behind, sending both of them tumbling into the grass. Wee gained her feet first and ran at Fur piling on to him, growling and snapping as he snapped and growled, fending her off. They rolled and tumbled until Wee went limp, realizing how dry her mouth really was. Fur pinned her there in the grass.

"Let me up," she growled. "I'm thirsty."

Fur grinned. "Not until you thank me for breakfast."

"Fur! Get up!"

He simply held her with an expectant look.

She turned her head to see Momma go around the barn. "Fuuuurr!"

He stared into his sister's eyes. "Well?"

She relented. "Oh, thank you Fur, for catching breakfast this morning." She kept her voice sullen and distant.

He stood slowly, looking satisfied.

Wee sprinted towards the barn waiting until she had put some distance between herself and Fur to yell, "Butt Slayer!" before disappearing behind the barn.

Fur grumbled and continued at his own pace. He was stronger than his sister, but her agility and stamina were greater than his. He knew that, but for the first time, he didn't care. He could hunt better all the time. They didn't need to sit hoping Roger would feed them some pitifully rare scraps or a small bit of milk. He would be able to take care of them and one day, he thought to himself, the coyotes themselves would fear his coming.

He reached the back of the barn to find Momma still searching for water. The troughs and dishes were still dry as the fall rains had not yet begun and Roger was not there to fill them with the hose. She looked everywhere that water usually was kept but found nothing. She looked towards the stream with longing, but she was still too weak to risk it. She trotted around the barn where the hose that Roger used had lay. It was still there.

Water dripped slowly where the hose attached to the spigot on the wall of the barn. Each drip took several seconds to form and as soon as it hit the dirt, it was absorbed by the greedy dry earth. She licked the connection where it was wet. That would take forever just to get anything. She whined softly and pawed at the hose. She could smell the water but knew that touching hoses was forbidden. She stared at the house for a moment as if somehow Roger would suddenly appear as soon as she touched the neatly coiled rings. She kept her eyes facing the door as she slowly picked up one coil and bit down firmly. Water began to spray through the holes, wetting her face, but of course the house remained silent.

She began to lap the water as it sprayed, slowly, still nervous. Though she knew Roger was gone, deep inside her psyche, she knew she was being a bad dog.

The pups moved closer and Momma looked up, as if noticing them for the first time. They moved in closer, eager to taste the cool, clean water. "Go ahead," Momma said softly. "It's ok. Roger is gone." It was more to herself than the pups who could barely wait. Both pups darted in lapping amidst the spray and loving every minute of it. They drank and played in it throughout the heat of the day as the leaking water made puddles and wet the grass all around them.

Momma watched them in between resting and napping and drinking for herself. Lost in their own silliness, they did not see the times when Momma would lay with her head on her paws, smiling gently at the antics of her pups. They could know a life of happiness that she herself had never experienced. They could have a life without fear. They could laugh and play and catch food and never again know the cruelty of humans. They could all be happy. This could be the life for all of them. And it will be, she vowed to herself. Never again would she live under the confines and harshness of man.

Momma stood, feeling somehow stronger and more determined. She would teach them how to survive. "Come," she said suddenly. "There are rats to be had for dinner."

She turned and trotted as well as she could up towards the house and its scrap pile. The pups fell in behind.

Chapter 7
Wild and Free

As the time wore on, the pups grew lanky and lean. Food was never plentiful, but even though the rats grew more scarce and more wily, the occasional trespasser ensured their survival. Momma also gained strength and although she was not young, she felt better mentally than she had for some time.

The occasional person would come to the farm. It was always the same. A talkative person who left behind the strong scent of human perfumes and soaps, would lead people around showing them the house and sometimes even the barn. The visits were infrequent and the dogs always laid low and waited for them to return to their cars and drive out again before coming back into the open.

It was a good time and despite the frequent bouts of emptiness in their stomachs, the pups often frolicked and rolled in the grass. Momma would sleep for hours in the shade of the trees as fears of Roger's return ceased to be a concern. The hose at the house had stopped running but a few good rains had left an ample supply of water in the buckets, troughs and dishes scattered about the farm. The air was cooler and the scorching heat of summer was gone for the season.

In the early hours of dawn, on a frosty day in early October, Wee awoke to find her mother staring intently out the barn doors. She seemed indecisive. Wee looked around the barn to see that Fur was already gone. She stood and walked to the barn opening to see what her mother was watching. It was an animal, something like a goat but alert and wild. Its ears twitched and it tested the scents on the wind. Wee was unsure what it was, but she was also no longer a tiny foolish pup and she made no sound and asked no questions. She simply stood beside her mother, almost as tall, but more narrow, and waited for some indication of what she was to do. The young deer tested some tender branches that had grown that summer where the goats had once fed. Everything about its movements, cautious and measured.

Whatever her mother had been thinking, the decision was made for them when Fur, by now taller than his mother and a decent novice hunter, came up out of the grass just a couple of yards from the young deer. Too late, she realized she had walked into danger. The young doe turned as if to flee but Fur's jaws caught the side of her neck and he held tight.

As the deer struggled to free herself, Momma had made her decision. She was already taking long strides to close the distance between the barn and her son.

Fur was losing his grip and he knew it, yet if he tried to get a better purchase, the deer would have her chance to escape. All he could do was try to clench his jaws tighter and try to maintain his tenuous hold. This was his first attempt at something larger than he was and try as he might, he felt his jaws slipping, his teeth tearing skin and muscle, but knowing his bite would not stop his prey from escaping.

Momma arrived just in time, leaping up and grabbing the flailing deer by the nose. Able to release for just a moment, Fur latched back on to the neck of the doe and gripped her tightly. Wee was unsure of her role in all this. She had killed rats and possums and a small coon once, but never anything like this. At a loss, she darted in and out, snapping and biting, grabbing and tearing. She moved to the rear and darted in again, biting at the legs and was awarded a sharp hoof to the face. Ignoring the pain, she ducked in once more, grabbing the leg and refusing to let go as it jerked and thrashed until she was forced to release it again. They lacked any real skill for such things, but the deer was young and inexperienced and they were determined.

In the end, by the time it was over, the deer lay still and the dogs stood panting and gasping for several minutes before they finally laid down next to their kill. Too exhausted to even attempt to eat, they lay there in the mess on the grass and rested.

When Wee awoke, it was to the sound of Fur gnawing on their hard-won feast. She stood up and began testing the area around one of the wounds she had inflicted. She glanced over at Momma who was still asleep in the grass. "Don't worry about her," Fur said softly. "There is plenty for everyone."
She looked back at their meal and realized this was true. She also noticed that at the moment, Fur was not acting proud or boasting about initiating the takedown. She looked at him standing with his head low, tearing at the neck where he had fought so hard to hold on. For a moment, she was looking at him through the eyes of a stranger and she realized just how much he had grown from her silly bumbling brother. This had taken all of them, working together. It wasn't his victory, it was all of theirs. She settled in to eat her share and for a time, she thought of nothing else.

At some point Momma got up to join them and Wee moved over so that Momma could eat where it was already opened. She knew her mother was not as young and she feared the struggle had taken a lot out of her strength. Momma accepted her offer without reservation and Wee knew she had been right. She was not sure that made her feel better.

All day, they picked and ate and slept, just enjoying the feeling of absolute gluttony. It was one of the first times they could remember being full and still having more food. It was a blissful day, despite the sore muscles and aching jaws. When evening came, they fell asleep like napping people after Thanksgiving dinner.

Wee was awakened by the low deep growl of a dog. Rising quickly, she realized it was the threatening voice of her brother. Momma was already on her feet, head down, lips curled making a low growl of her own. Even before she saw them, Wee smelled their scent and her blood ran cold. For a moment, she was a small pup again, running along the fence looking for safety with the sound of her mother's angry snarls still audible in the night. There were at least five of them. Less than there could have been but they were still outnumbered. She looked to her mother and at Fur and realized they planned to fight.

Perhaps it was their success that day or perhaps the strong desire to feel full again tomorrow but Wee knew they were going to hold their ground. She too lowered her head and growled at the would-be thieves. Momma advanced and they fell in, beside her. The coyotes hesitated to cross the fence. They had lost these fights before, many months ago. They knew this white she-devil and one of them bore the scars to prove it. The pups, though young, were no longer hapless babes and Fur at the very least, though inexperienced, was now much larger than his canine cousins.

Momma could see their hesitation and watched their indecision. For a moment, she felt a great pride as this was the life she had once known. A life where coyotes fled the white death, which were her and her brethren. Perhaps, one day, they would again not dare to step foot on the fields of her and her kin. And all the while she was recalling her days of glory, she was advancing. The pups, keeping pace on either side, slowly moved apart to engage the invaders. It worked. Whether or not they'd have won, the coyotes were sure to incur injuries and their run-ins with the new men and their loud sticks that took a life in a second, the ones who actively hunted them, the way they hunted prey, had already impacted their numbers. If the takeover would not be easy, they were wise enough not to risk it.

As the coyotes slunk off into the shadows, Wee breathed a small sigh of relief. Momma stood proud and silent and Fur huffed a snort of disappointment. If Wee hadn't felt a little shaky, she'd have made a comment about his getting too sure of himself. Instead, she said nothing. They silently returned to their kill and began to gnaw on various bones, not out of any real hunger, but just because they could.

In the days that followed. They ate less but it was sufficient. They gained some weight off that kill and their coats grew thicker and shinier. They laid in the chill morning air and enjoyed chewing the marrow out of every last bone. They even caught a few would-be scavengers to add to their meals. They played and slept and for a time, that was enough.

Chapter 8
Life On The Outside

As the mornings grew colder, a change had
come over the dogs. They felt more confident in
their surroundings. They worried less about
what might come from beyond their fence line
and spent more time claiming their territory. The
helpless pups were no more. Although they
were by no means adults, they were large
enough to make an impression, as their brief
run in with the coyotes had shown. So with that
new confidence, when the food began to run
low, they began to watch what they could see
beyond their fenced boundary.

It was Fur who made the first excursion late one
evening when he could see something moving
the tall brown blades of grass in the unused
field. He paced along the fence, trying for a
better view and finding none, he put his feet up
on the top and silently went over.
He returned with the possum to find his mother
watching him. She looked tense. He walked
over and dropped the small body on the
ground. "Next time," he said, looking Momma in
the eye, "we should all go together." His
mother's solemn nod said he hadn't sounded
too smug about knowing what she was going to
say.

They shared the possum and spoke little. They were all considering their options. If the food was going to be out there, they would have to go get it. They all knew it. Although it meant more possible dangers, none of them were willingly going to go back to the days of struggling for a few morsels. They would have to risk their safety if they wanted to do more than to exist, hoping some small critter would wander into their domain.

It was Momma who spoke first. "We will stay in the area by the stream. There, if necessary, we will be able to retreat back here to avoid both coyotes and man."

"Perhaps," replied Fur, "The coyotes should be retreating from us."

"Do you know why the coyotes retreat?" Momma's gaze was serious, as she spoke.

"Because they are mangy cowards."

Momma hesitated. They were that and she loathed them with every fiber of her being.

"Yes," she said. "But coyotes also know that if they can not hunt, they can not eat" she paused for a moment, "and neither can we."

Fur wanted to argue. He wanted to boast with every fiber of his adolescent pride. His mother's missing eye and the scar going across the head, made him stifle the words he wanted to say. He might risk his safety, but he would not risk hers. If they were going together, he could not put her in unwarranted danger.

Wee quietly watched the exchange and was surprised her brother had not let his ego get the better of him. Sometimes he was mature at the most unexpected of moments.

She stood up and looked to the fence line. "It's probably too late now. At least we had something. Maybe tomorrow we can go out."

Fur suddenly found an outlet for his pride. "And who made sure you had something to eat?"

She rolled her eyes. He was instantly a little boy again. "You did, oh mighty Fur," she said with a slight bow. She couldn't help it and started to giggle. Fur leaped on her growling and as Wee squirmed out from under him, they were off tumbling and wrestling on the dry grass.

The old dog smiled inwardly and made her way up to the barn to lay in one of the forward most stalls. It had been her place, back when things were different. As much as she missed the comfort of the days when she knew what each day would bring, the lack of humankind was also very peaceful.

After a short bout of play, Fur and Wee instinctively trotted along the perimeter of the fence checking along the wooded area and back up towards the house. When all was quiet and there was no smell or sound to signal any possible intruder, they joined their mother in the barn. Fur took up a spot of old hay, not far from his mother and Wee lay near the doorway looking out over the fields. There they dozed until the early morning hours.

Wee awoke to the sound of quiet voices - human voices. She lay as still as the straw on the floor and watched the two men. One of them was bent down looking at the hole under the fence.

"Hey, Luke! What do you make of this?"

The other man approached and knelt down. He pulled a few loose hairs off the wires. "It certainly isn't coyote hair."

Barry pulled a few hairs off as well. "You think something is living in the old farm?"

"I doubt it," Luke replied, standing back up. "The old man had dogs, but I heard they went with the sheep. It's probably been there for quite a while."

"I guess," Barry said. "Were they white?"

"Yep. They were some kind of guardian dog."

Barry turned away and then paused. "You ever think about getting some of your own? Then we wouldn't be out here chasing coyotes all night."

"Hell, no!" Luke looked disgusted. I've seen them things out on ranches. A bunch of feral, vicious beasts. Tina and I wanna have a family. I don't want to have to worry about some giant dogs attacking my kids."

Barry sighed. "Wishful thinking we could sleep, I guess "

"Believe me," Luke said, rubbing the back of his neck, "I'm as tired as you, but every ranch out here has lost something. Goats, sheep, even a few calves. We haven't since the first week. The only thing keeping us from being in the same shape as the rest of them is being out here."

Barry sighed again. "I know Lucas. I know."

Wee watched as the men faded off out of sight, still talking quietly. She backed up slowly and stood to her feet. She turned and looked to see Fur standing to her left, just slightly behind.

"Did you see them?" She realized she was shaking slightly.

"Fur whispered in return. "I heard them. Do you think they were looking for us?"

"I don't know. They were looking at our hole. They stayed outside the fence though."

Momma joined them. "We just have to stay out of sight. Humans can't smell so if they don't see us, they won't know we're here "

Fur looked at his mother in disbelief. "They can't smell anything?"

"Well, maybe if something is really dead or if the milk is really soured, but they can't smell much."

"How do they hunt?" Wee asked.

"They use sight, Momma said. They look for tracks or….

"Flattened grass?" Wee interrupted.

"Yes, said Momma. "Those kinds of things. But in the dark, they can't see much at all unless the moon is very bright. They have to use lights, like Roger did when he came to check at night."

Wee walked back to the doorway. She could neither see, nor hear the men who had come to the fence. She sighed. Humans may not be able to smell or see very well, but they were awful. Just when things had seemed peaceful, they had to ruin it.

She slowly left the barn and headed out along the corral. She was careful in case they were hiding. Her mind flashed images of Roger trying to get her to come in the barn. They were sneaky, when they wanted to catch you.

She made her way along the fence, sniffing the air and listening for any sound. Cautiously, she made her way to the hole. She had been afraid it would be blocked, like the way Roger had blocked under the shed. It wasn't though. They had left it, the way they had found it, though their awful smell still lingered in the air.

She felt Fur's presence and was glad he had followed.

"They may not smell, but they certainly stink," Fur said quietly.

"They sure do." Wee whispered back. "I hope they just stay away. "

She didn't like the way they made her tremble inside. She didn't like their loud sticks that killed things far away. And she didn't like that they always seemed to hate them. She decided coyotes were better than humans.

Chapter 9
Into The Night

Early that evening, when the sun started to set, the trio slipped out under the fence and into the field beyond. As Wee passed through, she stopped and looked back. The hole seemed awkward now. The freshness of the man smell had already begun to fade and yet the space seemed less safe, as if their presence had left a permanent mark. She shook off the feeling and followed her mother quietly to the stream.

The human smell was there as well, but Wee ignored it. They were out here for a purpose and the sooner they achieved it, the sooner they could retreat to safety. If they were going to eat tonight, she had to stay focused.

She looked up from drinking and saw Fur watching her. "They're gone," he said. She wondered if he felt awkward too.
"I know," she replied quietly. Let's find something to eat"

They headed off, neither far apart, nor closely bunched together. Each was sniffing the wind and the grass and hoping to catch the scent or sound of something that would diminish the rumbling in their stomachs.

Wee continued along, trying not to pay attention to the human smells and trying to ignore the feeling that they were the trespassers. She headed off along the edge of the field that bordered the wooded area on the other side of the fence. The chilly night air brought many scents and as the light disappeared from the day, she forgot about the humans and what their actions might mean.

After a short time, she curved back and followed the natural winding path of the stream. It was not long before she saw movement along the top of the banking. It was a short, wide creature, digging and scratching in the dirt seemingly nibbling this and that as it found what it was looking for. It was neither possum nor raccoon but surely, it must be edible.
She moved in slowly trying not to frighten it before she was close. It moved a few yards further and began digging again. She was quite close and beginning to crouch for the final dash when it looked up at her. It made small noises and turned its back to her. "This will be easy," Wee thought to herself. "It doesn't even run." She darted towards it suddenly and as she opened her mouth to grab it, she was hit by the most foul, awful cloud. Her eyes were suddenly on fire, her throat was on fire, even her nostrils were on fire. Unable to see, she back pedaled and fell down the embankment and into the

stream. She sputtered and made her way up the other side where she fell gagging and retching on the opposite bank. She rubbed her face in the grass, over and over, whining softly and trying to regain some composure.

"What did you do?" Fur asked, coughing slightly at the fog which surrounded her.

She did not answer. She just continued to try to get the burning sensation to cease and her eyes to stop watering. Fur sat back and said nothing.

After several minutes, when the worst part of the agony had lessened, she made her way back down the embankment and began to drink. It wasn't pleasant. The water did nothing for the awful burning in her throat and eventually, she simply wandered back up onto the grass and lay down. When she looked across the stream, there on the opposite bank, the wretched creature was still digging up small roots and eating them.

Fur saw it as well and started to move forward.

"Don't," Wee said weakly. "That is what did this."

Fur looked at her incredulously. "That? That, did this to you?"

Wee nodded. "Yes."

"It looks so… so stupid."

"I know," Wee told him. "I know. I thought it would be easy."

A sharp yip carried through the silence. Momma was calling them. Fur looked at his sister. "Can you make it, stinky?" She would have glared, but at the moment, she was too miserable to care and simply nodded. He turned and headed in the direction the yip had come from as it sounded again. Wee got to her feet and padded sullenly behind him. Fur did look back once or twice before deciding she was capable of following and headed off into the night.

When they reached their mother, she had killed a rather large possum. It was something at least. Momma looked at Wee, who stood with her head hung. "You have to sneak up on them and grab them by the head," she said softly. Fur snorted in disgust. "Who would want to eat that anyway?"
Momma chuckled. "It's not so bad if you do it quickly." She paused, then said, "Come on, let's eat."
Wee shook her head and then flopped down with her head on her paws. She didn't want to eat. She didn't want anything. Everything tasted bad. She just wanted to feel better. She watched them eat their dinner, feeling somewhat sorry for herself.
When the pair had finished eating with a forlorn Wee looking on, they quietly made their way back to the space under the fence and returned to the barn to sleep

Chapter 10
A Change Of Course

When morning came, Wee finally felt better
about the events of the night before. The sting
had diminished, and she was extremely thirsty
and hungry. While there was little she could do
about the hunger at the moment, she could go
get herself a drink. She slipped out of the barn
into the frosty morning air and headed down to
the space beneath the fence. She was
cautious. It was almost daylight, a time when
humans seemed to be on the move. Seeing
and hearing nothing out of the ordinary, she
continued down to the water's edge and drank
without that terrible taste that had coated her
mouth and throat the previous night.

She came back up from the stream and looked
around. She wished she had eaten the previous
night but between the retching and her desire
for self-pity, she had foregone the simple meal.
Instead of crossing back under the fence, she
began searching the grass between the fence
line and the water, much as she had the night
before. She was hoping to encounter some
small bit of food that would lessen her hunger
until nightfall. Her efforts paid off as a tiny field
mouse darted through the grass in front of her.
She pounced, caught it under her paws and

snapped it up in one gulp. It was something at least. A few more and she would at least feel less empty.

It wasn't long before she found herself much where she had been last night. She could smell the odor and moved further away just in case that thing was still around somewhere. She passed on and as she made her way around a bend in the bank, she stopped short. Wee slunk down onto her belly and lay as still as could be. Her heart started racing but she dared not move. About fifty feet or so, ahead of her were the human men, focused on something that was on the ground. The smell of what they were looking at, reached Wee. It was a delicious smell, one that stirred a rumbling in her stomach, but she dared not move.

Lucas Porter looked at the wounds and punctures on the partially eaten goat. He felt angry. It didn't belong to him, but it was just one more loss for the local people. His brother stood up. "I guess we can tell Benson, they don't have to search for this one. How did it end up way out here?"
Lucas sighed. "I'm guessing a 300lb Boer was no easy kill, especially with part of the pack after the does. They probably harried and chased it until they were able to take him down.

Just when I think we're making a difference, it seems we've made no difference at all."

Barry ran his hand over his nearly trimmed beard. "Look. I know you want us to take care of this problem, but we can't defend everyone. The Wyman family is blaming us for their latest losses. They say we're riling them up and chasing them down their way."

Lucas spat. "Then why don't they get out there and protect their own flocks."

Barry began to move away from the goat looking for signs of what had led up to the buck's fate.

"Maybe," he said after pausing to look at blood droplets on the ground, "some people like to sleep at night."

They kept moving away, following the trail back the way the buck and his pursuers had come. Wee, lying silently upright, motionless in the weeds, breathed a sigh of relief. As soon as there was some distance between her and the men, she slunk back towards home, forgetting all about her hungry stomach and slipped under the fence and trotted directly to the barn.

When she arrived both Fur and her mother looked anxious.

"Where were you?" Fur asked her.

She went further into the barn as if feeling not quite safe in the doorway. Then she told them both all that she had seen.

Momma was quiet as Wee told her story. She wished the humans would just stay away. She feared one day, the men would get curious and cross the fence.

She looked at Wee. "I know you were thirsty, but we can't go out in the daylight. Not ever. If the humans find us, they will likely not be satisfied with leaving us alone."

Wee felt disheartened. She wished there were no humans and no sticks that go boom and that they could just live in peace, but such was never the case. With a huff, she sank to the floor. The barn, which had been their sanctuary, was feeling something like a prison.

Chapter 11
Things In The Night

By the time dusk began to creep in and the trio felt safe to leave the barn, Wee felt no better. She had spent the day lying in the barn and had barely spoken to Fur at all. She didn't feel much like hunting for food despite having missed the meal from the previous night. She just wanted to sulk.

Momma led the way down to the fence and slipped under. When they reached the stream and had drunk their fill, Momma looked at Wee. "Why don't you show us what the humans found? Maybe there is something left."

Wee crinkled her forehead. "You want to go where the humans were?"

"You said it smelled wonderful. I'm sure the humans are long gone and we'll be careful." Momma said the last part more softly.

"Okay. Maybe we'll find something." Wee didn't feel like searching for food and maybe this would be easier. She turned back up the bank and led the way along the stream.

When they reached the place of the skunk, Wee still gave the area a wide berth. Momma may bite their heads but she wasn't risking any encounters. Once had been enough for her.

As they rounded the bend where Wee had crouched in the grass earlier that day, she stopped and looked across out towards a slight incline. "It's up there," she whispered. Momma could already smell the scent, but she told the children to stay and circled out about the area. She stayed close to the ground, half crouched, looking for any sign of man or beast.

After circling around and finding no sign of anyone, she came back to the two pups. "Come on," she said softly. "Let's go get some food." She led out, still coming around from the other side and testing the wind. The night was relatively silent except for the distant sound of a barking dog.

They reached the goat lying in the grass and for a moment she hesitated. She sniffed it over. Once, this could have been one of her charges, but now, there was nothing she could do to protect it. She shook off the moment of awkwardness and looked up at the waiting pups. "Let's eat."

"Wow, said Fur. "There is so much!" Even Wee couldn't believe how much food lay before them. It was a feast and then some. They could eat for days.

It took little time before all three fell to eating and it would be some hours with their bellies bloated, that they finally had eaten all that they could. Despite the desire to sleep, the lingering smell of both coyote and man was enough to make them finally leave the incline and make their way back to the barn as the moon rose high in the night. Once there, they collapsed on the barn floor and slept. There had been few times in the pups' lives that they had not felt hungry. They slept as well as they had eaten. And as the moon rose high into the night, the coyotes moved quietly, cautiously up the incline and helped themselves to the remains.

And while the dogs slept well into the morning, three men would stand over the scattered remnants of the goat carcass.

Lucas, looking tired and as annoyed as the day before, was surveying the scene the coyotes had left behind. "Looks like they came back for it, Mr. Benson. There was a lot more yesterday."

The older man frowned and shook his head. "That goat cost me $1600 plus the cost of bringing him from Missouri. Now, the only thing I got is the hopes the does don't miscarry after all that running. I don't even think they was all bred."

"It's a terrible thing, Sir," Barry said quietly, seeing the strain in the old man's face."

The old man looked towards the direction of the barn where the dogs were currently sleeping. "You know," he said. Roger wasn't the easiest man to get along with, but he had at least half a dozen dogs out here at one point. They were feral as the dickens and you sure didn't want to come up here, but they kept these damn coyotes in check. When Roger decided to retire, he sold off them dogs with the sheep and now, I swear, the damn yotes are running unchecked and fearless to boot."

Barry Porter looked up and asked, "You ever think about getting some dogs?"

"I would if I could," the old man answered, "but I don't have that kind of farm. I don't take my stock to auctions or markets. My buyers come to the farm. They wanna see what they're getting and how it's kept. I can't have some wild dogs running around. Someone gets bitten and there goes the whole place. But you guys, you got plenty of room. Hell, I'll bet Roger would sell off some of this. He's had the place up for sale, but ya know, it needs some repairs and the house ain't nothing fancy and not a lot of people want to get into ranching these days. They want things that'll make money. You guys though, you could have dogs."

"Nooo!" Lucas said immediately. "Tina and I want a family. I'm not gonna have to worry about some crazy dogs going after one of my kids. I knew some people and their kids weren't allowed anywhere out in the fields. I want my kids to be able to help out, learn to drive the tractor, learn about shearing and to take care of the lambs. Those dogs aren't for me."

"Well, just make sure the coyotes don't eat your kids instead," Mr. Benson said bitterly. "It doesn't seem to be getting better."

Lucas tried not to react, knowing how much the loss of the new buck was affecting the old man's mood. "I'll get them coyotes under control. It's just gonna take a little time."

The old man began to walk back the way they had come. "Maybe next time, you can come around and chase em out your way, instead of up towards mine."

Lucas felt the blood rush to his face as the anger crept in. "I ain't running em anywhere. I'm dropping em where they stand. They just know my place is more dangerous. Maybe if I had someone else losing a little sleep over it, we'd get it done faster."

The old man slowed and hung his head, "I know," he said. "But I ain't got it in me to go traipsing around in the dark all night, anymore. And people like the Wymans just don't get it. They don't realize it was the dogs that kept things mostly peaceful. They think if they leave the predators alone, they'll leave the stock alone. They're blaming you, but it ain't that. They know they have nothing to fear."

Lucas quieted his anger, knowing the old man was just frustrated. "I know it hurts. I've lost stock too. I won't give up on this. I'll get their numbers down and the losses will drop. The Wymans can think what they want but in the long run, I'm helping them too. They'll have to see it eventually. And if they don't, it won't matter. Let them think it's God's grace or nature's majesty or whatever they want to come up with. I'll be helping them either way."

Inside, Barry sighed. Apparently, a good night's sleep was not in his future.

Chapter 12
The Beginning and the End

When the dogs finally awoke, all was quiet and still. The frost from last night, still laying on the shadowed places and the air was crisp and cold. They lazed around for the better part of the day, still feeling content from the previous night's meal. They had eaten a lion's share of that goat and no one was inclined to move much further than a comfortable distance to relieve themselves.

When the light began to fade, it was thirst and not hunger that drove them to duck out under the fence and return to the stream. Returning to the crest of the bank, the wind brought to them the smell of coyotes. They had been here at some point, not right here, but close.

Fur was the first to speak. "I'll bet they came back and ate the rest of our food," he said, sounding annoyed.

Momma sighed. "Most likely. It was their kill, after all. We would never do such a thing," she said, her distaste evident in her voice.

"But.. We kill things all the time," Fur sputtered.

His mother looked at him reproachfully. "It is our duty to protect the animals of man. We do not harm them and a dog who does, will suffer the same fate, as I did, for biting."

"Then why did we eat it?" Wee asked. "If it's forbidden, why would we touch it.?"

"It was already gone," Momma said, simply. "Nothing we did or didn't do would change that."

"So," Fur said after a moment, "It wouldn't be wrong if we snuck up there and grabbed a bone to chew on or something?"

Momma shook her head. "We can. We should just be careful."

They headed out with Momma in the lead this time, moving out through the brush filled areas and circling around through a stand of trees to come out onto the top of the incline. The smell of coyote was everywhere and even fresher was the scent of man. What had seemed like a good idea, to quell their boredom, seemed less safe now.

The bones were scattered here and there and it was hard to smell if anything might be close due to the overwhelming scent of death and coyote and the stench of sweating, perfumed human. Suddenly, they did not want to be there. Momma whispered, "Grab a bone and we'll take it with us. I don't want to stay."

The pups did not like the idea of staying either and even looking for a good bone with some shreds of meat still attached seemed too long to be there. They all kind of hurriedly grabbed something and they went back down the way they had come, instinctively moving slightly crouched and making no noise. None of them felt comfortable until they were back, not only inside the fence, but inside the barn. They didn't even really want the bones now. They hadn't truly been hungry and the feelings of danger had stifled the desire for mindless chewing. They spoke little and eventually dozed off yet again, leaving the bones for the following day. Wee awoke in the middle of the night with a whimper. In her dreams, she had been trapped in the barn. The doors were shut and she was being hunted by a man with the face of Lucas Porter and carrying Roger's milk pail. She shuddered at the still clear images of trying to hide somewhere in the barn, while he followed from spot to spot.

She picked up her bone and brought it to the old hay to try to calm her mind and give her something else to focus on. Her mouth was dry from her imagined terror and her fears from earlier in the night. She wanted a drink. Giving up on the idea of the bone, she crept out into the field by the barn. She licked the frozen dew on dried leaves and stuck her tongue in old troughs and buckets. It was all just a tease and made her even more thirsty. She looked down towards the stream and then up towards the barn. Maybe she should try to awaken Fur. She knew she'd never hear the end of it, if she did. She could just go. It wasn't that far. She could just hurry down and back and it would only take a minute. She looked at the barn again, half hoping to see Fur appear in the doorway so she could pretend to allow him to tag along. When he didn't appear, she finally made her decision. She exhaled heavily and made her way to the space beneath the fence. She sniffed the air testing for some scent of danger. There was nothing but old leaves and frozen ground. She tucked her head and pushed out into the field beyond.

Staying silent as could be, she made her way down to the water's edge. As she bent to drink, her toes broke the thin ice along the shallowest part. She hesitated, but hearing nothing, she bowed her head and finally drank from the freezing cold water. It tasted so good. She drank until she was finally content and told herself she'd better get back. As she lifted her head, she saw a small movement on the top of the opposite bank. It was a small, dark creature with long ears, that hopped cautiously along the bank, nibbling little bits of dry grass. "What in the world is that thing?" She asked herself. And as suddenly as it had appeared, it moved off the edge and out of sight. Wee looked back towards home. Then she looked up the opposite bank where the thing had disappeared. Okay, just a small peek over the other bank. She crossed the water and crept up the opposite side. There was nothing there. She scanned the empty expanse before her.

Just as she was about to turn back, she saw it move. It was being very cautious. Its ridiculous ears turned this way and that. It would take a few bites and stop to look for danger, sometimes standing upright on two legs, before dropping back down and resuming its eating. Wee, hunched in the grass on her stomach, suddenly felt a desire to catch it. She had to be careful though because this thing was terribly alert. Wee wasn't very hungry, she was fascinated. She wanted to put her skills to the test. If she could catch it, she could bring it back to Momma, who would surely know what it was. Then she would also have bragging rights because she was quite certain that Fur had never seen one either. And if Momma agreed that they were hard to catch, that would be even better!

Every time the creature turned away and put its head down, Wee would inch forward. Sometimes, she would move a good bit and other times, it's head would come up before she'd barely moved at all. She closed in slowly wanting to be sure she could grab it in a short sprint. Suddenly, it moved forward, half a dozen hops. Wee almost gave herself away in her desire to sprint after it, thinking it had seen her. But she held her position. It apparently hadn't seen her. It was just weird. She continued her small movements when it wasn't watching.

Some part of her wanted to just dart and let it scurry away, so she could just go home to the barn, but her pride kept her there. Fur would be so surprised and surely Momma would be impressed.

She kept at the game. Using stealth and patience, she made her way closer and closer. Occasionally, it would hop further, but she didn't panic about it now. It was alert, but oblivious. Finally, it hopped a few short hops back in her direction. Wee knew this was the best chance she'd get. Like a flash, she leaped forward and the creature darted sideways. It was skilled in its own way, a master of escape. Wee hit the ground, already banking towards the fleeing rabbit and in two bounds, she grabbed it between her mouth and her paws. The scream of the rabbit was like nothing Wee had ever heard and she almost dropped it. In her attempt to keep a hold, she tightened her jaws quickly and the rabbit went limp and silent. Wee stood there breathless before dropping her prey. She sniffed its still warm body. It looked kind of simple now and she hoped Momma would back her story about the difficulty of killing it. Still, it was strange with its long ears and she hoped Fur would be intrigued by its appearance.

She picked it up in her mouth and looked out across the field. She had come quite a ways more than she'd realized and it took a moment to determine which way home actually was. Getting her bearings, she began to trot back in the general direction of the fence gap. She wanted to drop the thing in the barn and maybe take a nap. Movement like a shadow in the darkness caught her eye and for a moment, she thought Fur had followed her when he awoke and found her missing, but it was not Fur and it was not alone. The coyotes had heard the squeal of the rabbit as they lay up on the incline chewing on the remnants of their previous kill. There was an intruder in their territory and it was alone.

Chapter 13
Enemies Abound

Wee stopped in her tracks. She was young, but she was not unaware of the danger she was in. She thought of Momma and Fur, so close and yet too far away. Maybe they would hear something. If they did, they would certainly realize she was missing and come to her aid. Very likely, the coyotes would not want to take them all on. Yet, she couldn't just stand there and let them attack.

She let the rabbit fall from her mouth. Fur was the prideful one, yet she had let her own ego bring her to this point. Her desire to have Fur marvel at her skills was her undoing. She should have been cautious. She should have been smart. She was no better than Fur at all.

She looked up from her thoughts and realized the coyotes were fanning out around her as they moved closer. She felt suddenly small and vulnerable. She tried to think of what her course of action should be. Then without warning, she turned and ran. Wee ran as she had seldom run in her life. It was not with direction or thought. It was all about speed. She sensed them behind her and knew they were giving chase. All she could do was keep moving. Surely, they would give up. One stupid pup wasn't worth their time and effort, was it? Her lungs were starting to burn. Seldom in her life, had she had a chance to build endurance. Most times were spent trying to move quietly and unseen. Wrestling with Fur was not the same as what she was attempting now. She couldn't hear them over the sound of her own breathing and the rushing of her blood in her own ears as she tried to keep up her momentum.

Wee saw a brief flash of something dark and she was taken off her feet, somersaulting across the hard ground before spinning around to face her attackers. She felt sudden pain in her leg and turned, biting and snapping, only to have her teeth close on nothing, and the pain to begin on her back. So it continued. Every time she snapped and tried to retaliate, the attacker would dart away and another would move in. Eventually, Wee managed to gain her feet and tried her best to fight back. Her growls became more high-pitched, and her snapping was accompanied by cries and small whines. She had no conscious thoughts. It was simply the struggles of a creature who knows it will not win, but can not simply give in, and allow the end to come. They were careful, efficient creatures and they had done this many times. Darting and biting to avoid risk of injury, while slowly causing damage to their intended victim.

Wee's cries became more pitiful and the growling stopped. She was tired and she couldn't find the energy to even turn around. She just tried to keep her feet beneath her. Her vision seemed blurred and she barely noticed the pain anymore. Finally, blissfully, everything went dark.

Chapter 14
Dark Times

When Barry made it to the front porch of his cabin, still holding his shirt in his hand, Lucas was already moving across the yard of the main house out towards the field. Barry grabbed his own gun from inside the door and raced to catch up. They didn't speak. They both had the same thoughts. The coyotes were close and they definitely had something.

As they made their way out into the field, through the herd of sheep, bunched at the gate, looking terrified and panicky, the men both feared the coyotes had breached the fence. Barry feared it most because he had pleaded with Lucas to take the night off and worry about important things like a hot meal and a good night's sleep. If they had lost stock because of it, he would never hear the end of it and he could forget about sleeping, ever again.

They pushed swiftly through the sheep and picked up the pace. The cackle of the coyotes was closer and they knew whatever they had wouldn't last long. The ewes were newly bred and any loss would be really two or three. Barry could hear Lucas's muttering as he ran. "One damn night. They couldn't give us just one damned night."

Barry knew that deep down Lucas had been just as happy to grudgingly have a night off. He and Tina had been chatting happily that evening, discussing the ranch, the future and all of their plans. They had sat together by the small outdoor fire looking content as they snuggled on the bench in the backyard. Now Lucas was regretting his decision and berating himself for living life for a moment.

They slowed their movements, as the coyotes came into view and Lucas was the first to raise his rifle and fire into the group. He did not miss. Barry's shot came only a second after. Lucas fired again as the coyotes began to scatter. They were in the open though, a big mistake on their part. More than half a dozen lost their lives and others were wounded. They moved to the scene of the kill, still keeping an eye out for any movement.

The men barely paused at the bloody lump lying against the grass. Lucas fired at the silhouette of an injured coyote trying to regain its feet. It collapsed silently into the dark. They kept moving. If they had any chance to do more damage to the pack, this was the time. They moved quietly, keeping each other in sight, but watching for movement in the other directions. They managed to take out a few more before they finally paused. The adrenaline and anger were wearing off and Barry was beginning to feel the effects of not having worn a jacket. It was cold and the sweat on his body was beginning to cool. He shivered slightly. Still silent, they began to make their way back.

As they came to the area where the coyotes had been, they noticed the light shining among the carnage. Tina! Lucas picked up his pace. If that was one of their new ewes, he knew she would be heartbroken. She wasn't a totally soft woman, but these sheep represented their dreams and their future. And Tina hadn't grown up on a ranch. She took the losses a bit more to heart. She was crouched down among the coyote bodies, looking over something on the ground. At their approach, she stood and held out something to Barry. "I thought you might be cold," she said softly. Barry took the coat gratefully and as he put it on, she bent back down to whatever she had been looking at. It was bloody and looked misshapen in the dim light.

"It doesn't look like it was a sheep," Lucas told her.

She glanced up at him briefly. "It's.." She paused. "It's a dog."

Lucas's voice grew cold. "Are you telling me there was a dog running with the coyotes?"

"No! No, Luke. That's what they were killing."

Both men moved in closer and bent down.

"I wonder whose dog it was," Barry said quietly. He could tell Tina was upset by the quarry being a pet.

Tina ran her hands gently over the body. "I don't think it's anyone's dog. At least, I hope not. It's nothing, but skin and bones." She touched it again gently. "And it's not WAS. The dog is still breathing."

Both men looked at each other, over the woman's head. They knew where this was going and there was no stopping it.

She glanced up at Lucas. "Will you go warm up the truck and find something to put on the back seat?"

Lucas stroked his chin with one hand and sighed. "Sure," he said quietly. "Let me go see what I can find."

Without another word, he headed back towards home.

Lucas was known as a stern man. He grew up on a ranch and was used to making the hard decisions. When he and Tina had met, there had just been something about her quiet manner and gentle ways. She wasn't weak though. She had an inner strength, as well as grit and determination. Yet, she brought peace into Lucas's heart and he felt a softness when he was with her. Yet, there were times when she would feel strongly about something. And although most times, she didn't argue with Lucas, there were sometimes when she would not back down. He'd known her long enough to know that this was one of those times. "If only she hadn't followed us." He thought. He probably would have simply ended the creature's suffering. He sighed again. Such was not to be. He started the truck and went into the house and looked around. He finally settled on one of the older blankets on the chair in the living room and carried it outside as the sacrifice for the woman he loved.

By the time he had laid the blanket out to cover the seat, he could hear Barry and Tina talking. He looked up to see Tina opening the gate out of the field for Barry to pass through with the limp, lump of a stray dog. Lucas almost chuckled at Barry's string of short, reassuring responses to Tina's constant reminders like, "Be careful,' "Watch its head" and "Go easy." Even Barry knew that this was not the time to argue.

When Barry laid the dog on the seat as gently as possible, Tina said, "You guys can sit in the front and I'll ride in the back with the dog." Barry rolled his eyes as he looked at his brother. Yep, it was gonna be a family affair. He walked around the truck and climbed in and as they closed the doors, Lucas shifted the truck into gear and drove out towards town.

An hour and fifteen minutes and a few phone calls later, they arrived at the emergency vet and Barry, already bloody, carried the dog inside. The receptionist stared at the mess in his arms, as Tina rambled on about the night's events. The receptionist made notes and asked questions while entering the information into the computer. The receptionist seemed disdainful of the people before her and hardly seemed to be paying attention to much of the story. Her demeanor remained cold and her questions succinct. She simply continued to ask for information in a monotone voice. "Boy or girl?" "I'm not sure," Tina replied. "It's badly hurt." "Any GUESS how old?" the receptionist asked. "No idea," Tina stated, the frustration beginning to creep into her voice.
Finally, she asked for the dog's name. Tina stared at her, blankly. Lucas leaned forward and sternly said, "She just told you we found the dog in a coyote attack. How would we know its name?"
The receptionist sputtered, "I have to put in a name for our records."
A red color crept into Lucas's face. He hadn't had much sleep and his patience was thin enough without the open distaste from the receptionist towards the trio, especially his wife.

"Make one up and get the doc out here, before this thing doesn't need saving."

The receptionist looked taken aback at his abruptness, but she typed in a few quick letters before looking up at Lucas.

"I put Jesse, since you don't seem to know if it's a boy or a girl."

Tina silently put her hand on Lucas's arm. She didn't want to get thrown out of the vet's office, no matter how abhorrent she found the woman. Fortunately, the woman seemed done for the moment and walked away to pick up the phone and have a brief conversation with low mumbled words, they were sure were about them, before hanging up and telling them the vet would be right out. Tina took that moment to check the dog and was almost surprised to still find a weak heartbeat.

True to the receptionist's words, the vet came out just a few moments later, accompanied by two techs. He looked over the dog, still limp in Barry's arms. "My lord," he said, "Did you have it out there all by itself?"

"It's not ours." Tina said quietly. "We heard the coyotes attacking something and went to check."

"Oh, I see." His tone did not sound like he saw at all. "I'm surprised you bothered to bring it in."

Tina sighed. "Look. I just felt sorry for it. I know it's bad but I hate those coyotes and I just didn't want to leave it."

The vet looked at the woman and then the two men, suddenly feeling like he had a grasp on the situation.

When he spoke to Tina again, there was a small measure of compassion in his voice. Let's bring it into a room and we'll see what we can do."

They followed the vet into the small room with vet techs in tow and finally Barry was able to set the limp bundle on a table. The vet put on a pair of gloves and began checking the multiple wounds and punctures. Looking up, he noticed the crowded state of the exam room and looking at the woman before him, he said, "I'm going to need some room to work. Maybe some of you could stay in the waiting room." Lucas met the vet's gaze and said, "We'll all go out. Let me know when you know something."

He ignored the vet's look of resentment. Lucas was well aware that the vet had wanted Tina to stay, for some reason and furthermore, the vet knew that he knew. Barry pulled the door open and Lucas waited for Tina to walk out before following behind her.

They sat in the waiting area not really speaking and ignoring the occasional looks from the receptionist. Tina would occasionally look down the hall towards the door of the small room where they had left the dog in the vet's care. Lucas looked at the clock on the wall. It was 3:15. Soon it would be morning and the day at the ranch would begin. After a moment, Lucas spoke to Tina.

"It's almost morning and someone should put out hay and water. Why don't you let Barry take you home and he can feed up. I'll take care of things here. It's probably gonna be a while and we don't know how things are gonna go."

He did not say the rest of what he was thinking, but the look on Tina's face said she knew. "I just…" she started to say, then stopped. "I just feel like it deserves some chance. Out there alone and so thin, left to be coyote fodder. I just…" She trailed off again. She was trying to make her feelings known, but she also knew that even if it were possible to save the dog, they knew nothing about it. And money on the ranch did not come for free. There was only so much she could justify asking Lucas to spend. Lucas reached over and cupped his hand under her chin, tilting her head back. He saw the tired look on her face. He kissed her gently on the cheek and said, "Let me see what the vet has to say. We don't know anything yet. Go home. Get some rest and Barry can pick me up when I'm done here."

Tina nodded quietly and he could see that she was trying to hide the tears in her eyes. The sheep losses in the beginning had hit her hard. It was part of what drove him to stay on the coyotes. He put his arm around her and gently rubbed her back for a moment. Then he nodded at Barry and stepped away. Barry stood up and put his arm around Tina's, he gently led her out of the vet building. When she glanced back, Lucas tried to give a look of compassion. He watched them both get into the truck and waited for them to pull out of the lot before he walked over to a row of chairs and sat down.

Chapter 15
A Thing Of Love

Not long after Lucas sat down, he realized the vet was standing beside him. The fact that he had not seen the man approach told him he had nodded off. He sat up straighter as the vet sat down beside him. The vet looked at him for a moment as if trying to judge the man beside him. When he spoke his voice was quiet. "Listen," he said. "The dog is criminally thin and has multiple injuries, including internal damage." He glanced around as if expecting the woman to reappear. "It might be best if we just ended her suffering. It would be expensive for the surgeries and there would be a lot of care required after the fact. I'm sure you aren't prepared to devote that kind of time."

Lucas was quiet for a moment before speaking. Everything about the man beside him said he disliked Lucas, and Lucas was not the kind of man to let such things go unanswered.

"If you fix the dog, what are its chances of survival?"

The vet looked mildly surprised at the question. "Well," he said, "it could likely survive, but it will be a long time before it would be fit to work again. And it would need proper care and proper feed. It would have to be kept clean and watched for signs of any infection."

Lucas tried to hide his irritation. The man spoke as if feed and care would be cause for the decision to euthanize the dog. He stood up abruptly, startling the vet. His voice was tense when he spoke. "Fix the dog," he said.

The vet stood as well. "You realize," he said, looking Lucas right in the eyes. "You will still be responsible for the bill, even if it's not YOUR dog."

With sudden clarity, Lucas finally understood the issues the vet had with him. The man thought Lucas was lying. He thought this starving, bloody wreck actually belonged to Lucas. Did he think him poor? No, he thought him cruel, Lucas decided. He, and the receptionist, thought they were the ones who had left this emaciated animal to be attacked and almost killed by wild animals. For a moment, he was unsure what to even say.

He stepped back, away from the vet. He glanced at the receptionist, who quickly tried to pretend that she hadn't been paying attention. He looked back at the veterinarian, the color creeping back into his face, as he felt a surge of anger. When he spoke, his voice was calm. "If your receptionist wasn't so busy making judgements," he said coldly, "She would have been able to tell you this wasn't my dog. My brother and I thought the coyotes had one of our sheep, but when we were done shooting, my wife found the dog among the coyotes." He paused, but his eyes never left those of the man before him. He continued on. "My wife was upset when we lost sheep to the coyotes and she felt bad for the dog. I don't neglect my damn animals." Then slightly more loudly, he said, "Now fix the damn dog. And don't worry, I'll pay the bill."

The vet looked at him for a brief moment, then lowering his head, he nodded and walked out.

Chapter 16
Questioning Life Choices

It was several hours before Lucas called Barry to pick him up. He had nodded off in the chair several times. When Barry arrived to get him, he looked far more rested and freshly showered. Lucas, on the other hand, was exhausted, had a crick in his neck from falling asleep in the rigid, straight backed, waiting room chair and he was questioning his pride and his sanity.

He remained silent as Barry pulled out of the parking lot and headed back towards the ranch.

Lucas knew his brother was waiting for some kind of an answer. He wasn't sure he was ready to give it. "$3800! I just gave a man $3800 to fix some half dead, mutt puppy. He wouldn't spend that kind of money for anything that wasn't a horse. There was simply no way to justify that kind of expense, for the sake of proving to the vet that he was not the kind of person he believed him to be."

Lucas tried to swallow the nauseous feeling in the pit of his stomach and tried to find something to answer Barry's questioning glances. Finally, he simply said, "It's still alive." He hesitated but Barry said nothing. He just waited expectantly. "And according to the vet, it's probably only about six or seven months old. And it's female, but the vet spayed it for next to nothing."

He paused again, expecting Barry to say something, but his brother just kept driving, looking straight ahead and giving no sign of his thoughts. "He gave it shots too. But it has to stay there for a while to make sure everything is alright. They are gonna keep it sedated for a couple days to let things start to heal and watch for any issues."

He stopped talking and looked at Barry who was still driving silently. "Look!" Lucas said. Suddenly, Barry started to laugh. He laughed as if he'd just heard the funniest joke. Lucas didn't find it funny. He was tired and stressed and the pain in his neck wasn't improving his mood. He glared over at his brother. "What the hell makes this so damn funny?"

His brother glanced over at him. "Mr. I don't want any useless animals because everything has to pull its weight, now has a dog."

Lucas rubbed the back of his neck. "I didn't say I was keeping the damn thing."

Barry, chuckled. "You think Tina is gonna nurse that thing back to health and then want to get rid of it? He chuckled again. "You're a dog owner now, sure as anything."

Lucas slumped down in the seat, looking angry and said nothing more for the rest of the ride home. He didn't even speak when he got out of the truck. As he stalked up to the house, still warring with his inner turmoil, Barry called his name. He turned, expecting one more last comment, but instead Barry jogged the few steps to catch up. He spoke quietly, the obnoxious younger brother attitude gone for the moment. "Just go talk to Tina. I know she's been wondering about the outcome and I think she feels guilty for making you have to make the choice. Then go get some rest. I'll take care of the animals for tonight."

Lucas bowed his head. "Thanks," he said. "I'll go talk to her."

With that, he headed to the door and Barry left to head to his own cabin.

Lucas walked inside and quietly shut the door behind him. Tina was in the kitchen. The smell of something delicious made Lucas realize how long he had been without a meal. He walked into the kitchen and stood silently watching her put food on a plate.

"You must be starving," Tina said, without turning to look at him.

"I am," he agreed. "And the smell is making me even hungrier."

Tina added some warm rolls to the plate and began to butter them. She still had not turned around or made eye contact with her husband. He reached past her as she finished buttering and gently took the plate out of her hand. He sat at the table and began to eat. He couldn't think of anything else for the next ten minutes. When his hunger pangs had lessened, he noticed that Tina was busying herself with wiping the counter and putting clean dishes in the cabinets, still not looking at him. After a moment, he said casually, "So where exactly do you plan to keep that dog when it has to leave the vets?"

Tina almost dropped the cup in her hand, but managed to catch hold of it again and set it back on the counter. She remained not looking at him and when she spoke, her voice cracked slightly. "Oh Luke!" Her words cut off and she bowed her head.

Lucas got up from the table and walked over to where she was standing. He gently put his arms around her and leaned in close. There was a slight hitching to her shoulders and he knew she was crying. He leaned in close. "Dang this woman" he thought. But when he spoke his voice was softer. "The vet says it's going to need care and its wounds tended and kept clean. Where do you suppose we do that?"

She turned to him then and hugged him, still not speaking. She buried her face in his chest and tried to hide the tears running down her cheeks. He continued to just hold her silently. For some reason, $3800 didn't seem all that bad. He'd make it up when the lambs went to market. He just hoped Barry didn't find out. He'd never let him live it down. Lucas sighed and stroked her hair. At times like this, when she seemed so feminine and so fragile, he felt the need to give her whatever she needed.

When they finally moved apart, Lucas turned back to the table and without even sitting down, picked up the plate and quickly wolfed down his now lukewarm food. He suddenly felt very tired. He looked at his wife who had gone back to putting away the dishes. "Barry says he'll do evening chores. I'm going to take a quick shower and get some sleep."
Tina nodded but didn't speak. He took his now empty plate to the sink and rinsed It before setting it down. As he reached the doorway, Tina finally spoke. "Lucas…"
He paused and looked back "Thank you," she said softly.
He started to move towards the bathroom. "For everything." She said, "The waiting. The talking to the vet. For not letting it die." She trailed off.
"It's a girl," Lucas told her. "And I guess now her name is Jess."
Then without another word, he headed to the shower.

As Tina watched him leave, she gave a small smile. She couldn't believe it. Lucas had never been much of a dog person and when he suggested that she and Barry head home, she was sure it was so she wouldn't have to stay and hear the conversation. Lucas was always so practical and paying money for useless things was never a consideration. What had happened there at the vet's? What had made him decide to do something so unlike him? She really hadn't thought the dog would come back. Now she truly did need to find a place to keep her. Some place where she wouldn't bother Lucas. Somewhere that she could make her a good dog. She knew he would never keep a dog that was unruly or that was a danger to the animals on the ranch. If she wanted Jess to stay, she was going to have to make sure that she stayed out of Lucas's way and out of trouble.

Some minutes later Lucas climbed into bed and he fell asleep wondering how he'd gotten himself into this. When he finally drifted off, he slept well into the wee morning hours.

Chapter 17
A Bad Dream

Wee struggled for consciousness. Her senses were assailed by strange things and horrible scents. She heard strange noises and she felt cold and uncomfortable. She felt something touching her but she could not wake up and she could not move away. She whimpered softly. Then she faded out into darkness once more. In her dreams, sharp teeth and yellow eyes haunted her. She was lost and alone. For the next few days, she rode through those moments of struggling to awaken, her vivid nightmares, and total darkness.

When she finally awoke, it was not much better. Her eyes struggled to take in her surroundings. She didn't understand any of what she was seeing. She was in a place of bright lights and harsh smells. She tried to get up but nothing in her body seemed to work. She couldn't even lift her head. She wanted to panic but she couldn't seem to move. Her mind was fuzzy and nothing seemed to make sense. Then a door opened and a young woman passed into the room. Wee's breathing became rapid. It was a human. There was a human moving towards her and she couldn't move. She wanted to, but no part of her would respond. The woman heard her whimpering and noticed her eyes were open.

"Hey there. Look who finally woke up." The young woman's voice was shrill and it echoed in the emptiness of the room. Wee could do nothing but whimper. "You make an awful lot of noise," the woman said in her high-pitched voice. "I don't really think all that is necessary." She opened a door in front of Wee and reached in, touching her here and there, as she checked her over.

Wee tried to force her body to respond. She tried to fight off the grogginess that kept her from moving away from this woman and her loud noises. Instead, she just made more panicked, whimpering noises until the woman finally withdrew her hands and closed the cage door.

Wee was forced to listen as the woman continued on, occasionally opening other cages and making her strange noises. Wee continued to try to rise and make her body do what it should. Her paw twitched but nothing more. She kept trying. She began to fight her way out of the fog. But the more she did, the more she began to notice the pain creeping through her body. She felt like she should know why, but she couldn't remember. This nightmare she found herself in was worse than the dreams of the coyotes. "The coyotes!" Wee thought to herself. That was the last thing she remembered. The biting and the snarling. She remembered the fear and the weakness and then, nothing. It didn't make any sense to her. Where was she? She was startled out of her thoughts as the woman walked back by and this time, when she tried to move, her legs actually made an attempt to get under her. She flailed for a few seconds before the woman kept going and out the wooden door.

Wee tried to tell herself to stay calm. She had to be smart. She had to think. Then the wooden door opened again and a man in a white top came into the narrow room. Wee forgot all about calm and smart and began to whimper and flail again. She still couldn't get up, but she was going to try. She was still struggling when the man opened the cage door and timing it just right, he managed to grab her flailing leg and held it still.

Wee wanted to defend herself, but her mother's face came into her mind, and with it, her mother's warning about biting humans. She whimpered, as if his hand was burning her skin, but she did not bite. The man deftly injected something into the tube attached to her leg and calmly held it still. Wee continued to try to pull away, still making high pitched whines. Then all of a sudden, she felt weak and tired, and fight though she may, she slumped to the floor of the

cage and in a few moments, her head drooped
down upon her paws and she knew no more.

Chapter 18
Life Goes On

They had just loaded up the lambs for market when Lucas's phone rang. He pulled it out of his pocket. The number was not one he recognized. He pulled one glove off and answered the call. "Lucas Porter."
It took a moment for his brain to register what the voice on the other end was talking about. "Mr. Porter. This is Nancy at the Lakeview Emergency Clinic. Dr. Riley says that as long as the dog will eat, you can pick her up this afternoon."

At first, he had thought it was a call from a hospital and he was afraid something had happened to someone he knew. He struggled to come to terms with it being something totally different.
"Dog?" He replied.
The woman hesitated before answering. "Yes, Mr. Porter. Your dog you dropped off." She hesitated again, "Umm, Jesse. You brought her in after she was attacked."
"It's not my dog." Lucas replied, but then said "I'll be in to get her."
The woman paused, obviously confused.
"I'll be in to get the dog." Lucas stated and hung up the call.

Barry snickered under his breath. Lucas gave him a cold look and walked up along the side of the truck. He reached into his wallet, took out some cash and handed it to the driver. "Thanks a lot." Lucas stated and began walking up towards the house.

The driver looked puzzled. Usually, Lucas would discuss the ranch and market prices and the man would talk about his other deliveries and what they had brought in. Barry stepped up beside the truck. "Don't mind him." He said loudly. "He just doesn't want to be late to get his dog."

Barry watched the slight hesitation in Lucas's gait, but he kept walking. He laughed heartily, but did not explain further. "Take care." He said to the driver, still laughing. "We'll see you in the spring."

He began to follow Lucas, while the driver, no less confused, pulled the truck out through the gate and headed down the driveway, out past the house and onto the road.

Barry hurried to catch up to his brother. When he reached him, Lucas turned suddenly. "Look! I don't give a damn about that dog. I don't give a damn what happens to it. What I do care about is my wife. I just want her to feel like she saved it, not how we failed with the sheep. And when it's healthy, we'll find it a home."

Barry turned serious. "I know, Lucas. I know. I'm younger than you, but I still remember." He glanced down at Lucas's arm. He couldn't see the scars with his jacket on, but they were there. There was another along his left shoulder and a couple more on his back. Barry could still remember running, screaming for their dad. He remembered thinking Lucas was dead. Yeah, he remembered.

Lucas sighed. "I know you do," he said. "If not for you, I probably would have died that day."

Barry looked at his brother, shaking off the childhood memories. "Listen. Maybe this dog will be terrible. Maybe it won't. Plenty of nice dogs exist in the world. If nothing else, you'll have something in common. You'll both have scars all over."

Lucas shook his head. In spite of everything, he had to laugh. "You idiot." He chuckled.

Barry grinned.

"Go let Tina know that you're going to go pick up your dog. You want me to ride with you or you think Tina will want to go?" Barry tried to look casual while calling it his dog.

Lucas gave him a look, but didn't rise to the bait. He was going to say he wanted Barry's company, but he felt a panicky rise of adrenaline. What if the receptionist mentioned the price or had any additional charges. He didn't want anyone to ask questions about what he had spent. He tried to look calm. "No. That's okay. I'm not going to waste everyone's day. Tina can make sure she has the place all set to put her and you can do whatever it is you do around here."

Barry raised one eyebrow. Whatever I do, huh? I'll tell you what. Tomorrow I won't do it and you see if you can figure it out."

Lucas laughed. He knew Barry would get riled by that, but it was his revenge for all the dog comments. "Really funny." Barry told him, knowing full well that Lucas hadn't meant his words. "Why don't you go get your dog. Don't forget, you're gonna need a crate."

He paused. "Maybe a pretty collar. Don't forget food. Maybe some treats."

Lucas made a face filled with disgust. He rolled his eyes. Unfortunately, Barry wasn't wrong. He couldn't just let the dog loose in the shed. He would need a crate and it would need food. More money, he thought. He sighed. "I guess I'd better get going."

Barry saw the mental struggle inside his brother's head written on his face. He knew how Lucas felt about dogs in general. He just nodded, deciding not to provoke him any further. Lucas turned and walked away.

After Lucas informed Tina and left for town, he found himself thinking about the dog. He had only seen it unconscious. What if it did try to attack him? He felt his anxiety start to rise. It wasn't that big, but still. He tried to push the thoughts away and focus on what he needed to do. Whether he liked it or not this thing was now his responsibility. He eventually reached the parking lot of the department store and went inside. He looked around. This was not the kind of place Lucas ever went. His clothing was actually made for work and he had no use for trinkets. He knew Tina came here on occasion. She liked to go to town for her own kind of outing, once in a while. He wished he had brought her along, but he hadn't wanted her to have to deal with the people at the vet's office and he didn't even know what he'd say if the vet brought up the cost of the dog. A cost that apparently was still on going.

He began wandering down the various aisles looking for what he needed. There was everything here. Every unnecessary, useless thing a person could want. Bright sparkly things, blankets in many patterns and colors and more kitchen gadgets than he knew what to do with. He found himself wondering if Tina ever wanted some of these things. He would have to ask. They did have a toaster and a coffee pot, but here, they had little ovens devoted to toasting and all kinds of other things. Many of the things he saw, he had no idea what they were used for. Maybe one day, he should go here with Tina and see if any of them caught her eye.

A voice shook him out of his thoughts. "Excuse me. Were you looking for anything in particular?"

He looked over to see a young woman in a vest with a name tag that read Shelly. "No." Lucas replied, but then remembered why he came. "I'm looking for a dog crate. Something, maybe wooden or metal. Something so a dog can't bite me."

The woman looked at him with shock. After an awkward moment she asked, "Is this your dog?"

"No." Lucas said. And then realizing the woman was looking at him oddly, he tried to explain. "It was a stray. It's kind of wild. I have to pick it up from the vet and I'm not sure how it will react."

The woman's face lit up suddenly. "Oh my god!" she said, suddenly excited. "You are so sweet. That is so nice of you. Come with me and I'll help you!"

"Thanks." Lucas told her, a little surprised by her sudden excitement and the high pitch of her voice.

Shelly led him across the store and down one of the aisles. There she pointed out a row of large plastic crates on display. "How big is the dog?" she asked, still acting excited and giddy.

"Not really big." Lucas told her, "but it's still a puppy."

"Do you know what kind it is?"

Lucas shook his head. "No. We found her injured in a field."

"Oh, that's so sad. Is it a boy or a girl?"

"Girl." Lucas replied. "The vet said it was a girl."

So, it went, with her leading him around the store all babbling and excitement. He nodded, replied and tried to ignore the slow creeping pain in his temples. Thirty or so minutes later, he was leaving with a large crate, a collar, a leash, some supposedly healthy food, dishes and $320 less in his bank account. He wondered how people have dogs, or why. All they did was cost money.

He stood outside his truck putting the crate together, fumbling with the bolts and plastic nuts. He wondered what idiot came up with this design. Maybe a child with tiny fingers. It was ridiculous. Minutes later, much to his dismay, it wouldn't fit without him moving the front seats up quite a bit. He grew more frustrated by the minute. Eventually, he got it situated, tossed the food in the bed, threw the leash and collar on the passenger seat and wedged himself into the driver's seat with his knees bent up. He just wanted to drive home and forget about the dog. Pushing against the crate, he managed to get the seat back a couple more clicks and give himself a little more driving room and tried to calm the throbbing in his head, despite knowing the vet's office would probably make it worse. When he parked, he searched both the console and the glove compartment, hoping Tina had something that would help his headache. Sure enough, he found a bottle of aspirin in one of the little compartments in the console and his thoughts went back to how grateful he was to have his wife.

Those thoughts helped him to calm down and reassess why he was so wound up anyway. It wasn't truly the dog. It was the vet. He hated the way the man looked at him. The way he spoke to him. He didn't know why the vet insisted he was lying. Lucas was known for his honesty, hard work, and his knowledge among the people who knew him. He was respected even if seen as a bit too straightforward. He wasn't used to being seen the way the vet saw him. He was a tough man, but a good one. He steeled himself for the interaction and went inside.

Chapter 19
Into The Unknown

As Lucas stood at the front counter at the receptionist desk, he was glad to see it wasn't the same woman. He hoped this one would seem less hostile. "Can I help you?" Asked the woman looking up from her computer.
"I'm here to pick up a dog." Lucas said.
"Your name?"
"Lucas Porter." He said, hoping she knew nothing about him.
To his relief, she didn't seem to and after typing his name into the computer, she simply told him someone would be right out. Then she picked up the phone and Lucas sat in one of the waiting chairs again. He felt slightly more relaxed.

A few minutes later a young man came out and approached Lucas. It was not the veterinarian. He glanced at Lucas and then around him.
"You're going to need a crate." He said.
Lucas was glad Barry had mentioned it. He would have been slightly embarrassed otherwise.
"You have to bring it in." The young man said, as if Lucas should have known. "She's really scared and she has no leash or collar."

"I have those too." Lucas said, hoping that would get him out of having to get the crate back out of the truck.

"She's still really weak and she has stitches on her neck. You might have to carry her out to do her business."

Lucas stared at him in mild disbelief. "Carry her?"

The young man nodded.

Lucas tried to imagine him carrying a strange dog outside. He couldn't exactly just set her down out there. Could he? He didn't even want to touch her. He stood abruptly to hide his fear and stated, "I'll go get the crate."

"Okay." The young man remained pleasant.

Outside, Lucas tried not to think about what would happen later. He moved his seat forward again and tugged and pulled until he managed to maneuver the crate back out of the truck. He picked it up by the cage door and carried it awkwardly across the lot. When he got it through both sets of doors and into the lobby, the man was still waiting for him.

"That's a big crate." He said as Lucas approached.

"It's what the woman at the store recommended." Lucas told him, feeling like he had to justify his apparent mistake.

The young man nodded and said, "We'll see if we can get her in it."

Lucas didn't exactly like the sound of that, but he followed the young man out back, while managing to get the crate through all the doors.To his dismay, the vet was there in the back room, waiting for him.

Lucas watched the doctor's expression turn sour, when he saw him. So much for an easy escape. The man in the white coat glanced at the crate. "You realize she has to go outside to go to the bathroom? The man paused as he watched Lucas's facial expression.

"I'll have to figure that out." Lucas said. He felt his indignation creeping in.

"It'll be a lot harder to reach her in a crate that big." The vet continued.

"Look! Lucas said, tired of the whole thing. "I went to a store and this is what the woman said I should buy, so this is what I got. It's gonna have to do."

The vet paused. "Don't you have a slip lead?"

"A what?" Lucas asked, feeling very frustrated at his inability to do anything correctly.

The vet walked down the hall, took a leash off the wall and walked back to Lucas. "This." The man pulled the rope of the leash through a small metal ring at one end and put his hand through the loop and pulled it tight. "It'll go around her neck, so she can't get away."

Inwardly Lucas sighed. It was just a looped rope with a handle. Like a lasso for dogs. Slip lead…

The vet handed it to him. "Take this one. You'll need it to take her out."

Lucas nodded.

"I sedated her some so it'd be easier. You want to try to get her in there?"

"No." Lucas stated bluntly. "I don't. "

He looked at the wild-eyed mess cowering in the back of one cage in the row of cages. He tried to imagine dragging the dog out of there. He didn't want to touch it.

The vet looked at him, seeming rather surprised at his refusal.

Lucas involuntarily took a step back. He felt a small rush of adrenaline. The veterinarian looked at him. Lucas was sure he almost smirked. "How are you going to take care of a dog, if you can't handle it sedated?"

"My brother." Lucas sputtered, not wanting to say his wife. "My brother will take care of the dog."

The man kept looking at him. Finally he said, "Perhaps your brother should have come to get it."

"He had things to do." Lucas lied.

The young tech seemed to take pity on Lucas. " I think I can get the dog in there by myself."

He said. "Why don't you go back to the waiting room and I'll try to get her loaded up."
Grateful, Lucas nodded and walked out.

Once back in the waiting room, he felt calmer and began to berate himself for letting the doctor see him get upset. He composed himself, determined not to let it happen again. He remembered the cowering dog. Apparently, they both felt the same way. It's just a pup, he told himself. Get a grip. He heard the sounds of the pup crying and squealing down the hall. What was he gonna do if they couldn't get it in the crate? Lucas cleared his throat. "I'm gonna man up and get it done. I'm not a kid anymore. " His own voice startled him. He hadn't meant to speak out loud. He glanced around but the receptionist was busy typing. She didn't appear to have heard him.

In a short time, the door opened and the young tech came out carrying the crate with a young woman. The vet followed behind them. They headed straight for the front door and Lucas stood up swiftly to follow. Once outside, he moved ahead of them and opened the door to the back seat. The two techs started trying to Get the crate back in and Lucas went around the far side to the back of the crate to help. He closed the door, then came around and closed the other door as well. "Thank you." Lucas said.

The sincerity in his voice was evident. "No problem." The young man answered.

Lucas looked the young man over. "You really should become a vet." He said. "You'd make a good one."

The young man smiled and Lucas shot the doctor a quick look, making sure his implication was noticed. He was glad to see it had.

They all walked back in and after some 15 minutes of instructions from the vet who constantly seemed to imply he wouldn't do them, Lucas finally escaped with printed instructions, three bottles of medicine and a receipt for an additional $112 paid. They had even charged him for the slip lead. But at that point, it seemed a small price to pay for escaping.

As he drove home, listening to the occasional shifting of the dog as he braked or took a corner, he thought about the shed where Tina planned to keep the dog for now. The vet has plainly stated that she had to be watched. They had to make sure she didn't mess with her stitches and watch for signs of infection. She needed meds twice a day. And according to the fine doctor, she should also have as much human interaction as possible, to help her be less fearful. Mentally, he was trying hard not to know the solution to the problem, but by the

time he made it home, he had accepted the
inevitable.

Lucas drove the truck into the driveway and
then backed as close to the house as he could.
Tina came out onto the porch and he could see
Barry coming down from the barn. When he got
out, Tina came to greet him. She started talking
about her plans and the set up she had in the
shed. He let her talk until Barry made it around
to the side of the truck. As Tina stopped talking,
Lucas spoke to Barry. "If I take the back of the
crate, will you take the front?"
This was not the time to tease his brother and
Barry knew it. He knew what he was asking.
Opening the truck door, Barry looked at the
shivering pup, who had braced herself against
the back of the crate. It looked utterly terrified.
"Yeah," he said. "I'll get the front."
As soon as they got the crate out of the truck,
Tina moved to lead the way, heading towards
the shed at a quick pace. Lucas whistled. She
looked back and he jerked his head towards the
door of the main house. "Get the door."
Tina stood for a second staring in disbelief, sure
that she had misunderstood. Lucas would
never! He made the motion again, ignoring
Barry's open mouth and his wife's shocked
expression. She walked towards the house,
hesitantly, as if waiting for him to correct her

thinking, but when she opened the door, Lucas and Barry were close behind.

As soon as they reached the living room, Lucas stopped. "Okay. Let's set it down.
As soon as the crate was on the floor, he walked past them and moved a small table out of one far corner and then slid the crate into the space. "Lucas?" Tina's voice was soft. He didn't answer as he went back out and came in with the bag of dog food. He set it in the kitchen and went back out the door. Neither Tina nor Barry spoke despite exchanging glances when Lucas wasn't in the room. He returned with the dishes, leash, collar, slip lead, some papers, and the small bag with the medicine. He set them all in a pile on the floor except the medicine and the papers. Those he held out to Tina. When she reached to take them, he finally spoke. "This is her medicine and the papers to tell you how much to give her and how to treat her wounds." He handed them to her and picked up the lead the vet had given him. "This is to take her out to the bathroom because she'll try to get away and she can't wear a collar yet." As he spoke, He pulled the leash through the ring and made a loop much like the vet had done.
As he spoke, Barry glanced at the paperwork and the receipt that was stapled to it. "112 dollars." He said. "That isn't bad. Does he do sheep?"

Lucas took a deep breath. "Actually, I gave him a deposit the first time. That was just the remainder."

He hoped Barry wouldn't ask what he had left and was thankful he didn't. Barry had amazing insight sometimes. He just said, "Okay, that makes sense."

Lucas looked at Tina. "The vet says someone has to make sure she doesn't pick at her stitches and watch for any infection and that if she's ever going to be handled, she needs as much time with people as possible." He paused trying to hide his emotional turmoil. "So, unless you are going to live in the shed, this is the only thing that makes sense for right now."

Tina nodded. She didn't want to make things more awkward. "Okay. "

He started to walk away and she spoke again. "Lucas…"

The man paused but did not turn around.

"Thanks. I don't really want to live in the shed."

He tried to smile at her. It wasn't much of a smile, but he tried. Then he continued to the door and walked out.

After a brief look at Tina, Barry followed him.

Chapter 20
No Escape

Wee sat against the back of the crate, trying to watch the people through the thin spaces on the side. She heard them talking but had no idea what they were saying. They smelled angry, stressed and unhappy, much like Wee herself. She wished she could wake up and find herself back in the barn, with Fur by her side. Momma! She would do anything to be with Momma again. Yet, for days now, she could not wake up. It was one ever changing nightmare, after another. She spent each day terrified and enduring changes that she could not understand.

She watched as the two men left out the door. She felt better when there were less of them. The woman stood silently for a few minutes after they left. Wee simply watched and waited for the next thing to happen to her. She did not have long to wait. The woman set the things she was holding onto a table and moved towards Wee. She tried to retreat further, but there was nowhere to go. She whimpered softly. The woman stooped down and looked at her. She murmured softly, things Wee could not understand. After a moment, the woman stood up and retrieved some things off the floor and the things she had set on the table and disappeared from view.

Wee listened to the sounds of the woman on the other side of the wall. After a moment, she snuck forward, still alert for any change. The quiet noises in the kitchen continued. She put her nose against the wire of the cage and pushed. It didn't open. She pushed harder, but it still held. She began to pull on it with her teeth. "Hey!"
Wee looked up to see the woman had come around the corner of the wall. She froze with the metal still in her teeth. "No!"
The woman moved towards her and Wee fled to the back of the crate. When the woman reached her she stooped down again. When she spoke, her voice was soft. "You can't do that. You'll hurt yourself."
Wee just stared. The woman did not sound angry. Roger had always sounded angry. The woman stayed there for several moments and Wee just stared back at her pathetically.
Finally, she moved away and Wee felt as if she could breathe again. Then the woman returned carrying something in her hands. She set it on top of the crate and bent down. Putting herself firmly in front of the door, she opened it just a bit and reached for the thing on top of the crate. She placed it inside the cage, spoke again, and closed and latched the door.

The aroma that reached Wee's nose was heavenly. Her mouth began to water and she sniffed the air. But she waited until the woman moved away across the room, before moving slowly forward. She kept her eyes on the woman, waiting for the woman to yell and come after her. Instead, the woman sat across the room and began to look at other things. Wee began to eat what was in the dish. It was marvelous. It was warm and crunchy and the liquid tasted wonderful. Wee gulped it down while never taking her eyes off the woman. They had given her something to eat at the other place with the strange smells, but nothing like this. She gulped it down and proceeded to lick up every bit of flavor. The woman never moved until Wee was done. Then she stood and took the things off the floor that the angry man had placed there. She disappeared behind the wall again and came back carefully carrying another dish. Wee stayed in the back, but hoped it was more food. The woman placed it in her crate and took the empty dish. When she stood and walked away, Wee immediately moved forward. It was not food though. It was water.

Wee was slightly disappointed, but after sniffing around to make sure she hadn't missed any morsel of her meal, she decided she was thirsty. She drank until the bowl was mostly empty and then moved back to return to her hiding place. Laying there, she realized she didn't hurt as much as she had. She hadn't even noticed she was hurting. She felt better though. She was warm and she had something in her belly. She tried to stay alert, but she grew more tired as the minutes passed on and before she knew it, she had fallen asleep in her enemy's house.

Chapter 21
Wild Thing

Lucas and Barry had finished chores and were talking for a moment by the truck before heading in for dinner. Barry had been careful to keep the conversation away from the dog. Never in his life would he have dreamed that Lucas would ever have allowed a dog in his house. He wasn't sure what had happened, but he knew it had to be more than just the dog's care. There was something going on and he knew better than to ask. He kept the conversation to chores and the plans for tomorrow. All of a sudden, there was a crash inside the house and then another. They looked up and Lucas began to head for the door. In his mind, he could see the dog attacking Tina and the panic welled up in his throat. He was already in motion when a firm hand grabbed his shoulder. "Wait!" Barry said. "I'll go take care of it." He rushed past his brother, was across the porch and inside the door, before Lucas could make a decision. Lucas ran his hand through his hair, hesitated in his stride, but then headed for the porch. As he reached the top of the steps, the door cracked and Barry's head poked out the door. "It's fine." He said. Then he looked at Lucas and said, "You might want to get off the porch."

Lucas went back down the steps and moved over by the truck. He was still unsure if he should have gone inside. Then the door opened and Barry's back appeared in the doorway. There was another crash and then Barry stepped out holding tightly to the handle of the slip lead. As he cleared the doorway, a white blur went past his legs and tried to bolt off the porch. It was hauled up short by the slip lead, but continued to flail and scrabble to get off the porch. Lucas moved away further down the driveway, as Barry rushed to catch up and Tina was close behind.

As Lucas continued to back up, he realized the dog was not trying to attack them, it was simply trying to get away. He continued backing up, while watching the struggling dog and Barry and Tina's efforts to figure out what to do. Lucas's anxiety began to rise and he moved further away. Eventually, he turned away from the struggling dog and walked back towards the barn. He walked until he could no longer hear the gagging, whining creature at the end of the rope. He did not return until Barry came to get him.

When they returned to the house, Tina was finishing putting dinner on the table. She still seemed a little shaken. A glance around the house showed everything fine and in order. He glanced towards the crate and through the cracks, he could see the eyes watching him. Lucas moved on towards Tina and washed his hands in the kitchen sink. "Anything I can help with?" he asked quietly.

Tina shook her head and then said, "You can help eat it."

Her smile was still a bit weak and he knew more than anything, she was worried about his feelings. He tried to be casual. He was embarrassed by his own inability to help when his wife was the one taking the risks. Yet, it did not seem like the dog had tried to turn on them. It was just wild and unused to humans. Maybe she'd never seen a human before. He looked at Tina, reaching for her arm. "Are you okay?"

She nodded. "I'm sorry." She said, "I didn't think that she had never been on a leash. She was so frightened and it was choking her and she didn't understand."

Lucas wrapped his arms around her and pulled her close for a moment before releasing her and sitting down at the kitchen table.

"So, did you get her to go?" Lucas asked, trying to ignore the awkward feeling in everyone's demeanor.

Tina sighed. "She did, but only because she was so scared and trying to get away from us. That wasn't quite how I wanted it to go."

"Did you get the lead on okay?" He wondered if the dog was willing to lash out.

"Yes. Although I don't know if she'll want it on again. She never tries to bite, even when she's terrified."

Lucas nodded. "Maybe she just needs to learn. At least, I hope."

Barry spoke up. "Think of it like a wild horse. Fortunately, it's a lot smaller."

Then the trio fell to eating and the conversation died down as they were each lost in their own thoughts about what lay ahead.

Wee laid in the crate listening to the sounds of dinner and marveling at the smells. She was still shaken by the events of the evening and the thing around her neck that would not let her escape. She was also aware that despite her panicking and knocking things over, the humans did not seem angry. If she had done that with Roger, she hated to think what would have happened. Thoughts of Roger also made her think of her family and Wee spent the rest of the human's mealtime, feeling sad and alone. She was so lost in her own misery, that she didn't hear the woman by her cage until she was bending down to open the door. Wee scrambled to her feet and drew back. To her surprise, the woman placed the bowl of crunchy food in her cage. It was covered in juice that smelled of the people's dinner. It was weird how they kept feeding her. She'd rarely been fed by a human and never so much or meals so close together. Usually, it was just a bit of milk and never enough to satisfy. She waited for the woman to walk away before diving in like she had earlier that day. The food made her tired, but it also took away the soreness. She fell asleep listening to occasional voices and the sound of dishes clanking in the kitchen.

Chapter 22
A Change Of Heart

For the next several days, whenever the dog needed care, Lucas would have something to do. No one mentioned his absences. The day Tina and Barry removed the stitches, Lucas went and checked the fence. Every time, Barry would go find him and without saying so, it let him know the task was done. In much that way, the next two weeks slipped by. Everything else was just the normal ranch life. Some nights, Lucas and Barry would spend looking for signs of coyote activity. Occasionally, they even found their quarry and other times, they just felt better knowing their scent was fresh, if the coyotes did come by.

Saturday morning, some two weeks later, Lucas came in the house from chores. Tina was tidying things in the living room, her hair pulled back in a ponytail and wearing her ranch clothing. He looked at the crate. The dog was quiet, but he could see her watching through the crate. He considered his options for a moment. Tina looked at him and saw him watching the dog. "She's doing much better," she told him. "She's gotten to understand the lead and she isn't as scared when I have to touch her."

Lucas ignored the meaning behind the conversation. He knew she was afraid that he would deem the dog a lost cause. When he spoke, the conversation was totally different than what Tina expected. "Aren't you going to town today?" He asked.

She shook her head. "No. Her meds are done, but she still might need to go out to the bathroom and …"

Lucas cut her off. "Can't Barry take her out if she needs to go? I mean, I'm sure I could manage to give her water. She hasn't eaten you yet."

The way Tina looked at him and the surprise on her face, followed by a look of gratitude, struck Lucas's heart. It always did. He knew her trips to town twice a month meant a lot to her. A day away from the ranch to socialize, get a few things she wanted and perhaps stop somewhere for a bite to eat, that she didn't have to cook, meant a lot to her. "I'm sure I'm capable of scrounging up some lunch. Why don't you head out?"

She went to him and wrapped her arms around his waist and buried her face against his chest. He held her close for a few moments and when he stepped back, he put his hand gently under her chin. When she met his gaze, he said, "Go get ready. We can manage just fine until you get back."

She reached up and kissed his cheek and hurried off towards the bedroom.

An hour later after more kisses and thank yous and goodbyes, Tina drove out of the driveway. Barry watched the truck drive out in disbelief. He thought about going up to the house, but decided not to interfere with whatever Lucas was trying to do.

Inside the house, Lucas paced a bit, stopping occasionally to cast a glance at the dog. It watched every move he made. He wondered if she did that when Tina was in the house alone. He looked at the empty dishes on top of her crate. Maybe that would be the best way to start. He found the food in the kitchen pantry and filled one bowl with it. Then he filled the other with water and carried them both into the living room. He set both dishes on top of the crate and unlatched the door. He stood slowly to get the dishes, without scaring the dog. The dog, while unsure, seemed to be looking forward to his offerings. As the dog moved inside, the crate door began to swing open. With his hands full and almost as a reflex, he quickly used his boot to push the door shut. The dog yelped and fled to the back. He stooped down dishes in hand and looked inside. The dog was pressed against the back wall and her body was quivering. Lucas started to feel anger well up inside. He was positive that the dog had expected Lucas to kick her. He wasn't a dumb man, and the only way this pup would expect to be kicked, was if she had been kicked. That meant she wasn't afraid of humans because she'd never seen them. She was afraid of humans because of what they had done. He didn't like that idea at all.

Lucas carefully set the dishes inside and latched the door. He did not retreat though. He sat down on the floor, with his legs stretched out and spoke softly to the frightened dog. "Hey, girl. Jess. It's okay. Easy now." He kept talking softly, trying to be reassuring. He didn't know why, but the idea of that starving animal, who had almost died from the coyotes, actually belonging to someone, made him really mad.

When the dog did not come forward, Lucas got up and went into the kitchen. He opened the fridge door and took out the leftover roast from the night before. He cut off some strips and picked them up in his hand and returned to the room. The dog who had been eating while he was in the kitchen, had moved to the back of the crate upon his return. He sat down again. Taking one of the strips from one hand with the other, he pushed it between the wire grates. He continued to hold one end. He continued to talk in a quiet, though gruff, tone of voice.

Wee stared at the man. She was confused. Moments before, he had seemed quick to try to strike her, but now he sat beside her, talking in soft, soothing tones. The smell of the food he held was alluring, but she was unsure about this whole situation. She liked the man's voice. It made her feel better, somehow. It made her feel calm inside, like Fur did when he would act more dog than puppy. She moved forward slowly, reaching out as far as she could. The man continued to talk, but he didn't move. Wee took a step. She reached out again and licked the meat and pulled back. The man did not change his voice or his position. She reached forward again. This time she nibbled at one end. She gave it a slight tug and the man let go. She retreated to the back of her crate to eat it, but the man simply took another piece and pushed it through the grate again. She was quicker this time to step forward and take it. He didn't seem dangerous or sneaky like Roger had been. When the meat ran out and the man finally stood, she was almost sorry to see him go.

Lucas went into the kitchen and washed his hands before using part of the leftover roast to make himself a couple of sandwiches. The growing positive response from the dog made him feel good inside. They were opposite sides of the same coin. They both had been hurt and both lacked trust in the other and they both were trying to reach an understanding. He put his sandwiches on a plate and carried them into the living room. He sat on the far end of the couch where he could see the dog. She paused from eating the food in her bowl when he walked in, but as soon as Lucas was seated on the couch and began to eat, she resumed eating as well. When she finished and had had a drink, she did not retreat to the back. She stood watching the food go into Lucas's mouth. He chuckled to himself. She apparently liked being fed.

Lucas had just finished eating when the phone rang. He answered, "Lucas Porter."
A man's voice replied. This is Dr. Riley from Lakeview Emergency Clinic. It has come to my attention that you haven't brought the dog back in to have her stitches removed. "My brother did it."
"Your brother did it?" The doctor repeated.
"Yes."
"You do realize if he missed any stitch, it could become infected."
"He didn't miss any." Lucas said with confidence.

There was a pause on the other end of the line and then the man said, "Is she back working yet?"

Lucas chuckled. "I got her a job at the auto parts store in Dalton, 9 - 5."

There was absolute silence on the other end of the line and after a moment, Lucas disconnected the call.

Outside, Barry, who had been trying to leave Lucas to hopefully sort out things with the dog, was being eaten by curiosity. He wondered if anything was going on or if Lucas was just enjoying some time inside. He didn't think so. Lucas seldom just hung around the house and never when his wife wasn't home. Obviously, something was going on. Maybe he should just go up there casually. Barry decided he should at least check in.

As he headed down towards the house, he heard the front door open. Lucas was talking quietly. Barry stopped in his tracks. He backed up by the shed and stepped out of view. He could not believe it. Lucas had come out the door with the dog. He glanced back at Lucas and then made his way back up to the barn. If his brother looked now, it would appear as though Barry hadn't seen him. When he made it inside, he found a crack that allowed him to see down by the house. He grinned. Well, I'll be

damned, he thought. He waited until Lucas
went back inside before making his way back
down and to his own cabin.

Chapter 23
Surprise! Surprise!

Tina had fretted most of the day about leaving Lucas with the dog. She didn't want to come home to hear of bad experiences or occurrences. She also knew that Lucas had been determined to give her her usual day in town, especially since she had missed the previous one. He always reassured her that everyone needed a day off, though he never took one himself. Really, she knew it was his way of making sure she didn't miss the life she once led. He was right. Although she loved her life with him, she did enjoy her day in town. It made her feel refreshed and it made her glad for the life she'd chosen at the same time. She had enjoyed herself, but as she had been making the drive home, the concerns she had pushed aside, returned in full force. She was later than she had meant to be. Service at the diner where she stopped to eat had been slow and although she had stayed and enjoyed her meal, she found all the what ifs running through her head.

When she finally parked the truck in the driveway, she didn't bother to take her purchases with her. That could wait. She just wanted to make sure everything was alright. She went up the porch steps quietly, trying not to seem frantic. She didn't want Lucas to think she hadn't trusted him. She opened the door calmly and walked inside, gently closing it behind her. In just a few steps, she could see the crate door was open. Her heart fell. What had happened?

Lucas looked up as Tina came into the living room. As she moved past the back of the couch, she stopped mid step. Lying on the floor, past where Lucas sat on the couch, adorned with both collar and leash, was Jess. Tina stared at the dog and at Lucas, open mouthed with disbelief. "Lucas?" She began, not knowing what to say next.

"Barry was right." He said. "It's like taming a wild horse."

Tina didn't know whether to laugh or cry with relief. While her emotions ran wild and she tried to figure it out, Lucas stood up, coaxed the dog back into the crate, unhooked the leash from her collar and closed the door.

When he stood up he found his wife in his arms, smiling and crying at the same time. He tried to hide his own rush of emotions and said, "What did you think was gonna happen?"

"I don't know." She sputtered. "How did you…?" She didn't finish. She didn't know what to say. Lucas stepped back. She was starting to make him feel embarrassed. He changed the subject. "Did you buy anything in town?"

She smiled, almost grinning, despite the tears on her cheeks. "Yes!" she said, sounding entirely too enthusiastic for it to be about what she bought. "Hang on. I'll be right back."
She hurried out the door to the truck. Lucas sighed. He felt foolish at her obvious excitement, but he felt good about it too. He had made her far happier than a day in town ever did. That, he felt, was quite an accomplishment.

By the time Tina brought her few purchases In and showed them to Lucas, it was past their normal bedtime. She hadn't bought much. She never did. She showed him her new scarf, a couple of new warm flannel shirts, a new drink pitcher and a new set of measuring cups. She also sheepishly showed him the new pad she had gotten for Jess's crate. "The towel is so small and it's always rumpled." She said. "I thought this would be neater."
The new kitchen items reminded him of his trip to the store. "Do you need more things for the kitchen?"
He would have been more specific, but he wasn't sure what many of them were.
"I got what I needed." She said. "What made you ask that?"
Lucas helped out in the kitchen, but it wasn't his domain.

He told her about his trip to get the crate and the things he saw in the kitchen department. She giggled at his lack of knowledge. "You know," she said. If I wanted things like that, I could get them when I went to town. I prefer to make things my way. I don't need all that stuff." She paused and then said, "It's sweet of you to ask, Luke. But I have everything I want right here."

God, he loved this woman. So unlike anyone he had met before. He didn't know how he lured her in and some days, he didn't know how he kept her. He was glad for it, just the same.

When they headed to bed, Lucas prayed for a quiet night without the coyotes. He had just laid down, when he heard a low whine from the living room. It was followed by another. He slipped back out of bed and went back down the hall to the living room. He bent down and looked at the dog. "Shhh, Jess!" He said. "You be good."

She stared back at him. "Quiet! It's bedtime." Then he stood and returned to his bed and his wife.

Wee listened to the man's footsteps fade away. She didn't know what he said, but the tone sounded a lot like Momma when she was disappointed in their behavior. She felt very lonely. For the first time in her life, it was the absence of humans that bothered her. It was a weird feeling. They were different from Roger. Every one of them. She wanted their presence to make her feel better. She thought of her momma and of Fur, she still missed the comfort and familiarity of their existence. Yet, she liked the gentle contact from the man, the soft voice of the woman and she liked the feeling of her full stomach every day. Maybe, just maybe, she thought, this life was not so bad. She sighed in a mixture of sadness and contentment, before laying her head down on her paws.

Chapter 24
Winter In Paradise

The weeks rolled past and life on the ranch continued much as it always did. Jess, as the humans called her, continued to put on weight and size. Her coat had grown in, thick and glossy, hiding all but the scars on her muzzle. The crate, which had once seemed almost ridiculously huge with the quivering, half-starved pup scrunched in the back had been remanded to the shed. Much to the surprise of some of the ranch residents, Jess had not. Though still sometimes frightened by quick movements and loud noises, she became more confident all the time.

Jess was beginning to learn all the ins and outs of the ranch. She often followed Lucas, on leash, out to the barn. The sheep, who had been moved much closer to home for the winter, were still somewhat nervous about having a dog in their midst. Jess did her best to be calm and reassuring, as she followed Lucas among them.

Lucas was amazed at her natural affinity for the sheep. She seemed comfortable among them. More comfortable than she often was around people. As she had grown, her origins had become impossible to miss. She was definitely a dog bred for stock. Lucas had feared those dogs. They were always watching with suspicion and an air of hostility. Jess, however, was nothing like them. He marveled at her good nature. She, though once fearful, was affectionate, caring and eager to learn. With reassurance and a lot of coaxing, she conquered her fear of new things and new experiences. Lucas found himself enjoying her company. She added something to the household that had not existed before. He didn't trust dogs, but Jess seemed different than what he had expected. She seemed to understand much more than he would have ever expected.

Tina met him as he was heading back from the barn. "I'm running to the post office to drop off a few packages. I won't have to go in. I thought it might be a good time to take Jess on her first ride to town."

Lucas had taken Jess around the farm in the truck a few times. She didn't really like it, but like with so many things, her skills were improving. Where it once had taken almost 30 minutes to coax her into the truck, it now only took about 5.

Lucas nodded. "Sure. It'd be a good experience for her. If you do take her out of the truck for anything, just remember to hold the leash tight in case something scares her. And don't let anyone touch her because I don't think she's really ready for that, especially in a strange place."

As he spoke, he stooped down and checked the tightness of the dog's collar. Tina brought her hand up to her mouth to hide her smile. You'd think he was sending his kid to a sitter or having a new person watch the ranch. I'll make sure she's fine, Lucas. If I do let her out to pee, I'll make sure it's away from everything."

"Okay. I just don't know what would happen, if she got away."

"I'll be extra careful." Tina promised.

Lucas walked Jess to the truck and coaxed her into the back seat. Then he kissed Tina goodbye and told her to drive carefully. As she pulled the truck out the driveway, she heard him yell, "And don't roll the windows down too much because she can squeeze through some pretty small spaces."

Tina giggled as she turned onto the road. She felt happy, almost silly. Never would she have believed she'd be riding off from the ranch, with a dog in the truck.

Tina had grown up in the suburbs. She had spent much of her life with the family dog. When she was a teen, she often took the dog when she went out because it made her feel safer. When she met Lucas, Tina was in college. When the topic of dogs had come up, he had made it absolutely clear that there would never be a dog in his household. As she had fallen in love with him, she had accepted his standpoint. He was unlike any man she had met. His quiet demeanor, the way he treated her and the way he made her feel, had made the decision to give up dogs relatively easy. But she had still missed it. Now here she was, riding down the road with her dog and the man she loved, waiting for them at home.

She pulled into the drive thru at the post office. She was sending a few gifts to people back home. Perhaps one day, she would have them come to the ranch for Christmas. Right now, they still had a lot to complete including a better house for Barry, whose cabin would become the guest house.

In the back, Jess let out a small whine. "It's okay girl." Tina told her. The dog had been unsure about the person in the window talking to Tina and handing things back and forth. On the off chance she did have to pee, Tina pulled the truck down to the far end of the lot where pavement met grassy field. There she got out and opened Jess's door a bit and took a firm hold of the leash. Then she coaxed the dog out and led her onto the grass. It took some time for Jess to relax a little and stop smelling around. When she finally did go, Tina looked up from the dog to find a man standing in the parking lot watching her. He was wearing a blue button-down shirt and dark gray, casual slacks, with black leather shoes. He looked vaguely familiar, but she couldn't place where she might know him from or match a name to the face.

Upon seeing her staring back at him, the man approached, and Tina tightened her grip on the dog. She pulled the leash up short to bring Jess closer, in case she got frightened. He seemed to notice and stopped about ten feet away. "Mrs Porter?" He asked while looking over the dog. "Yes. Mr. ..." she trailed off.
"Dr. Riley."
Oh of course. She had only seen him that one night and without the lab coat, she hadn't known where she had seen him. He was still looking at the dog. Tina reached down and gently rubbed Jess's head. "Looking good, isn't she?" Tina said, her voice slightly cold.
"Umm, yes." The doctor said. "Are you still with...?
"Lucas." Tina stated, feeling her anger rise in a way it seldom did. One thing she wouldn't tolerate was someone speaking badly of her husband. If Lucas had been there, she would have let him handle it, but now, she could take matters into her own hands. "Yes, Doctor Riley. I'm still with my husband and I'm a little tired of the way you speak about him and the way you

speak to him. He's a good man. He brought the dog in that night because I asked him to. He paid for her care, her food and helped take care of her."

The doctor looked taken aback. She had seemed so meek and quiet that night. Tina, though, was not done and she continued on, "I told you and he told you the dog wasn't ours. I haven't had a dog since I was a teen, and he has never owned a dog. We took responsibility for her and she looks this way because this is how we take care of our animals. I don't know why you have a problem with ranch people or my husband, but I've had enough. We told you we found her up back in a field because we found her up back in a field."

The veterinarian was quiet for so long that Tina had decided to put the dog in the truck and leave. He just stood with his head down. When she opened the back door, he spoke. When he did, his voice was quiet and soft. "I became a vet because I cared about animals. My first real job was further out west. I thought doing farm calls would be good experience for me. I was wrong. I saw a lot of things on the ranches out there. Many of them take good care of their stock because that's their money, but the dogs, especially the dogs like her…"

He paused as if remembering. Tina could hear the emotion in his voice. Her anger died as suddenly as it had risen. "The dogs were often starved, had infected Injuries, and no one cared. I saw a dog with flystrike once, still trying to do his job. We couldn't have caught them to treat them and we wouldn't have been allowed anyway, because the ranchers wouldn't have paid for it. I left that practice because I had to, for my own wellbeing. I worked a few places in more populated areas and eventually I set up my own practice here. I guess my experience made me assume and you're right. I have a problem with ranch people. But I was wrong about you and your husband. I'm sorry."

There was a long pause and finally, Tina spoke.

"I'm not." Tina said, her voice as quiet as the doctor's.

"I am not sorry."

He glanced at her, questioning and she continued, head down, not making eye contact. "When my husband was a child, he lived on a ranch. He was attacked by a neighbor's dog. Not one of these kinds of dogs, but a big one just the same. It was killing sheep and it almost killed him. If his brother hadn't run for help, it probably would have. His father had to shoot it to save him. He spent weeks in the hospital, had skin grafts, multiple surgeries. He still bears the scars. I grew up with dogs, but he hated them. He said he would never own a dog." Tina was holding back tears now, but she continued. "I accepted that because he's a great man and I understood. That night, he only brought her in because of how much he loves me. He's terrified of dogs. But Jess, she was different. She'd been hurt too. He started trying to earn her trust and he started to trust her. They are learning about trust together and for that, I can not be sorry."

Tina opened the truck door and called Jess inside. The dog, as if understanding something was going on, did not hesitate. When Tina shut the door and turned around, the doctor was much closer. He reached out and rested his hand on her arm. For a few moments, they stood like that. Two people who both needed comfort but didn't know each other well enough to give it.

Tina found her voice and looked up at the doctor. She said, "Thank you. Thank you for listening to me."
Dr. Riley brought his hand away trying to break the moment. "If you need anything for her," he said, glancing towards the dog, "you are welcome to bring her to my clinic any time." Tina gave a small smile in return. "I appreciate that. I will."

They moved apart and the doctor walked away without looking back. Tina waited until he had gotten in his car to get into her own truck and head home. When she did arrive at the ranch, she did not tell Lucas about her conversation with the doctor.

A few days later a dumbfounded Lucas stood on the porch holding the envelope from the vet's office tucked between two fingers looking at the check for $1900 that he held in his hand. With it was one single piece of paper with the Lakeview Emergency Hospital letterhead and one line that had his original payment amount and a second line that read, discount for stray dog - $1900. He stood there for some time wondering what had happened and why the doctor who had talked to him with such disdain, every time they met, suddenly seemed to have a total change of heart. He put the papers back in the envelope and tucked the envelope into his inside coat pocket. He did not tell Tina about the letter from the doctor. He did confide to Jess that she had gotten a whole lot less expensive.

Chapter 25
Predators In The Night

The sound of Jess barking brought Lucas upright out of bed. In all the time she had been with them, she had made many noises, but she had never barked. Jess was at the window, looking out over the barn. She lowered her head submissively when she heard Lucas's approach. He reached down and gently caressed her head. "Good girl." he said softly. Lucas peered through the glass out into the dark but could see nothing. He walked into the kitchen and grabbed the headlamp flashlight. In the living room, he heard Jess growl.

When he went back to the living room, Tina and Jess were both looking out the window. "What is it?" Tina asked Lucas. "She's never done this before."
"I know. I'm gonna go take a look."
He went back to the kitchen, pulled on his boots and coat, then grabbed his rifle from by the door. Jess was still growling. "I'll go check it out. Stay here with the dog." Lucas said, as he opened the door to go out.
Much to his surprise, as soon as the door opened, Jess tore out through the gap and ran out into the night.

Lucas went out the door, yelling Jess's name. She had never been outside, off leash and he had no idea if she would return or flee back to the life she had known. He called her name again. "Jess! Jess. Here girl."

For a moment there was nothing. He looked around the yard, the headlamp, lighting up the night. Suddenly, Jess's bark sounded. It was coming from down by the barn. Lucas jogged in that direction, still carrying the rifle and feeling a bigger sense of relief than he would have ever thought he'd feel about a dog. Jess was there at the gate to where the sheep were kept for the winter. Her volley of barks rang clear in the cold night air. When he reached her, he realized he should have brought the leash, but he had been too worried that Jess would run away.

He opened the gate and again, Jess raced through without looking back. He heard the door open to Barry's cabin, but he followed after Jess, leaving Barry to catch up. On the far side of the sheep enclosure, he caught up to her again. She was standing back about 10 feet from the fence line, growling deep in her throat. Lucas moved his head slowly, letting the light pan out across the field beyond. He couldn't see anything out of the ordinary. He turned back at the sound of Barry's footsteps on frozen ground. When he turned back to the dog, he saw something move in the edge of the flashlight beam. Without thinking, the rifle came up as he turned his head. Sure enough, a coyote moved to escape the light. Lucas fired as it disappeared. He heard the yelp and felt some satisfaction that he hadn't entirely missed. "Lucas!" His brother's voice sounded stern. He turned around to ask what was wrong, but he saw for himself. Jess had retreated some distance back towards the sheep. She was crouched down on the ground, shaking with fear. When Lucas said her name and stepped forward, she bolted across the field and disappeared among the sheep. Damn it! He thought to himself. He'd forgotten that she probably knew nothing about guns. The loud noise had scared the hell out of her. Lucas looked towards the fence and then back towards the dog. He made his way down among the sheep, but Jess was nowhere to be found. He shined the light across the yard. He didn't know if she could jump the fence, but maybe if she was frightened enough. He couldn't see her within the range of the flashlight or in the light from the porch.

He continued looking among the groups of sheep where they were bunched up near the gate and the barn. They obviously didn't like the proximity of the coyotes either and the noise of the rifle would be anything but reassuring to the sheep. Barry, now beside him said, "Maybe she went in the barn. She goes in with us often enough that it might feel safe." Lucas nodded and moved in that direction. He didn't know what he'd tell Tina if the dog was gone. He didn't want to admit how much he didn't like the idea either. He pushed his way through the milling, frightened sheep and made his way to the barn doorway. In the back, he could see her eyes reflected in the flashlight beam. "Jess. Hey girl. It's okay." he said in a calm, steady voice. He took a step forward.

Jess watched the silhouette of the man with the rifle fill the doorway of the barn. The light was in her eyes and she could not see. In her mind, she was a small puppy and the man in the doorway was Roger. He carried the boom stick and he had her cornered. She whined pitifully, her eyes darting back and forth, searching for a means of escape. Suddenly, the light went out and for a moment she was blind. She lay there listening, trying to hear something besides her own stressed panting. When her eyes began to adjust, there was no longer Roger. The man in the barn was stooped down, the rifle laid aside. "Come on, girl. You're alright. It's okay.
A low, but gruff voice reached her ears. "Easy, hon."
She whined softly in indecision, but the man continued. Jess tried to calm herself. This was not Roger. It was Luke. Lucas. Not Roger. She

whined again as the man kept talking. His voice, always calm and reassuring. She inched her way forward. "Good girl. It's okay, Jess. You're okay." He continued.

She made her way to where he was crouched, his hands empty. He reached out slowly, with his hand palm up and she sniffed it. "Good girl." He said.

She stepped forward and pressed her head against his coat, still whining softly. He ran his hands down over her head and rubbed the fur on her sides gently. You're alright, girl. You're okay."

Jess melted her head and chest into his lap and let the relief consume her. He was not Roger. He was the man that made her feel safe when things were new and frightening. He didn't get mad.

Lucas stayed stooped with the dog for a while, until the fear faded and the sound of his voice got a slight tail wag. Then he stood and tried to act as if everything was normal. "Come on, Jess. Let's go."

He didn't know if it would work without a leash, but he was going to try it. When the dog fell in beside him, Lucas gave a slight smile.

Whatever just happened, she still trusted him. He continued out of the barn like it was any other day. As he passed Barry, he said, "Do me a favor and once we're gone, grab my rifle."

Barry nodded in understanding. "Yeah sure. I'll leave it on the porch."

Lucas continued back to the gate and called Jess through. He knew he was taking a chance, but she had already shown that running away was not the first thing on her mind. Jess continued to follow beside him as she so often did on a leash. Lucas liked the idea that maybe she would hang around and he wouldn't forever be hooking her leash to something while he worked.

Tina was, of course, waiting for him on the porch. She was wearing her winter coat but still in her pajamas. "Go on in." Lucas said. "I want to get Jess inside." She opened the door and stepped in with Lucas and the dog close behind. When the door closed Lucas felt he could truly breathe again. "I heard the shot. What happened?" Tina asked anxiously.

Lucas took a deep breath. "I was afraid she'd run. But she went down towards the barn, still barking. I let her in with the sheep and she headed up back to the grazing area and was upset about something on the other side. I started shining the light and I saw a coyote and without thinking about Jess, I shot. It scared her and she ran."

"She probably had no idea what that was." Tina mused.

Lucas thought for a moment trying to find words to explain what he felt. "She fled to the barn, but here's where it got strange. When I got to the barn, she acted terrified. Not just about the gun but scared of me. She acted like I was some monster. I don't know. But when I got her to realize it was just me in the doorway, she practically climbed into my lap. She was whining and shaking. It was just really weird. But she was willing to follow me up here and into the house. In the barn though, she acted like she was the one being hunted."

Tina moved and put her arm around Lucas's waist. "I wish she could talk. She could tell us what was going on."

Lucas chuckled. "Just what I need, a talking dog. Where are you going, Lucas? What are you doing that for, Lucas?"

Tina giggled and wrapped her arms around him tighter. "Why don't we go back to bed, Lucas?" She said in much the same voice he had used when making the dog speak.

Laughing, he took off his coat and boots. He placed the headlamp on the charger in the kitchen where it always stayed in case he needed it. Suddenly, he remembered his rifle and he stepped out, while being careful that this time the dog would not follow. He went in just as carefully. Setting the rifle in its usual place by the door, he walked across the kitchen, picked Tina up in his arms and carried her back to the bedroom, where he dumped her, laughing, unceremoniously on the bed. Jess, who had followed, stood in the doorway absorbing the scent of their happiness and cheer, her fear almost forgotten.

When they were settled under the covers, Tina asked, "How were the coyotes in the grazing area?"

"I don't know. Lucas said. "We'll have to check fence tomorrow. I don't like that they came this close. I almost feel like something must be making them uncomfortable where they usually are."

"You think one of the other ranchers has been working on them too?"

"Sadly, I don't think so. I just find it odd."

"How do you think she knew something was out there? I mean, not that it's a bad thing, but how could she have heard them indoors?"

Lucas thought for a moment. "I don't think she could hear them. She couldn't have seen them either." He paused, considering the possibilities. "Maybe it was the sheep."

"What do you mean?"

"Well, if she couldn't see or hear the coyotes, then it had to be the sheep's behavior that made her realize something was wrong."

They were both silent for a minute as they considered Lucas's explanation.

Finally, Tina spoke. "If that is what happened. This could be a good thing. You'd know if the sheep were in danger, without having to be out there all the time."

Lucas thought about that. "That's true. At least until they go back out to graze. Then she wouldn't be able to see or hear them either."

"But…" Tina said quietly. "For now, we could possibly get some sleep."

Lucas rolled over and wrapped his arm around her. "That is not the worst idea you've ever had."

Tina laughed. "What about saving the dog?"

Lucas picked his head up and looked at Jess lying silently in the doorway of the room. He put his hand over Tina's face. "You just hush. We'll see about that."

She pulled his hand off still laughing.

He wrapped his arm around her again and pulled her close. They drifted off and all three of them slept peacefully until morning.

The next morning when Barry came up to the house for coffee, Lucas told him about their thoughts of the previous evening. After some discussion, Barry said, "I think it would be really good if you could get her over the fear of the gun."

"Why's that?" Lucas asked him.

"Okay. Now if she hadn't been there last night, even if we'd heard the sheep making a commotion, we wouldn't know which side they were coming in from. We could waste a lot of time figuring it out. She can tell us where they are, but then we can't shoot because she'll get scared. "

Lucas interrupted. "So if I can get her used to the gun fire, she can be our eyes in the dark, so to speak."

"Exactly." Barry said.

"How do I get her used to it without terrifying her?"

Barry thought for a moment. "Maybe start with something smaller. Shoot rabbits or squirrels. You have your .22, don't you? Maybe she'll learn to like it, if she gets a snack."

"That's not a bad idea." Lucas agreed. "Let's go up and check fence and see where they got in."

Out in the field, they found blood from where he had shot the night before, but no body. Lucas didn't like the idea of having left an injured animal, but at the time, Jess had been more important. Searching along the back fence line, they found a spot where the coyotes had come in under the fence, not over. He pulled a few hairs off the bottom fence line and for a moment, the image of Barry doing the same, up by the old man's place, flickered through his mind. This was not white though, it was gray and brown. Barry interrupted his thoughts. "Pickings must be getting slim, if they're digging in out here. Maybe the neighbors also have their stuff pulled in for the winter. You heard from anybody?"

"No." Lucas said, letting the hairs blow off into the wind, his thoughts forgotten. "I haven't seen much of anyone since the cold set in."

"No news is good news, right?" Barry said hopefully.

Lucas nodded agreement. "I'm sure we'll hear if something goes wrong. Even if it's to blame us." They spent time finding some larger rocks and filling the gap, before returning home to do chores. And for a time, there were no more incursions.

Chapter 26
Roger Returns

Over the next several weeks, Lucas would take
time out whenever possible, to work with Jess
on her fear of gunfire. It took giving her some
distance at first and a lot of calm reassurance,
but Barry had been right in that it didn't take
long for the dog to understand the correlation
between the treats she was given and the
sound of the gun. When she was more relaxed,
Lucas moved to using Barry's .38 and
eventually, he moved back to using his rifle.
Each time he changed firearms, he'd hook her
some distance away, but close enough to see
what was going on. When using a new weapon,
he always made sure his first shots got some
prize for Jess, but as she became more
accustomed to the noise, he would sometimes
fire randomly. She didn't really like the noise of
the gun, but at least she didn't panic over the
sound.

On a cold March morning, Tina was checking
new lambs in the barn, when Lucas and Jess
came back from a short excursion up back for
gun practice. Jess trotted right up to one of the
lambs that Tina was toweling dry. It was one of
triplets and the mom had been exhausted by
the time the last had been born. "Be careful!"
Lucas said suddenly. Both Tina and Jess

looked up at him. "I've been feeding her all kinds of stuff. I don't want her to think it's dinner."

Tina spoke to the dog. "Easy. See the new baby."

She could see the anxiety in Lucas's face. Jess sniffed the baby all over. "Jess!" Lucas said sternly.

"Take it easy." Tina said. "How is she supposed to learn if we keep her away?"

She continued toweling the lamb and turned its face towards the dog. Jess sniffed the lamb's face and gave a couple of short licks. Her tail wagged slightly. "I think she likes it." Tina said. Lucas released the breath he had been holding. His visions of her grabbing and shaking the lamb like a squirrel, began to fade. Jess was curious, but with a little guidance from Tina, she was very polite and gentle.

Suddenly. Jess made a low, deep growl and before either one of them could react, she swept past Lucas, snarling and barking. Lucas looked up to see an older man standing right in the barn. He had been so focused on the dog, he hadn't even heard him approach. "Jess!" He yelled, taken by surprise by both the man, and the dog's reaction. As he moved forward to grab the dog, the old man swung his leg and tried to kick her. Jess dodged the boot and backed up, still barking. Lucas grabbed her collar and pulled her back. Tina, who had been just as in shock, jumped to her feet, pushed the lamb into the open stall and grabbed a lead hanging in the aisle of the barn. She stepped forward and clipped it on Jess's collar and pulled her to the back of the barn. Tina tried to calm the dog, while Lucas tried to get his emotions under control. He was shocked at the dog's reaction, but still angry about the man trying to kick her.

"Can I help you with something?" Lucas asked, more sternly than he meant to.

The man was looking past him, still glaring at the dog, who had ceased barking, but continued to growl. "You know, you shouldn't have one of them dogs, if it attacks people." The old man said, not even trying to disguise the angry contempt in his voice."

"She has never reacted to a human like that before." Lucas said defensively. "I think you scared her."

"Well, she did it now." The man was angry and his voice was hostile. "It's me today. Might be you tomorrow."

Tina started forward, determined not to let this old stranger stir Lucas's fears, but Jess stepped across her path, blocking her from going forward, and never taking her eyes off the man in front of her.

Lucas, however, was getting annoyed.

"Perhaps," he said, "You shouldn't be sneaking

around in people's barns uninvited. Now did you need something?"

The old man met his gaze with a somewhat haughty look. "I'm Roger Allen. I heard from Mr. Benson that you might be interested in my place."

Just then, Barry appeared in the doorway. "Oh, hey. We have company." He said in a conversational tone.

Lucas had an idea that Barry had heard some of the conversation and was trying to salvage the possibility of them buying more land. Lucas was grateful because he had been tempted to send this man right back where he came from.

Barry approached and held out his hand. "Barry Porter, sir. Nice to meet you."

Roger shook his hand before saying, "Where did you get that dog?"

"It was a stray." Barry responded before Lucas could speak.

"Where did you find it?" Roger asked, staring at Jess.

"I got it from the vet." Lucas said quickly. "It was in pretty rough shape."

The old man was silent, watching the dog.

Lucas said calmly, "If you think you know who it belonged to, I'd like to know. I have a hell of a lot of vet fees and some board and feed they can pay me for."

The two men locked eyes and Lucas did not look away. It was the old man who lowered his gaze first. "No." Roger said stiffly. "No, I don't. But let me tell you. I had an old dog like her once. She had a couple pups. We were trying to round them up to move them to a new ranch in the southern part of the state. That old bitch turned on us and attacked a man. I shot her right where she stood. If I were you, I'd do the same thing with that one."

"So what happened to the pups?" Lucas asked, his voice cold as ice and his demeanor stiff.

"They took off." Roger said, bluntly. "They either starved or were coyote food. Not that it really matters. I don't need 'em. I'd already lost the money on them."

Again the image of the white hairs that Barry had picked off the fence flashed through his mind.

Lucas turned red in the face, but Barry stepped in again. "You here to talk dogs or are you here to talk property?" Barry asked, his voice still conversational. "Why don't we go up to the house and talk business?"

Barry led the way and Roger began to follow. On the way out, he mumbled. "Don't say I didn't warn you!"

Tina stared at the back of the old man, until they were gone out of sight. Then she looked down at Jess. She brought the dog in the stall with her to make sure the lambs were all okay and that the mom was caring for all of them. The ewe wasn't happy about the dog's presence, but Tina was careful to stay between them. When she was done, she took Jess out into the aisle and sat down, holding the dog close. She petted her gently and talked in soft tones. Her emotions were a mixture of anger, pity and fear. She hoped that horrible old man would not change Lucas's mind.

If Tina had been able to join the men up at the house, she would have been shocked at her husband's behavior. Lucas was usually very polite in his business dealings. He wasn't a pushover, but he would listen to the other person's point of view and even make a few concessions, if it made both people walk away happy. He knew good relationships were better than a few hundred dollars sometimes and that if he gave in on occasion, he could get the other person to do the same, another time. He had a way of making people feel like they got what they deserved, without giving too much. Today was not that day.

When they sat at the table, Lucas had no idea what Mr. Benson had said to Roger, but "selling him some land" had Roger thinking he could get Lucas to buy his whole place. Lucas conceded nothing. He was direct and to the point. He let Roger explain the ranch and the upgrades over the years, (some of which had been done several years before) and why he felt the ranch was worth his asking price. When he finished, Lucas looked him right in the eye and said, "I don't want your ranch, Mr. Allen."

Roger looked at him and started to speak, but Lucas cut him off. "I want 500 acres, bordering my property. That's it. Nothing else. I'll pay a decent price and you can take it or leave it. That will still leave you with enough acreage to still sell your place as a ranch and will help me be able to expand."

Roger looked offended and surprised. Whatever he had heard about Lucas, this was not what he had expected. He opened his mouth but no words came out. He closed it again, shifted in the chair a bit and finally spoke. "I'm not sure I want to cut my ranch into two pieces."

"Then we have nothing to talk about." Lucas stated flatly. "You can have a good amount of money now and still be able to sell your ranch or you can wait and hope for all the money later."

Roger's eyes flared with anger and he remained silent for a few minutes. Lucas said nothing.

Finally Roger's shoulders slumped. "You know you have me over a barrel." he said sullenly.

"That may be true, but I'm offering a more than fair price for it. So, what do you want to do? I still have work to get done."

"I'll do it." Roger did not meet his gaze.

"Good. Have the paperwork drawn up and let me know when to come sign it."

Lucas stood up from the table. He said, "My brother will see you out." Then he put his coat back on and walked out the door.

Barry stood as well. "Come on, Mr. Allen. I'll walk you to your car." He knew the man must need the money because his face said he'd like to be able to say a lot of things to Lucas. Barry just ignored his expression.

When he had stood and waited for the man to get into his vehicle and close the door, he started to turn away. The old man spoke, "You know, your brother…"

Barry cut him off. "You should have shut up about the dog." Then he turned and walked back towards the barn, where he was sure Lucas was talking to Tina. He heard the car start and drive away into the distance.

Barry reached the barn in time to hear Lucas say, "It has to be. "That's the only thing that makes sense. Benson said Roger was the only one around here with dogs. He abandons two pups and we find one attacked by coyotes."

"But that would have been months before we found her." Tina said, her voice filled with disbelief. "How would she have survived?"

"Well," Barry interrupted. "She sure seems to know what to do with squirrels and gophers and whatever you've given her. Maybe she was catching a few herself."

Lucas raised his eyebrow. "You are not wrong. She definitely knew they were food."

"So where is the other pup?" Tina wondered out loud.

Lucas and Barry were both silent. Lucas reached out and put his hand on Tina's shoulder. Then he reached down and stroked Jess's furry head. The dog was back to her usual self. She fawned over Lucas and the attention he was giving. "That night, we weren't really looking for dogs. It's possible it was somewhere in those fields. Maybe she was just faster, outran them longer or put up more of a fight. Or maybe the other never made it that long. It's hard to say." Lucas hated to say it to her, but it was likely the truth.

Tina put her hands together and stared at the floor. "Poor thing." She murmured. "I'm surprised all dogs don't want to bite him."

Barry scratched the dog on the head and between the ears. She wiggled with excitement. He always had a way of winding her up. "We got this dingbat, though. Barry started to laugh. "That is, of course, unless someone wants to pay us for all the vet bills and the feed and care."

Lucas smiled. "That ended that conversation, didn't it?"

"Yep." Barry said. It sure did."

Lucas's face turned serious. "She sure was protecting you though." He looked at Tina. She nodded. "It makes me feel safer. She is always so sweet to us, but she has proven she'll protect us too. And the sheep." she added after a moment's hesitation. She was still nervous Luke wouldn't trust her now.

Lucas stopped and scratched the dog. He watched her as he did. He brought his face level with hers, looking for some sign of the aggression she had shown earlier. It wasn't there. Her eyes were soft. Her body was relaxed and there was no trace of that hardness in her posture. Finally, he said to Jess, "Don't worry. I didn't like him much either. And you know him better than me."

He stood and looked at Tina, who was looking at the dog. "But we are getting more land!" Barry said, ignoring the tension in the barn walkway.

Tina looked up quickly, excitement filling her eyes. "Wait! Seriously?" She asked.

"Yep." Barry told her. "Your husband here drove a hard bargain; one Roger couldn't refuse."

She looked at Lucas with her eyes shining. This was so important to the growth of the ranch.

"How much are we getting? I mean, not that it really matters. It will be something!"

Lucas looked almost embarrassed. "Half the old man's land." Barry answered for him. "500 more acres. We can have as big a ranch as we want. Maybe bring in a few horses."

Tina was jittering with happiness. "Oh my god!" She said, putting her hands to her mouth. "Really?"

"Slow down, you two. Wait until we actually have it, to plan out the rest of our lives. One thing at a time." Lucas told them while shaking his head. "We want to grow slowly. Make sure we're ready."

Barry nodded and Tina said. "Of course."

But Lucas could see they were both still planning in their heads. "Come on, Jess!" He called, walking to the door of the barn. At least the dog was content with the way things were.

Chapter 27
A Working Class Dog

As the days began to grow longer and winter began to lose its grip, the ewes, who had been mostly kept in the large open areas of the barn, were allowed to take their lambs outside. They were old enough to be able to find their mothers, amongst many others. The morning air was filled with the sounds of sheep crying for their breakfast and the softer cries of lambs calling to their moms.

Jess followed Lucas among the sheep. She had gained the trust of all but the most crusty old sheep. Those, the dog would skirt around as she wove between the rest, moving among them with nary a ripple. Lucas often found himself watching her as she checked in with ewes and lambs alike. Her presence wasn't just tolerated. She was accepted.

Most days, Jess hung out with Lucas as he went through the barn and got grain for the sheep. Occasionally though, she stayed out among them as they waited and paced impatiently. At first, Lucas had worried that the frolicking of the lambs might be taken as a signal to play, but Jess only watched their antics with passive curiosity. He was constantly surprised by her instincts and attentive nature.

She had been learning not to fear simple objects, like a shovel or a rake in human hands, when it was swung or scraped along the barn floor. She no longer worried about Lucas throwing snow. She was confident in her environment and had become quicker to adapt to new things. As such, Lucas seldom did chores without her. She had become as much a familiar part of chores as his brother.

Jess watched him as he moved among the sheep putting grain in the feeder. Occasionally, when he looked at her, her tail would wag involuntarily. She enjoyed being with all of them, but the early morning chores when Barry was busy with other aspects of the ranch, like using the tractor to move snow or bringing round bales closer to the barn, and Tina was in the house making sure no one went hungry, was for the two of them, alone. She felt safe among them and although sometimes at night, she would dream of another place and different comforts, she barely remembered a life without them. Once in a while, when out in the field, images of other dogs would flutter through her thoughts. For a time, she would sniff the wind as if she might actually catch their scent, but these days, she just pushed them aside and focused on the people who made her feel safe and protected, even from the bad man in her dreams.

The snow began to recede and more often, the warmest part of the day, turned the snow into a sloppy mess that froze again at night. Dried weeds from the previous year began to stick up in clumps between the frozen remains of the snow. The sheep began to move about, and they seemed restless and bored in the confines of the small field where they had wintered to keep them safe. It was a warm day and Barry and Lucas headed up to check fence in the large field beyond. With the melting of the snow, there were beginning to be things that the sheep could eat. Small blades of short grass had begun to creep out between the dried brown grass. The sheep were tired of winter, tired of the close quarters and the growing lambs were not making it better.

Jess had been with Lucas for chores, but when Barry met up with them to go into the larger pasture areas, he had questioned whether or not they should bring the dog closer to the place of her origins. Lucas had hesitated, unsure himself. In the end, he had decided to take her. She seemed to have little desire to leave their ranch or the people themselves. "There is nothing there for her anymore and nothing good ever came from that place anyway." He had told Barry.

He had not been wrong about Jess's desire to stay with her people. As they walked along the fence fixing any sagging places and pulling branches that had fallen during winter storms, Jess had followed along smelling along the fence and keeping a watchful eye on the open land beyond. "Boy, she really pays attention," Barry said watching the dog scanning the area beyond the fence.

"She sure does." Lucas said. "If there was anything out there, she'd see it, even if we didn't."

"That will really be helpful when we start replacing the old fence where Mr. Allen used to own." Barry said Mr. Allen with disdain in his voice. That was not the kind of man they would normally have any dealings with.

Lucas cast Barry a sideways glance. "At least that's done and over with and I don't think he'll show up at our barn anytime soon."

Barry chuckled. "I'm not sure if he's more worried about you or the dog."

Lucas and Barry had gone to town to sign the paperwork and buy the land. They had not been contacted by Roger, only his agent. He had not shown up at the meeting either. He had signed the papers with the lawyer who had written them up, before their arrival. Really, Lucas had been relieved. As much as he could certainly handle the old man, it was far easier not to deal with him. To his credit, Roger had not tried to alter anything from their original talk. The 501.3 acres now belonged to the brothers along with anything on it. It would take time and work to get the fields cleaned up and properly fenced. Yet it would not only give room for expanding, but to be able to have their own hay cut, with the ability to sell the extra. Barry was right. It would make It economically sound to have a few horses, which would make it far easier to check and move the sheep and to check the fence. Besides, like many young girls, Tina had always dreamed of having a horse. He would feel much more comfortable about her going riding, if he could teach Jess to follow her when she went. With the dog by her side to alert for trouble, and a good horse, he would feel like she was safe. Tina had also gotten quite good with the 9mm that Lucas had once bought her for Christmas when they first started the ranch.

Lucas and Barry spent most of the day fixing damage to the fence line, in preparation for letting the sheep out there. It was great for the welfare of the sheep, but it also put them back closer to the coyote's domain. They would have to spend some time at night, reminding the coyotes that breaching the fence was not a good idea. Barry had enjoyed sleeping most nights and was not looking forward to the change.

A few days later, after spending a few hours the night before patrolling the area, they decided to let the sheep up in the grazing area, even if they brought them back in the evening. Lucas opened the gates and he and Barry began pushing them up towards the opening. It didn't take long. As soon as the first sheep realized the gates were open, they began to pour through like water released from a dam. There was some chaos as lambs lost their mothers in the rush. The sheep seemed to have forgotten them in the moment, while they ran from one place to another grabbing small bits of green grass.

The cries from the lambs were ignored and to the men, every one felt like a beacon of encouragement to the coyotes. But there was nothing to be done about it except to wait until the ewes had gotten over their initial excitement. As they got the lost lambs into the main grazing area, they closed the gates to keep everyone together. When things began to calm and the mothers began to notice and call for their young, Lucas finally realized that Jess was nowhere to be seen. He looked out into the winter area, but the dog was nowhere in sight. "Barry. Did you see Jess come out?" He asked. "Umm. No." He also looked towards the small field that they had just left. Then, like Lucas, he began to scan the area with the sheep. "Maybe she got spooked and headed for the barn." He suggested, remembering the night when the gun had frightened her.

Lucas sighed. "Stay here. I'll go look."

He crossed the half frozen, muddy area near the barn and stepped inside. The dog was nowhere to be seen. He checked the sheep areas and the grain room, but she wasn't there. He walked back and scanned the drive going up to the house. Just then, he heard Barry whistle. He was looking towards Lucas and waving his arm in a comeback motion. Lucus trotted back as best he could on the slippery ground. As he got close, Barry moved his hand in a hurry up motion. Lucas came in the gate and Barry simply said. "Shhhh." And motioned Lucas to follow him, up over the gentle slope of the land. When he could see over it, Barry pointed.

Following Barry's gaze and his hand, Lucas looked out across the field. There, on the far side of the sheep, was Jess. She was standing alert, looking out into the land beyond. She sniffed the air and scanned for any potential movement. When she found nothing, she trotted further along and repeated the behavior. Barry and Lucas stood watching in wonder. As the sheep moved, she moved with them, always ahead of them and always watching further out.

The two men watched in fascination, for quite a while until Lucas suddenly realized that Tina would have no idea why they hadn't shown up back at home. He looked at his watch. It was already 10 am. "Holy." He said. "We better get down there before Tina thinks we ran into trouble."

Barry looked at him and then at his own watch. "Oh, we are already in trouble."

"Jess!" Lucas called. "Jess! Let's go!"

The dog started to come to him, as she usually did, but when she reached the point of leaving the sheep, she stopped and looked back.

"Jess! Here!" Lucas called again.

The dog lowered her head, but again, she did not come to him. Lucas moved closer. He was trying to get down to the house and explain about missing breakfast as there was no phone signal out here in the field. Now was not the time to have the dog suddenly refuse to listen. As Lucas approached, with clear aggravation in his demeanor, Jess dropped flat to the ground. He bent down and petted her head to reassure her. And then spoke in a softer tone. "Jess. Come on. Let's go."

The dog stood and began to follow. Only ten or so steps later, he glanced back to realize the dog had not continued. In fact, she had turned back towards the sheep and was moving back to where she had been. "Damn dog." Lucas muttered.

Barry's hand on his arm stopped him. He looked over at him. "She is protecting the sheep." Barry said. "That's what those dogs do. She doesn't want to leave them out here alone." "She isn't like those dogs. She's nothing like them!" Lucas spat.

"Maybe because she wasn't raised being kicked and starved." Barry reminded him. She doesn't have to be like a wild animal to have the instinct to protect. Do you think she would protect Tina if she'd been raised like those dogs?"

Lucas thought for a second. "No. No, she wouldn't." He paused watching her. "So what do I do?" he asked, looking to Barry, now that he'd come to some kind of terms with the difference between Jess and other dogs he'd seen. "Maybe we should leave her." Barry said hesitantly, as if still considering.

"What if the coyotes come while we're gone?" Lucas asked but he didn't sound adamant about her going.

Barry thought for a few more seconds. "Okay. First of all, in case you hadn't noticed, she isn't a little puppy anymore."

Lucas had to admit that that was true. Though she still looked young, she was quite a large dog. Far different than the half-starved pup, they had brought home from the vet. "And"

Barry continued, after a moment. "Look at the way she watches. She'll see them long before they actually get here. If she barks the way she did the other time, we'll certainly hear it, and we can come take care of business."

He could tell Lucas liked the idea. He was worried, but this could actually be a real game changer. It was like having an alarm system for the coyotes. That would be far easier than checking all the time.

Lucas ran his fingers through his short beard, thinking it all through. Tina might not like the idea, but Barry was absolutely right. They could bring the sheep back to the winter area at night, let them graze all day and know that if there was an issue, Jess would let him know. He just hoped she was as good with the sheep alone, as she was in his presence.

"You really think she'll be okay?" he asked, not wanting to voice his actual fears.

"Look," Barry told him. She obviously understands the need to protect them. Besides, she'll be earning her keep. You always say everything here has to earn its keep." He grinned at his brother.

Lucas looked at Barry from the corners of his eyes. His mouth twisted up into a wry smile. "Okay. Fine. We'll do it your way. But…" He paused just for a second. "You can come up and have coffee and explain the idea to Tina."

Barry laughed out loud. "I'll come have coffee and listen to you explain it."

Lucas looked up to where Jess was standing. He made his way to her and stooped down. She lowered her head, as if she did not want to have to disobey him again. He told her she was a good dog and stroked her fur. "Don't let me down, girl. Okay?" He said quietly. Jess just stared at him with her soft dark eyes. After a minute, he returned to his brother and with a last look back, they made their way down to the house, still arguing lightheartedly, about who would tell Tina. They had also, each without saying it, both come to the conclusion that this, barring some catastrophe, this was the way it was going to be. It would change so much about their lives.

Tina met them on the porch, so she had obviously been checking for them. "Is everything all right?" She asked them anxiously. Then almost immediately after, "Lucas, where's Jess?"
Her eyes filled with worry and Barry was the first to speak. "She's fine. Absolutely fine."
Tina looked at her husband. "Lucas?"
"Look. She didn't want to come back. I called her and she refused." Lucas said, trying to explain and failing badly.
"So, you just left her!" Tina exclaimed.

"Wait. Wait! Barry said quickly and Tina flashed him an angry look.

"You two, just left Jess somewhere?"

Lucas put his hand up in a stop position. Tina was silent for a moment. "We didn't abandon her. When we took the sheep up, she didn't want to leave them alone. She wanted to stay. So we let her." His voice was deliberately calm. "Did she say, no thanks, guys. I think I'll stay here?"

Lucas chuckled. Not a good idea when she was worried, but he couldn't help it. Barry just stared at the floorboards on the porch. "When we went up there, she immediately took up a position between the sheep and the fields beyond. She was walking with them and looking for any sign of danger. We watched her for a while, because I'd never seen a dog act like that. Then I realized the time and we went to leave, but Jess wouldn't. I even went up where she was and tried to get her to follow, but when we got past the sheep, she went back."

Tina was quiet for a few minutes; unsure her voice wouldn't crack when she spoke. She was not hysterical or flighty. But sometimes she worried when they were gone that something bad would happen. She was glad to see they were fine, but then noticed the dog was missing. She still worried that something bad would happen between Jess and Lucas.

Something that would ruin his trust forever. It was her biggest fear. She wanted so much for Lucas to see the good in a dog.

Having calmed a bit, she could finally ask. "Do you think she'll be okay? I mean, if the coyotes came?"

This was the part Barry was good at and he spoke first. "If she barks, we'll be able to hear it, no problem. We will grab our guns and go protect her and the sheep."

"Seriously?" Tina asked, her voice sounding hopeful.

Lucas nodded; glad Barry had this under control. He was not always the best at explaining.

Barry said. "With all the lambs up there, it's sure to attract attention."

"I know." Tina answered.

"But you had to see her." Barry continued before she got worried again. "It was amazing. She is scouting the whole area and looking for any movement. Instead of having to wait for the sound of screaming sheep to know something is wrong, she'll bark, way before the coyotes get there."

Tina thought about that and being an intelligent woman, she could easily understand that this made sense. This way, the dog would be safe and so would the sheep. "What about at night? Will you leave her out there then?" She asked.

"No." Lucas's response was immediate. "At night, we'll use some grain to bring the sheep back and Jess can come home."

Tina smiled. "I like that idea." She answered. Then realizing they were all on the porch, she said. "Why don't we all go in and have lunch?"

"I like THAT idea!" Barry said with a laugh.

"Me too." Lucas agreed while giving his brother an appreciative look.

They were not wrong about Jess's capabilities. Several times over the next month, she would sound off. Her deep bark would ring clear over the distance and Lucas and Barry, who had taken to keeping their rifles near to where they were working, would race out to the field to back Jess. In the beginning, they would definitely take the coyotes by surprise. They managed to take down a few. However, the coyotes weren't dumb, and it didn't take long for them to learn that the barking of the dog, meant the arrival of the men. The coyotes went from brazen, to hesitant, to leery. In a few weeks' time, the intermittent visits came to an end. Every day they would leave the sheep in Jess's protection and at night, they would bring them in, and Jess would happily come to the house. Each time, Tina would check her all over and make sure all was well. Then Jess would eat and join the family in the living room as she had all along.

Chapter 28
Worth Every Dime

The Porter's were all in the barn, when they heard the sound of a horn. Lucas looked outside to see a truck in the driveway. He motioned to Barry to follow and they went to meet the visitor. They were surprised to see Mr. Benson behind the wheel. "Good morning." Lucas said, in a friendly tone.

"Morning." Mr. Benson replied.

"Everything been okay, over your way?" Lucas knew the man had to be here for a reason. They were neighborly enough when they saw each other, but neither went out of their way to make that happen.

"Did you hear what happened to the Wymans?" The elderly man asked solemnly.

Lucas had known there had to be some news for the man to show up in his driveway. "No, I haven't seen much of anyone since before winter." Lucas told him honestly. "It's been pretty quiet around here."

Mr. Benson nodded. "I figured I'd come make sure you knew."

Lucas just waited as Barry moved just a little closer to make sure he could hear. The man said, "Last night, something got into their sheep. They had let them out to field to graze a few weeks back and everything had been fine. Went up this morning and there were sheep, injured, dead, lambs torn apart. Some of them died from exhaustion. They had to put down some of the injured. They tore the guts right out of them and left 'em alive."

Lucas felt his heart drop. The story was familiar. Barry recognized the description as well.

"That ain't no coyotes." Lucas said, his voice suddenly colder. Coyotes might run a few, but that…"

Mr. Benson finished for him. "It was dogs."

Lucas shuddered. He felt sick in the bottom of his stomach. He had seen, firsthand, the damage dogs did.

"Do you know who they belong to?" He asked. The man in the truck shook his head. "No idea. They were gone when they found the sheep, but their tracks were in some of the muddy places. I didn't see them, but they said the tracks were pretty big. Of course, they had to be to cause that kind of damage."

Lucas's face had turned pale. Dogs were worse than coyotes. They killed for the thrill of the chase without rhyme or reason.

"If I see them." Lucas told Mr. Benson. "I won't treat them differently than any other predator."

"I was kind of hoping you'd say that." The man said, his voice devoid of emotion.

Barry, who had stayed silent through the conversation, had to ask a question. "Did the Wymans ask you to come talk to us?

Lucas hadn't thought of that, but he also wanted to know. Especially after all they'd had to say last fall. The man in the truck adjusted his hat, he looked out the passenger window and down at his lap. He shook his head. "No. They didn't. They asked me not to tell you. They said it wasn't the dogs' fault. It was the owners who were to blame. Lucas and Barry looked at the man in disbelief. "Are you damn kidding me? Lucas said, raising his voice with vehement disapproval. "They don't want me to know? What if it ends up being my sheep next?"

"That's why I'm telling you." Josh Benson lowered his head again. "Well, honestly, not just for you. I'm also telling you for me. I'm not as fast as I used to be and my eyesight isn't great either. I'm hoping you can get them. I'm hoping those dogs just don't come home one day." Now Lucas understood. He put his hand on the old man's shoulder. "I'll damn make sure of it." He said.

Lucas straightened up and looked at the man. "Things can happen with dogs roaming at large. If they don't come home, who knows what could have happened to them."

The old man looked grateful. "Thank you. You're right. Any number of things could happen. They just might disappear like the knowledge of this conversation."

He tapped the truck. "You bet."

Lucas and Barry stepped back away and with a nod, Josh Benson backed out of the driveway.

Barry could see the grim set of his brother's jaw and he knew this was going to be personal for Lucas. When they reached the barn, they told Tina all about the conversation. She shook her head. "Those fools deserve to lose everything they have." she said bitterly. She hadn't started as a country girl, but she couldn't imagine being that naive. "If they come here, it will be their fault."

"At least we have Jess for a warning." Barry said, once again genuinely happy they had her. But Lucas looked more worried. "You don't think she'd join them, do you?"

"Lucas! Don't be silly. Why would she?" Tina said, sounding defensive.

"Dog's sometimes get excited by things other dogs are doing. I've heard about dogs egging another on. Pack mentality." Lucas was already imagining the worst-case scenario.

Tina didn't know what to say. She too had heard of terrible stories. What if he were right? Barry was the voice of reason. "Now hold up. She sees anything moving out there, she's going to go off. She's not gonna wait until they are inside the fence. Even if they run straight in, we'll already be on the way."

Lucas's shoulders sagged with relief. He was right. Barry was absolutely right. Tina felt relieved as well. So relieved, she could almost cry.

"Maybe we should just go check on her." Lucas said. "Take a look around while we're up there." Knowing it would make Lucas feel better, Barry agreed. When they had gone, Tina let her emotions have their way and she silently sent up a prayer to anyone who might listen. She prayed that that would never be Jess's fate.

Jess had been fine when the men had gone to check. And things remained that way for several days. They'd had a few alerts from Jess, but when they arrived, whatever she had seen was already gone from sight. Each time, Lucas would actually climb over the fence and have a look around. He was torn between not wanting anything to happen and hoping he'd get a chance to take care of the problem.

It was late one afternoon, and the men had been working on some of the old fence on the eastern side of the ranch. It was warm and cleaning the old branches and new scrub away from the fence had been back breaking work. This is where he wanted to keep the horses when they were ready for them. Suddenly Barry, who had walked up to grab their water jug, stopped in his tracks. "Lucas!" He yelled. Lucas turned and looked up. Barry yelled one word. "Jess!" Then he turned and ran across the field towards the back of the barn. Lucas dropped the tools in his hands and ran after him.

When Barry came around the side of the barn, he almost ran into Tina, who had been running to find them. She stepped back against the side of the barn as Lucas rounded the corner. As each man ran by, he grabbed a rifle from the barn doorway. Tina watched them go, hoping the sound of the washing machine had not covered the barking for too long.

The men were thinking much the same type of thoughts. Barry had not heard the dog until he had walked closer to the barn. How long had it been? They continued towards the field, their tiredness forgotten in their panic. When they reached the gates, the sheep were crowded near the fence and Lucas threw open the gates as Barry went through. The sheep began to flee past them to the safety of the barn. He saw one lamb go by with blood on its ear and a ewe with blood on her haunch and a gash on her face. The men ran further and up over the slope of the hill. They stared down across the expanse, seeing nothing at all. "Jess!" Lucas called. There was no response.

The two brothers spread out looking for signs of the intruders. Barry went down along the western side. As he moved along, he saw wet blood on the grass. He kept moving, looking for bodies of sheep or lambs. Lucas had gone the other way and was moving through the scrub brush that grew in clumps in various places. It gave pockets of shade to the sheep in the warmer months. Now it was a hindrance to his line of sight. As he passed into an open area, he saw something dark lying a ways further down the slope, in the grass. There was blood around it. He moved quickly down to it, rifle at the ready. He glanced around as he went, but he could see no sign of Barry and no sign of Jess.

When he got there, he was looking at a German Shepherd sized dog. It poked it with his boot, but it did not move. He stooped, setting down his rifle and grabbed the limp dog by its collar. He pulled its head around and looked at the tags. It had a rabies tag, much like Jess and another that said Jack with a phone number. The blood on Jack's face and on his throat said he wouldn't be coming home today. Lucas felt annoyed. If people were just responsible, Jack could be home, lying next to the couch. He knew the Wymans were right about it not being the dog's fault. Unlike the Wymans, he wasn't going to give the dogs or their owners a second chance.

Lucas stood up and turned around to look up the hill for Barry, as he did, he heard the low growl. He wheeled around to see a dog lying next to some scrub. Blood ran down the side of its head and one lip was torn. Blood was running down his neck from that too. It looked to be some kind of mix. Husky maybe. He wasn't sure. Lucas stepped back, over his rifle, his eyes never leaving the dog. The dog started to stand, as Lucas stooped to pick the rifle up. It was going to be a close one if the dog came for him. As Lucas brought the rifle up into his hands, he watched the dog curl its lips back, showing blood-stained white teeth. He saw the movement out of the corner of his eye but before he could register what it was, the white mass slammed into the threatening dog at full speed. The dog rolled sideways from the brunt of the impact and for a moment the two animals tumbled over two or three times, before they halted with the white dog on top.

Further up the hill, Barry, who had seen Jess race by him, watched, frozen in amazement. Then he spied Lucas standing rifle in hand, looking just as shocked, and made his way down to his brother. Lucas glanced at him and back to the fighting dogs. Jess slashed and bit at the other dog, as the two came up on their hind legs. They were both fighting to gain a grip on the other to give them the upper hand. In that moment, suddenly, Lucas's fear disappeared. He moved across the distance with hurried strides and with a carefully placed aim in the chaos, he slammed the butt of the rifle into the side of the dog's head. Its head went sideways, and the dog lost its balance. Jess wasted no time. As it fell onto its side, scrambling to regain its feet, she dove in, grabbing the dog by the throat and clenching her jaws with all her might, using her weight to pin its body to the ground. The men, unable to assist further, watched in horrified fascination as Jess ended the other dog's life. When all movement had stopped, still Jess held on. Lucas took a step forward and to his surprise, Jess let out a small growl. He froze. "Easy." Barry said. "Let her be. She's just all wound up. You've been in some fights. Did you want a hug, right after?"

"I don't want one right now." Lucas said breathlessly. It did make some sense to him with his own adrenaline rushing through his system.

After a minute or so more, Jess did let go. She sniffed the dog over and avoiding both men, she went to sniff the other dog. Then she went back to the first dog and smelled it again, before heading up the hill and disappearing from sight. "I guess she still doesn't want a hug." Lucas said, trying to calm his own nerves.

Barry gave a half-hearted chuckle. "I guess we better get rid of these." He said. "I don't want some angry city dweller mad at Jess for doing her best to keep things safe."

"Agreed." Lucas said.

He headed for the bigger dog and grabbed its collar. Its tag said Jill, with the same phone number. Grabbing the other one, Barry asked. "Where do you want to take them?

With a slight laugh, Lucas looked up towards the top of the slope and said. "Up the hill. Where else."

Barry gave him an odd look when Lucas laughed and for some reason, that made it funnier. He dragged the dog up, still chuckling to himself as Barry looked totally confused.

After they'd stashed the bodies for later disposal, off the ranch, they made a quick sweep to ensure they hadn't missed any injured sheep. When they were heading back to the barn, Lucas shut the gates. That was enough for one day. Tina already had the injured ewe and her lambs in one of the barn stalls and was tending their wounds. Jess was pacing in and out of the barn, trying to check on the ewe and the herd. Tina looked at them. "How bad is it?" she asked, having no idea what they had found. Lucas looked over the stall door. "Is the injured lamb in here?"

She nodded yes.

"Did you see any others injured?"

"No." She had started to look annoyed at his lack of an answer.

"That's all we saw." Lucas finally answered.

She looked up at his face. "Are you serious?" Both men nodded.

"Well, Jess might have some" Barry said, remembering the blood on the dog.

Lucas walked towards the barn door. "Jess! Come here."

This time she came to him. He knelt down and began to check her over, cataloging each injury in his head for when he actually doctored them. He found some scrapes and a few punctures, but certainly nothing detrimental. Jess was patient and very tolerant of whatever pain he might have caused her. As he tended to her wounds, with Barry hovering close by, they relayed the story to Tina. She listened with both awe and fear. Though she would not say it, part of her awe was Lucas aiding Jess in the fight. You'd almost think he loved that dog she thought, chuckling silently in her own head.

When they had done all they could for the ewe and lamb, who seemed like they would survive and Lucas had finished with Jess, they made their way to the house. The dog was hesitant to follow at first, but with a little coaxing, they managed to get her to follow.

Once they were seated, Tina explained that after they had left and the sheep came down, Jess had come down as well. It was her checking over the sheep and licking the ear of the lamb and the face of the ewe that had brought their injuries to Tina's attention because they had been hidden among the flock. When she had gone to try to separate them from the herd to get them indoors, Jess had run back to where Lucas and Barry had gone. Lucas shook his head. "Somehow, we missed her entirely. We didn't see her until she attacked the dog."

"That's crazy." Tina said. "I wonder what made her go back."

Barry shrugged. "Obviously to save her chore buddy."

Tina smiled. "So now what?"

Lucas said. "As soon as it's dark, we're gonna get them off the property. If someone does ever find them, they'll think wild animals did it."

"That's a good idea." Tina said in agreement. "They might not be very happy with us, if they knew."

"They certainly wouldn't be happy with Jess." Barry added.

"Better if they don't know." Lucas said quietly. "And on the way back, we'll drive by Mr. Benson's."

After they had placed the dogs in a wooded area, off of a sideroad, where no one would notice a parked truck, they headed to the goat farm owned by Josh Benson.

When they pulled in the driveway of Mr. Benson, they stayed in the truck, not wanting to have a conversation in front of his wife.

It took a few minutes, but the old man came out on the porch wearing an old flannel coat and rain boots. He stood hesitantly on the porch, peering into the dark driveway. Lucas stepped out and took a few steps into the light of the porch. As the old man made his way towards Lucas, he retreated back to the darkness by the truck. When Mr. Benson reached him, Lucas was casual. "How's things going?" He said.

Mr. Benson sighed. "A little tired, up every couple hours all night every time there is a noise. Hoping you have some good news."

Lucas scuffed his boot in the dirt. "I think you'd be fine getting some sleep tonight."

Their eyes met. Mr. Benson smiled a tired smile. "I was hoping you would say something like that."

Lucas nodded. "If the wife asks, we were just looking for directions."

"Thank you. I appreciate it." The old man said before turning and shuffling back towards the porch. Lucas got back in the truck and got back out onto the road.

They were silent at first but then Lucas said.
"Did you look at the tags on the dogs?"
"No." Barry said. "I didn't. Why?"
"Jack and Jill." Lucas answered.
"And? Barry asked, wondering what had to do with anything.
"That's why we took them up the hill."
Barry laughed and rolled his eyes. "You friggin idiot." He paused, chuckling regardless. "I'm supposed to say the dumb shit."
Lucas just laughed.

Barry looked over at Lucas in the darkness of the truck. "I guess the vet bill isn't such a big deal, huh?"
Lucas felt his face flush. He kept driving, staring out at the road. Finally, he said. "How long have you known?"
"Always." Barry said. "I let you make the financial decisions, but I still know what's going on. "
Lucas sighed. "I bet you're regretting that now."
"I don't think so." Barry said, seriously.
Lucas glanced his way with his eyebrow raised. Barry continued his thoughts. "I'd have chosen to just put the dog down. It would have seemed like the logical thing to do. But you didn't. Now, although she was an expense all winter, this spring she has been our salvation. How many sheep did the Wymans lose? How many lambs?"

"I don't know exactly." Lucas said, still slightly embarrassed.

"We'll say 10. The average price of a market lamb is around $350. Then you add in all the times she's alerted us to coyotes and that any one of those times could have cost us ewes and lambs. I'd say she has saved us more than she cost us by a long shot."

"Did you know the vet gave back half the bill?" Lucas asked, trying to save some face.

"Wait! Seriously? Was that the $1900?"

"Yeah." Lucas said. "That."

"What did you say to him?" Barry asked, wondering if Lucas had finally told the man what was what.

"That's just it." He replied. "I didn't say anything else. It just came in the mail one day."

"Well, don't that beat all." Barry muttered.

They drove the rest of the way in silence with Lucas feeling grateful that Barry had not given him a hard time, when he was so stressed about the whole thing. It wasn't that surprising though. Barry had always been the one person Lucas could count on in his life. Everyone saw Lucas as the strong one, the leader, but behind the scenes, it had often been Barry, despite his ready wit and easy demeanor, who helped hold things together.

Chapter 29
Fair Thee Well

The weeks wore on and things had been pretty quiet. Jess continued to spend her days with the sheep and her nights with the humans. The men continued to work on fencing projects and some necessary repairs to the barn. It was a relatively hot day and they decided to break for lunch in the coolness of the house. When they came into the kitchen, Tina had been sorting the mail and was holding a booklet in her hand. She looked up at Lucas as he walked over to the table. "The Springer Fair is starting next week." She said, in a casual tone.

Lucas looked up. "Isn't that like 3 hours from here?"

Tina nodded. "Yes. Something like that."

She began putting lunch on the table, setting the pamphlet on the counter. Barry and Lucas exchanged glances. "Did you want to go?" Lucas asked Tina.

He felt something was up because Tina usually was not so vague. Lucas had never stopped her from doing things she enjoyed. Instead of answering his question, she said. "They are going to have some livestock sales going on." Now both Lucas and Barry were paying attention. They knew, if she was mentioning it, there was a reason. "Is there something we need?" Lucas asked her, letting her string them along as they ate.

"They have some sheep going up for sale." Tina said.

"We have sheep." Barry answered. "Lots of sheep at the moment."

She hesitated before saying, "It says they're selling off some of Jacob Fournier's bloodlines." She had a slight smirk on his face. She knew these were something they would definitely want to have, The Fournier family had been ranching for over 100 years. Their sheep were well known for reaching market weight faster and for having good saleable fleece. Although the Porters had certainly worked hard to acquire good sheep and to improve them, these would be a fantastic addition to their herd. They did not come up for sale often. In fact, it would be unlikely they'd come across this chance again any time soon. They usually kept their genetics under very tight rein. Lucas and Barry had stopped eating and were looking from Tina to each other. There was no doubt now that they were going.

They finished their lunch with Tina while she read them about the other fair events. Unlike the men, she was more interested in the booths and events than the sheep. She understood the importance and knew the details, but going to the fair was more about enjoyment. When the men went back to work, Lucas wanted a chance to talk to Barry alone. Once they were down in the field he said. "She wants to go to that fair."

"You think?" Barry said. "I don't think I've heard her get that excited about something, ever."

Lucas started clearing. His mood had drastically changed during their time in the house. "So what's wrong with her going?" Barry didn't understand why Lucas would have an issue.

"I want you there to help make decisions on what we buy." Lucas said, still sounding troubled.

"Well, of course I'm going."

"So, who is watching the ranch?" Lucas said in a dry tone.

Barry hadn't thought of that actually. Now he understood the problem. Tina never asked for much and Lucas never said no. She'd do it. She'd stay home. But Lucas didn't want her to have to.

He was pulling old fence up where Lucas was cutting brush off. It all had to be replaced. It was old and from the previous owner. As Barry worked, he thought about how they could all manage. He knew Lucas was as well. He mulled some stuff through his head and thought his idea would work. "Look." Barry said "Hear me out. We haven't had any issues. The coyotes know that once the dog sees them, we'll be there soon. So here's what I think. We'll do chores that morning and let the sheep out like we always do. Once they're gone out there grazing, we'll put grain in the feeders and open the gates to the barn again. We can leave out and be to the fair about 10 or 10:30."

He could see Lucas thinking about what he had said.

"We'll take a look at the sheep and make notes about what we want. That'll give us 4 hours to do the things Tina wants to do. The sheep go up for sale at 3. We'll go to the sale and she can keep shopping or whatever. The sheep are used to getting grain at night so when we aren't there at dark, they'll start coming to the gate. It'll be open. They'll come down, eat, bed down. The coyotes certainly won't come down here. We'll load up the sheep and come straight home. Even if it's 8 or 9, it won't be that late. We can check everything. Close the gates. Bring Jess in the house and the sheep on the trailer can stay put until morning. Everyone gets what they want."

Lucas took a deep breath. "What if the coyotes did come? I know it's not likely, but I'd hate to go get sheep and lose sheep."

"Lucas." Barry shook his head. "Jess isn't a puppy anymore. Did you see her with that dog? A couple of coyotes come in, they're going to wish they hadn't. She'll jack and jill those suckers."

Lucas chuckled. He felt It was a solid idea. He also didn't know how not to worry. "She really is pretty capable."

"Damn straight." Barry said. "I wouldn't have believed that if I hadn't seen it."

"You're right. Really it would only be a couple hours later than usual and we haven't had a real attempt in weeks." Lucas's voice was still hesitant, but Barry also knew he was likely to agree.

"It's one day. Jess was a gift of fate. She is what we needed and we need to realize that it's different now. We might not always have to leave the house in shifts." As Barry talked about it, he realized how true it was. Yes, they ran up every time to help the dog, but she didn't really need it for a couple of scouts. They wouldn't want her up against the whole pack, but they hadn't been seen near the fence in any numbers since Jess started staying out there. At this point, the few sightings were often in the distance and many times, by the time they got there, they didn't see anything at all.

Lucas nodded. "So if nothing changes before then, that's what we'll do."

That night at dinner, they discussed the plan with Tina. He could see her excitement. She began looking at the pamphlet again after dinner and planning what exhibitions she would have time to see and talking about the various booths and events. They had a western horsemanship competition at 2:30 and although it ran pretty late, Tina decided she would go to that while they went to the sheep sale and simply leave whenever they were done. When Barry had left for the night and Tina and Lucas lay in bed, she was still mentioning things about the fair. Lucas was happy they were all going.

The rest of the week went by quickly as Tina made plans and put together food and drinks for the trip. The men spent every night at dinner discussing the sheep and what they could mean for the ranch. By the time the day came, they had everything ready and all their plans set in place.

Monday morning they started chores early and they let Jess and the sheep out onto the grazing area. After they'd put out grain and the sheep had meandered off out of sight, they quietly opened the gates and went back up by the barn. As Barry had suspected. The sheep were off like any other day and none of them paid any attention.

They made it out of the driveway at 6:45, with the stock trailer in tow. After stopping for gas and coffee, they headed out onto the highway and settled down for the long drive. As they went, they chatted about everything from sheep to horses and foods they had at the fair. They ate the breakfast sandwiches Tina had packed, while they drank their coffee. Occasionally, the conversation would fade and they would just watch the road until someone would start the conversation again. They made pretty good time once the normal workday traffic faded away and they pulled into the fairgrounds just shy of 10:00. After pulling around the back to find a place to park the truck and trailer, they paid the entrance fee and with Tina's guidance from the booklet, they made their way to where the sheep were being kept.

Fournier's weren't the only sheep being sold and Lucas felt bad for the people who had also brought sheep to sell. Some of them were nice, definitely respectable, but the ones they were after were easy to recognize. The others would sell. But the comparison would probably lower the final sale price.

The sheep were divided up into lots and that is how they would be sold. Lucas and Barry agreed on a group of about 30 young ewes that were in with a large ram. The ewes all looked to be one or two years old. They weren't going to go cheap, but they were willing to spend good money on good stock. They even looked at some of the other sheep and decided to bid on a lot of ten, if the prices were right. They were good sheep, bloodlines they wouldn't mind having, according to the paperwork on the pen, just not Fournier sheep.

Once decisions had been made, they let Tina take the lead. They followed her around as she took them through exhibits. They went from booth to booth and Tina, caught up in the fair atmosphere, bought a delicate, handmade necklace with a dog pendant that somewhat resembled Jess's silhouette. She also bought a new cap for Luke and made him put it on, stuffing his old one in her bag. They bought onion rings and fried dough, and Tina bought cotton candy. As much as the men rolled their eyes and Lucas would occasionally tease Tina for her enthusiasm, they were all having a good time just getting away. Though each of them, at various points, would think of things back home, none of them mentioned it out loud to the others. It was a nice day and no one was willing to risk ruining it. Afternoon came and eventually, around 2:00 Lucas and Barry bought drinks from a booth and headed back down to where the sheep were penned and Tina headed off to the horse arena, carrying a bratwurst in one hand and an ice tea in the other.

There were several prospective buyers there now and they were glad they had already registered to bid. They moved their way through the crowd, looking for a good seat. They found the best they could expect at that point. Sitting on the hard bleachers against the wall, in that section of the sheep barn. The other end housed show quality sheep of various breeds. Those people had little interest in the type of sheep being sold here. They were there for the competition, the points and a ribbon for their barn.

Barry poked Lucas. "Look over there."
He nodded his head off to the left and further down the bleachers. Lucas scanned the people sitting in that direction until he saw someone he recognized. Sitting lower down on the far end of the bleachers was Mr. Wyman, his wife and their two sons. Lucas sighed and drew his head back. "I hope they don't see us." He said, making a half scowl.
"Oh, come on Lucas." Barry said. "How will you know what you're doing wrong? Have you patted the coyotes lately?"
Lucas rolled his eyes. "They're here to buy the coyotes some dinner."
"Well, that will keep them away from us." Barry chuckled quietly.

When the bidding got underway, the chatter stopped. People were focused and the bidding was heavy. Although Barry shifted his legs on

occasion, Lucas was totally still. When the
sheep they wanted were driven out into the
pen, Lucas sat up straighter. He waited for
some of the people to drop out and there were
only a few serious bidders left before he raised
his paddle for the first time. To his irritation, he
noticed the Wyman's were among the few. Of
course. He continued, raising his paddle each
time and hoping that if he did have to drop out,
it wouldn't be to Lyle Wyman.

When Lucas won, Barry breathed a sigh of
relief. It was cut short by the auctioneer saying,
"Lot 119, goes to 11817, Lucas Porter."
They could see Lyle Wyman's head come up
and his wife start scanning through the crowd.
Lucas stifled his desire to duck and just stayed
the way he'd been sitting. As the next group of
sheep was pushed out, he saw Mrs. Wyman,
find him in the crowd. They locked eyes for a
moment and then she was tapping her
husband's shoulder and pointing up at them.
Other people turned to look and the brothers
just pretended not to notice.

They had spent more than Lucas had hoped,
but less than his limit, which meant he could still
bid on the small group from the other ranch. He
glanced at his watch, which made Barry look at
his. It was only 4:35. They still had some time. It
wouldn't take that long to load the sheep. They

waited patiently hoping the group would come out soon. When they heard the auctioneer say that Lyle Wayman had a winning bid, the wife gave them a smug gloating look. Barry leaned close to him. "Hey. They beat you at the ones you didn't bid on."

Lucas groaned. He didn't understand why they just couldn't mind their own ranch. For him it was business, not a competition. Perhaps they should try at the other end of the barn.

It was 5:15 when the other sheep they had hoped to buy, finally came out to the pen. Many of the bidders had left and Lucas figured this would go pretty quickly. He waited, just like before, but there were not a lot of bidders. He lifted his paddle. As people were dropping out, Barry saw Mrs. Wyman follow the auctioneer's gaze and then nudge her husband. He glanced up at them and then lifted his own paddle. Barry glanced at Lucas, but he was focused on the auctioneer and hadn't seen.

When the bidding reached their agreed limit, Lucas hesitated. "Going once..."

Barry nudged Lucas and nodded his head to let him know he shouldn't drop out. Lucas, who had no idea what was going on, raised his paddle and the auctioneer continued. Barry encouraged him twice more and when the auctioneer continued, Lyle Wyman, who, by the look of things, was going against his wife's wishes, did not bid again. Barry could see Mrs. Wyman chatting furiously, as she berated him for giving up. Then the auctioneer announced Lucas's name again and the woman shot them a dirty look. Barry struggled to keep his face expressionless. "You think it was worth going that high? Lucas asked his brother.

It wasn't a bad amount, really, just more than they agreed upon and Barry usually didn't say anything unless Lucas looked his way.

"Oh, it was definitely worth it." Barry said. Lucas looked at him questioningly, but Barry said nothing more.

It took them longer than they had hoped to pay their bill and get the sheep loaded. Lucas had been afraid the Wymans would seek them out, but when he saw them, Mr. Wyman looked away and his wife gave them a cold stare. When they had left the barn, they realized it had rained at some point. He texted Tina to make sure she was doing alright. She told him the rain had been short, and they had just stepped inside while it passed. After they had parked the truck back where it had been and had made sure the doors of the trailer were padlocked, they headed out to find Tina was waiting, still watching the horses. It was just after 7. As they walked down to the horses, Barry burst out laughing. Lucas looked at him. "Okay, what is going on?"

Laughing the whole time, Barry explained about Lyle only joining the bidding after they realized Lucas wanted those sheep and his wife's demeanor. Lucas laughed and shook his head. "Was it really worth it?" He asked.

"Oh definitely." Barry answered.

They were still chuckling when they reached the area where the horses were.

Having just left the truck, they had come up on the side of the arena where the barns were. As they walked by a pen with horses for sale, Lucas stopped. Barry backed up a couple of steps. "What did you see?"

Lucas walked to the corral and glanced at the clipboards with paperwork for each horse. Finding the one he wanted, he tapped his finger on it and handed the clipboard to Barry. Barry glanced down at it for a moment and then up at Lucas who pointed to a horse on one side. It was a bay, probably just shy of 15 hands, sturdy looking, but not bulky. Its mane and tail were long and its face had a thin white blaze. Barry looked at the paperwork more in depth. The little mare was 7 years old. She had worked on a sheep ranch and was used to trail rides. It said she had been the horse of a 15 year old girl. "You gonna ride that?" Barry said, already knowing the answer.

"Tina's birthday is in two weeks." Lucas said, knowing his brother knew damn well.

Barry snorted. "Fine. Fine. We'll spend more money. How you gonna hide that?"

Lucas climbed over the fence and approached the mare who didn't seem to mind. Barry hung up the clipboard and joined him. They checked her teeth and hooves and walked her around, finding no obvious issues.

"I can't hide it for two weeks, but if we get her and you take her back to the trailer, he looked up, it's probably going to be dark by that time. Chances are we can drive home, get Tina in the house and get the horse in a stall until morning."

Barry smiled. "Alright. Let's find the owner and give her a test drive."

Lucas was seldom spontaneous. But they both knew how happy it would make her.

Lucas looked at his phone and saw the "Everything alright?" text.

He texted back. "We ran into the Wymans at the sheep barn."

"Oh lord." She replied and Lucas could picture her facial expression.

Now that he had her stalled thinking they were stuck listening to Lyle and his wife, they headed into the barn and found someone who worked there. They told him what they were looking for and 15 minutes later, he came back with a man with graying hair and a western hat. He looked at both men. "Who's it for?"

"My wife." Lucas replied.

"Ohhh. What can i do for you?"

"I just want to take It for a quick ride." Lucas told him, not knowing how long the Wyman story would delay Tina.

The man grabbed the saddle and bridle and the brothers followed him out. "Is she a big woman?" The man asked, having no idea how to be diplomatic,

"Oh no. She's a dainty little thing." Lucas replied.

"Had to ask." The man said. "I had a lady here earlier who weighed pretty near as much as the horse. I had to turn her down."

Lucas pulled out his phone and showed the man the picture of Tina on the screen. "Be perfect for her. It was my daughter's horse, but she's in college now and probably gonna get a job in the city. Hate the idea of a good horse wasting away. I'd rather put money in her college funds."

Lucas sensed the man's attachment to the horse was connected to missing his daughter. He wondered for a moment if Tina's family had something that made them think of her.

"My wife was a city girl. He said. "Now we're out here running a sheep ranch."

"What about you?" The man asked.

"We grew up on a ranch." Lucas said. "I took some animal husbandry courses at a college and met my wife."

"She doing alright out there?"

"She loves it." Lucas said. "We're expanding the ranch and I'd like for her to have a good, trustworthy horse she can go out on."

The man led the horse out and handed the reins to Lucas. Lucas pulled himself into the saddle and gently rode around the parking lot, getting a feel for what the horse was like. She was easy-going and calm, but when Lucas gave her a tap with his heels, she picked up the pace without hesitation. He spent some time trying various things before he brought her back to the owner.

"What do you think? The man asked, looking hopeful.

Lucas slid off and looked at Barry, who nodded.

"We'll take her." Lucas said.

"You want the tack?" He asked.

"Sure." Barry told him before Lucas could answer.

Ignoring the text on his phone, Lucas went with the man to the office at the end of the barn, praying he wouldn't walk somewhere that Tina might see him.

When they were done and the paperwork was in Lucas's hand, he gave the envelope to Barry, who had been holding the horse while Lucas paid. Once Barry was out of sight he rushed through the barns and out towards the arena, where the last of the event horses were being led out for the night. He scanned the fence line and saw Tina's figure in the growing darkness. He hurried across to the fence and called her name. She turned around looking rather anxious. "You alright? Lucas said, feeling guilty. "Is everything okay? I was starting to worry. It was getting so late and you said you ran into the Wymans and I started thinking that maybe you got in an argument or a fight. Got arrested." Lucas pulled her to him, hugged her and laughed. "Come on." He said. I'll explain on the way."

"Where is Barry? She said suddenly.

"Oh." Lucas replied. He's staying with the truck. There's a lot of money in sheep, on there right now."

"How did it go? she asked, still feeling like something wasn't right.

Lucas, knowing she felt like something bad must have happened, began to tell her the whole story of Wyman bidding on the same flock and how they announced his name and then the petty bidding on the other sheep. He knew she didn't like them anymore than Lucas himself did, and that she would expend her angst, being aggravated about their behavior. He hated that he had made her worry, but he also hoped tomorrow, she would understand.

He was right about her directing her emotions elsewhere and she was so annoyed she got right into the truck without even glancing in the stock trailer. Barry, who had opened the door for her, to encourage her to hop in, added fuel to the fire when he got in the back seat. He told her about the dirty looks and Mrs. Wyman's smug glares and whatever else he thought might distract her. Lucas had to try hard not to smile.

"Did they get anything?" she finally asked.

"Yeah." Lucas said. They did get a group of older Fournier ewes and they bought a few of the other lots of sheep."

"Did they say a lot to you guys?" Tina was nothing if not protective and she wanted all the details.

"No." Barry said. "We were just trying to get out of there. They acted like we came there just to compete with them."

"So, what took so long?" She asked.

Barry thought a moment before answering.

"Well, every minute we were delayed, meant more people getting in line to pay and then that put them ahead of us to load up."

That statement wasn't totally untrue, although it wasn't particularly the Wyman's fault. He was desperately trying to ride the line of not lying. Lucas stepped up to change the course of the conversation. "They're just mad we don't pet the coyotes enough. Or maybe they're blaming my shooting for their losses. It's hard to say with them and we were trying not to wait around and find out."

Tina nodded. "I hope the coyotes eat all their stuff and they sell."

Lucas laughed. "Well, we aren't buying their land. I'll be fencing until I die."

"Speaking of dying, do we have any food in here?" Barry asked. "We missed dinner in all that."

Immediately, Tina forgot about the Wymans and started digging sandwiches out of the cooler on the seat between her and Lucas. She passed a couple to Barry and unwrapped one and handed it to Lucas. She then unwrapped one for herself and for a while, they were silent as they ate.

As they drew closer to home, they began to notice small branches and tufts of leaves in the road. After coming upon a larger one that Lucas had to swerve to avoid, he said, "Wow. It rained a bit at the fair, but it looks like it got pretty windy out here."

"Maybe, we had a thunderstorm or something." Barry said, while also peering out onto the road."

"I hope everything is okay at home." Tina said in a quiet voice.

"Oh, I'm sure it is." Barry said. "Worst case scenario, the power will be out. But even that, you'd think would be fixed by now."

"I would think so." Lucas agreed. "It probably passed by some time ago."

It was nearly 11 o'clock when they drove past the road to the veterinarian's office. The chatter in the truck had ceased and the occupants just wanted to be home.

Chapter 30
Three Of A Kind

Jess had spent most of the morning lying in the shade at the top of the slope of the hill. She had spent some time patrolling and moving with the sheep until the day got hotter and most of the sheep had found their own shade. It was a lazy kind of day and nothing much had moved in the land beyond their fields. When the sun passed overhead and her shade had disappeared, she wandered up to where the water trough for the sheep was and took a long drink. She spent some time wandering the fence line again and then sought out some of the sheep and their lambs in the places that they had sought refuge. Eventually, with nothing to do, she found a new shaded place and lay down again.

While she lay there, a breeze began to drift across the field. She sniffed the air. It was different now. The wind grew and the dog felt restless, though she couldn't really give a reason. Jess stood and wandered along the top of the slope. The sky began to grow dark and the wind increased. Off in the distance, the sky rumbled. She trotted down where the sheep were lying, but they didn't seem to feel her unease.

In a short time, the dark clouds blotted out the sun and the wind gusts swayed the tops of the trees along the fence line. The rumbling grew louder and further afield, light flashed across the sky. Jess moved among the sheep, encouraging them to get up. And then the sky opened up and the rain began to fall. The thunder roared and the lightning flashed. Wind bent the tops of the trees, and the scrub was laid almost flat by the gusts. The sheep began to move up the slope. Hail came down from the sky, plinking like small rocks. The sheep finally decided it was time they began to move up the hill towards the gates, slow at first, but faster as the hail hit their nose and their face. Jess wandered among the brush, making sure no one was left behind. At the top of the slope, the sheep began to hurry for the barn. It was their place of safety. The lightning cracked the sky. Jess moved with them as they went. A heavy gust of wind blew, followed by a loud cracking noise. The last thing Jess heard as they fled for the barn together, was the crash of something large falling to the ground. Then she was through the gate and they raced to the barn together.

Once in the barn, Jess wandered among the sheep, checking in with some and avoiding those who demanded more space. She wasn't really frightened. Her instincts had said they should move. Her instincts also said not to leave the sheep. She hadn't been sure how to accomplish both and so she had waited for the sheep to make the same decision. Now in the safety of the barn, despite the wind blowing through and the noise of the rain on the roof, they felt comfortable.

They stayed there until the winds diminished and the rain began to lighten. The sun began to peek through the clouds, and in no time, they were standing in the heat of a sunny day. The sheep began to wander and upon discovering the grain in their feeders, were all too happy to oblige. When the feeders were empty and their desire to eat grew, they slowly began to make their way back to the grass beyond the gates, with Jess wandering off ahead to check for any signs of danger. Finding none, they resumed their normal routine of grazing and resting when it got too hot.

As the sun began to crawl towards the western horizon and the heat began to fade, the sheep began to graze in earnest. This was the time to eat. They worked their way down the slope and up the other side, nibbling as they went, instinctively looking for the best shoots and greenery. It was boring and eventually Jess simply lay along the top of one slope and laid her head on her paws. The light continued to fade slowly, as it did in the summer months and

Jess began to listen for the sound of her humans. She wasn't impatient. Her clock just told her it should be soon. Her stomach was telling her as well. She stood up and stretched, ready to do another patrol when movement outside her territory caught her attention. She stiffened, then relaxed as she realized it was just a sheep. She scanned out across the field and noticed there were also other sheep moving out there. It picked up its head and called. Other sheep, closer to Jess, answered. Something began to stir in the back of her mind. It made her uncomfortable. The sheep began to sound upset. Jess moved to find them. Lambs began to cry and the dog picked up her pace.

When she found the crying sheep, they were calling out to the sheep outside the fence. As she watched, more sheep headed out into the fields beyond their border. She went to the corner where the sheep were leaving. She knew it was wrong and began to bark at the sheep, telling them to move back, but they ignored her. They were trying to figure out how to get to the other sheep. Some of them were making it. Jess moved in and realized that part of the fence was not on the ground. It was like a gate had opened out into the world beyond and as more sheep escaped. Lambs who no longer needed their mothers, but still kept track of their whereabouts, were noticing them missing. The ewe were calling them and they were responding and little by little, the sheep were filing out through the gap and the more they did, the more other sheep took notice. Jess started barking furiously, the sheep were too busy trying to find the opening to pay her any mind.

She ran to the opening and pushed her way among the sheep. She ran out into the wilds and began to bark at the sheep who were moving further and further away. They moved, but not in the direction Jess had wanted them to go. This was fresh, untouched grass and when she barked, they would just run 10 or 15 strides in some direction and begin to eat again. The dog became more frantic, running to this sheep and that, barking and even snapping, trying to turn them back. The sheep were not willing to leave their newfound pastures and all the while, more sheep were finding the opening and fleeing out into the grasslands beyond the fence. The sheep were spreading out and eating as they moved along finding the best new grass. The more that found the space, the less frantic the sheep became and Jess began to accept that they were all okay. She ceased her efforts to turn them back and settled for staying with them as they grazed along. It grew dark and quiet and the sheep, who were enjoying the cooler night air, had no desire to turn back. On occasion, they would call to one another, but it was just a normal type of communication as they moved along.

Jess set out ahead, looking for danger. She was uncomfortable with the situation, but not as uncomfortable as she had been when they were upset. They were calm now and she could focus on her job of keeping them safe. Jess kept herself between the sheep and the world beyond the fence, but as the time wore on and the sheep began to stray farther, the fence became less of a barrier between them and potential danger. By the time the sheep had gotten over their excitement for new grass and they had decided to rest, Jess was more than willing to take up a position on the top of a small bit of higher ground and lay down to watch. There she dozed on and off, listening for any sound of something awry.

It was not sound, but the smell that would wake her in the early morning. Jess picked up her head, scanning the expanse of open land. Some of the flock were on their feet, grazing quietly. Everything looked calm and serene. But the scent reaching her nostrils when the wind blew was one of danger and Jess got to her feet.
She sniffed the air again before silently moving out around the sheep and out into the open.

She stared out into the gray light of morning, searching for what she knew was coming. She saw the first movements out between some scrub type trees and she began to bark. The coyote moved back into the shadows and Jess moved along keeping herself between the sheep and the enemies she knew were out there. She barked again, letting them know the sheep were not alone. She could smell them, even if she could not see them. She saw movement off to the left and ran in that direction, barking as she went. Out ahead in the scrub, she saw movement too. She moved back in that direction and let out a volley of barking.

The sheep could also smell the danger now. They were picking up their heads and calling to one another. They started to move restlessly and push closer together. Jess moved out around them, using her presence to tighten up the throng of sheep. She was running solely on instincts now. Thousands of years of breeding had honed her abilities for moments like these. She circled the group of milling, panicky sheep and would stop to bark to her advancing adversaries.

Out in the distance, she could see not one, but two advancing coyotes. They were moving slowly, picking their way through the darkest of the shadows. Sometimes, they would fade from view altogether, but she knew they were out there and on the move. The sheep were beginning to become unruly. As the scent blew to them on the wind, they wanted to flee and Jess kept trying to hold them. She wanted to move out to meet her adversaries, but the sheep would flee into the open land. She could do nothing but wait and try to keep the sheep from following their own desire to run. She looked out to the left and saw nothing, but she knew it was out there too. Jess, held there by the sheep, could only wait for them to make their move. She could not protect the sheep, keep them together, and go on the attack.

When they did come, it was not from the direction she had been watching. While she had been watching what she could see, the pack had been making its way around, coming over the top of the very slope that Jess had been sleeping on. They were masters of the game and she was but one dog. The sudden presence of the pack was too much for the sheep and they fled down the slope and into the open, right towards the waiting coyotes in the shadows that Jess had been watching. She turned to follow but then stopped again and wheeled around. If she raced to defend the sheep from the coyotes down below, she left them open to the pack coming in from behind and if she faced them, the ones waiting would be able to get to the sheep. They had her and she knew it.

She watched the pack fan out as they moved towards her. She would bark and charge but did not engage. If she went after one, the others would use that moment to slip away and join the ambush or to attack her from behind. She kept up her facade of attacking, all while backing away further each time, trying to move towards the sheep. It was an exhausting game and she knew that she would lose, but at the moment, she could think of no other options. She heard the sudden strangled cries of a sheep and everything in her being told her to go to its rescue, yet she knew she could not. If she turned her back, the pack would attack her or run off to join their succeeding counterparts.

The sheep, scared and under attack, fled back to Jess and upon coming to the point of being able to see the coyotes ahead, finally turned towards home. They were running as prey does, with no thought but escape. When they went by, the coyotes turned to go with them and Jess had to move to intercept. She ran alongside the sheep, veering off to lunge after this coyote or that trying to prevent them from making an attack. Finally, the sheep made their way back to the fence, but not near the opening where the tree top had fallen. They, by now, had no idea how they had come to be on the other side of the fence, so they simply bunched up along the fence line, running back and forth in a tight group.

For Jess, this was at least a help. She at least had something at the back of the sheep to keep the coyotes from circling. In the stillness of the dawn, both predator, prey, and their protector froze as the choking, snarling cries of a coyote tore through the morning air. The coyotes were suddenly nervous and they looked to the sound of the cries. This, Jess thought to herself, was her chance to make a move.

She dashed forward, driving her weight into one of the coyotes grabbing ahold of the side of its neck as it stumbled from the force of the hit, she sank her teeth in as hard as she could and shook her head, tearing through skin and flesh before the others could move in. She heard them move behind her and leaped back, letting go of her quarry. She too, could dart and slash. She was not a helpless puppy anymore. When she leaped back, she spun around, lunging for one of the coyotes behind her. Again, she used the force of her weight, to knock it to the ground. She missed its neck but latched onto its face, tearing its lip and driving her teeth through the top of its muzzle. She felt teeth on her haunch and she whipped herself in that direction, snapping her teeth on air, as the coyote darted backwards. She was not afraid and she was determined to force them to stay and fight. She moved around them, pushing them towards the sheep. They made no effort to hunt now. They were being forced into battle. There were seven of them and only one of her, but Jess was not worried. They were filthy cowards, preying on those under her protection and she would not let this go.

Jess kept them on the defensive, moving in, growling and biting, only to retreat out of their grasp. The coyotes faced her, heads down and teeth bared. She growled deep in her throat, looking for an opportunity to move in.
Jess heard a rush of movement behind her, and as she moved to turn, she was struck from behind with enough force to send her flying sideways, into one of the coyotes, as she scrambled to keep her feet, and face her attacker, she snarled in warning. As she turned, she found herself staring at a large white dog. It was not paying any attention to Jess. It had a coyote by the throat and was vigorously shaking it like one would shake a rabbit.

As Jess stood, awestruck, the coyote behind her took advantage of her distraction and grabbed her from behind. She wheeled to face it, shaking it off and lunging forward. She grabbed the side of its face and it snapped its teeth, flailing to pull away. She pulled it down underneath her, still holding tightly, but it was ripped from underneath her. She turned again to find the white dog, who had pulled the coyote away, slammed it to the ground and tearing and biting with deep baritone, growls. As it ceased to struggle and the remaining coyotes were attempting to flee the white death among them, the dog turned to face Jess. Things long forgotten came rushing to her mind, with the scent of the creature before her. She didn't remember the fight or the sheep or her enemies. She was half crouched, reeling with the images in her mind, before she finally found her voice. "Fur?" She said in disbelief. As if she were waking from some dream and yet dreaming.

The dog stared back at her, also struggling with what stood before him. "Wee?" He said in astonishment, his voice barely a whisper.

She stood up slowly, taking a step forward on suddenly shaky legs. She moved to him, pressing her head into his bloody chest and breathing in the scent beneath. He responded in kind, laying his head across her back and pressing gently against her. They stayed that way for several moments, not speaking.

A whimper broke through the moment and she stepped back from him. A few feet back was an old dog, with one eye and missing part of one ear. She was bloody as well and moving with a slight limp to her step. "Momma!" Wee cried, moving to meet her, whimpering and sniffing her mother's face. The old dog sniffed her back, making small noises in return.

"We thought you were…" Furs's voice trailed off as if he couldn't say.

Wee struggled to explain what she could not understand. "I don't know. I …" She struggled to regain the memories she had forgotten for so long.

"I went to get a drink. I was so thirsty. I saw an animal." She blushed thinking how silly her actions had been.

"I wanted to show it to you, Fur. I wanted you to be surprised." She hesitated again. "I caught it. It was so silly. It was hard to catch, but easy to kill. It had big stupid ears. It screamed when I caught it and the coyotes came. I ran and I ran, but they caught me." Her voice was choked with emotions from long ago.

"I tried, Fur. I tried to fight, but… They were too strong and there were too many. Everything hurt and I felt weak. And then it all went dark. Maybe I did die."

"It's good to see you." Fur said quietly. He could sense the anguish and fear in her emotions.

"We looked for you. We followed where you

went. We found the rabbit. They really are pretty silly." His own voice was deep, but heavy with emotion. "We found the dead coyotes and the smell of humans and … He paused, trying to find words.

"We found where you had been attacked." Momma said, continuing the story. "But we could not find you."

Wee struggled to find a way to explain what had happened and how she lived. There were many things in her memory of the days following the attack that were blurry and others that she didn't understand. She gave up for the moment and simply enjoyed their presence. She moved between them, rubbing against one or the other. They nuzzled and pressed against her in return. Their reunion was far more important at the moment. More explanations could wait.

When they had come to accept the joy of being together, Fur broke the silence. "We should get going." He said.

Chapter 31
Home At Last

While Jess had been finding a place to doze, far off on the lands Lucas had purchased from Roger Allen, the porter family had pulled into the driveway, finally home from their long day. Lucas helped Tina carry the things she had bought and the leftover food in the cooler, into the house, saying that she could look over the sheep in the morning and that he and Barry would shut the gates to the sheep and bring Jess in the house. While he was talking to her inside, Barry was attempting to get the horse out of the trailer quietly, without letting the 10 sheep who had been with her, escape into the driveway. He finally managed to get the horse to step out, off the trailer, to the end of her lead while he blocked the sheep from following. As he stepped out and pulled the door In close past the horse, Lucas stepped around and took the horse's rope. Barry closed the door as quietly as possible and the two men hustled to move the horse to the barn, silently hoping it would not call out into the night. They went into the barn through the back to avoid Jess possibly barking and possibly spooking the horse. She had certainly never seen one before. A short time later, they had the horse in a stall with hay and a bit of grain to keep it quiet.

Then they went out and around to get Jess and lock the sheep in the lower pen for the night. As Lucas turned on his headlamp, He saw the eyeshine of sheep and felt a rush of relief. So many things had occurred in his mind on the last leg of their trip home. When he entered the gate, with Barry close behind, all dreams of a quick five-minute excursion were sadly brought to a halt. As Lucas panned the flashlight, they realized that most of the sheep had not come down to the corral. "So much for them eating the grain and staying here." Lucas said in tired annoyance.

Barry shrugged. "We are a little later than we expected."

"We had better go get some brighter flashlights." Lucas groaned. "They could be bedded down anywhere out there or still grazing."

Barry certainly understood how he felt. It had been an exhausting day, and it was hours past their usual bedtime. As they headed back out, he was thinking of nothing but sleep. "You know," he said, trying not to yawn. "Everything seems quiet and fine. We're going to be out there in a few hours."

Lucas stopped and looked at his brother, the headlamp unintentionally shining in his eyes.

Barry bent his head down and shielded his eyes. Lucas looked away and then shut off the light. "What are you thinking?" Lucas asked him, half hoping it was what he thought.

"I'm thinking I can't see." Barry said, still seeing the dots of light in his vision. "Okay, so Jess is obviously out there. She's apparently given up on us coming back too. It's only one night. We can come out here as soon as it's light and we'll go check them. It's not gonna kill them to spend one night grazing. If anything happens, Jess is sure to make a fuss."

Lucas stood there, warring between what he wanted and what his sense of responsibility said he should do. He looked back towards the sheep and sighed. "You really think they'll be okay?"

"They'll be fine." Barry said reassuringly. "You really do worry too much."

"Fine. We'll be out here at 6 and hopefully. they'll have come down anyway." Lucas grudgingly agreed.

"If not, we'll go check and come right back. I mean, you don't want Tina finding her birthday present without you."

He nodded and headed back to the house, turning on his light. Barry walked behind him, surprised that Lucas had gone along with his idea. Maybe having Jess really was making Lucas feel more relaxed. Barry went inside his cabin and closed the door, not wanting to give

Lucas time to reconsider. He did stand and watch Lucas continue to the house before taking off his boots and crawling into bed.

Lucas stepped inside the door knowing Tina would ask about the absence of the dog who slept in their bedroom doorway every night. She looked up when he came in. "Everything alright?" She asked immediately.

"Seems quiet out there." Lucas answered. He tried to sound reassuring when really, he had no reassurance.

"Where's Jess?" she asked, glancing past him. He certainly didn't want her to worry. "The sheep apparently ate their grain and wandered back out when we didn't come back, so some of them are down here, but some aren't. We figured it would be hard to find them all and get them down here, so we figured we'd just wait until morning." He waited for her objections but none were forthcoming. They were all exhausted. She simply nodded. So he took off his boots and in a very short time, they were all asleep.

The two were not awake until about 6 the next morning, when Barry knocked on the door, before letting himself in. They scrambled up and out of bed with Lucas looking sheepish, like he'd been caught doing something wrong. Barry assured him that all was still seemingly quiet, so Tina had made coffee before they headed out. Lucas drank it as quickly as possible before pulling on his shirt and boots and heading outside. Barry was right behind him as they headed out through the sheep pen and up towards the field.

The sheep that had been down by the barn that night had headed out to graze leaving the pen empty. As Barry and Lucas walked they noticed the fallen branches and broken boughs. "There must have been a much bigger storm here than where we were." Lucas said, looking around. "Sure was." Barry said. "This looks more like the road on the way home. Maybe that's what made the sheep go back out."

"Could be. Or they just realized they could eat double time."

As they walked through the gates out into the field, they noticed one side had blown back closed. And there were more bits of debris from small trees. They picked up the pace so they could see over the sloping hill that began the long rolling fields beyond. When they reached the top, they could see sheep grazing. They continued along though, wanting to make sure everything was okay. The sheep they could see didn't even make 100 head, much like the sheep that had been by the barn the previous night. As they scanned the field, still walking, Barry reached out and grabbed Lucas's arm.

"What the hell?" He said, pointing out beyond the fence line, way out in the field on the western side, and to the south of their field. Lucas stopped short. Far in the distance, were the sheep, looking formless and indistinct from the distance, but there was no mistaking it. There were no gates to out there yet, because they hadn't done much with Roger's land since buying it. They were working on their own land, ensuring it would produce hay to be cut for the winter, replacing fence and cleaning up the newly growing saplings. and any undesirable or toxic weeds they came across.

Deep down inside, they were glad to see the sheep seemed fine. But they were also tired and it was the last thing they had wanted to see. The two of them headed for the fence line closest to the sheep and moving almost at a jog, they made their way over the fence, looking for where the sheep may have gone through. They found it with little trouble. Lucas and Barry stood looking at the break in the fence and up where the top of the large pine had fallen. When it had hit the post, where the land started to rise, it had broken it off, driving it forward. That had pulled the posts at the bottom of the slope up out of the ground, lifting them almost three feet in the air. To the sheep, it had been like an open line, stretching more than twenty feet. They both ducked underneath and headed off towards the sheep. Neither Barry, nor Lucas spoke as they moved. They each had their concerns and both wanted to make sure all was well before really feeling like this was just an annoyance. Their concern increased when Lucas stopped short and they both saw the dead coyote in the grass. The way its neck was bent, was a clear indication it was broken and the unnatural way it was lying seemed more like it had been tossed there. "Dammmn." Barry said in a whisper, as they stooped and looked at the wound on its neck.

The scene had an eerie feeling that made the hairs stand out on their necks and arms. They stood again, this time trying to be silent. Lucas, who had been about to call the dog, suddenly realized he had not brought a weapon as he had headed out still half awake. His only consolation was that he had seen Barry had at least brought a pistol. Still, they moved quietly, going out around the stand of small trees and brush, to make sure they would not be taken by surprise, like Lucas had the day with the dog.

As they moved around the brush, trying to keep visibility, Lucas saw the furry figure next to some old limbs and short scrub that had grown up between them. He took a few steps towards the dog and said her name. "Jess!"

The dog came to its feet, spinning in midair as it did to face the intruder. It snarled as it touched ground before backing up, looking shocked and confused. The dog was far larger than Jess and Lucas had frozen as it had come up all bared teeth and raised hackles. Barry though had drawn his weapon in a flash. He was no longer a child and he didn't need to run for help this time. He had drawn and taken aim right by Lucas's side, almost as fast as the dog had moved.

Like a flash, Jess suddenly dashed between the men and her brother. She backed against him, barking in a high-pitched tone. Barry breathed, grateful he hadn't fired and hit their own dog. He felt Lucas's hand on his arm. Pushing it down slowly, but firmly still looking straight ahead. It was not Jess he was staring at, or even the large dog with the shaggy head that was retreating backwards, ever since Jess had jumped between them. He was looking past them at the dog who had been laying next to a severely injured, bleeding lamb. The one who was standing over it now, shaking slightly. It was an old dog with one eye. It had a line of fur missing across its head. Lucas stared at her in pity and disbelief. The conversation with Roger Allen replaying in his head and he knew. He knew the truth. "Put the gun away." He said to Barry.
When Barry hesitated, Lucas glanced over. "Put it away!" He said more firmly.

Barry pushed away the feelings that had made him react so quickly. He took a deep breath and holstered his weapon. Lucas stooped down. "Jess. It's okay. Good girl."

She had stopped barking when Barry had lowered the gun, but she had stayed between them and her family. They were standing together, the old dog hesitant to leave the lamb she'd been protecting.

Barry backed up a few steps to give Lucas a little space and to regain his composure. He wasn't quite sure what had made Lucas suddenly confident, but he knew something had. "Jess." Lucas said again softly. The dog looked at Barry as if to judge what he might do. Seeming satisfied that they weren't in danger, she slowly moved to Lucas. He reached out and stroked the top of her head. "You're a good girl." He told her before slowly standing up and backing away.

"Lucas?" Barry said questioningly, unsure if he meant to leave the dog behind or what he was thinking.

Lucas retreated some more, motioning for Barry to do the same. When they had moved enough for the old dog to look less scared, Lucas finally spoke. "It's them, Barry. It has to be."

It's who, exactly?" Barry asked, knowing he was missing something.

"What did Roger Allen say? He was trying to get the pups and the mother tried to defend them, so he shot her. I asked what happened to the pups and he said they probably died. I knew Jess had to be one, he has to be the other. Look at her. Doesn't that look like she got shot?"

Finally, Barry had all the information he needed to understand. "So, what are we going to do?"

"I don't know." Lucas answered truthfully. "Let's go look around and try not to scare them off entirely.

Chapter 31
The Ties That Bind

While Lucas and Barry went off to try to put together the events of the previous night, Wee stood with her family. Lucas had not commanded her to do otherwise, and he had, in fact, given her the same kind of quick petting she usually received when he was leaving. She looked at Fur. "See! I told you they would listen to me."

When Fur had wanted them to go back to Roger's, Wee had been forced to tell them the whole story then and there. She told them about the cold place where she woke up after the coyotes had gotten her. The place with the funny smells where she kept falling asleep. She had also told them about the humans who had taken her home and cared for her. She explained about the sheep and her duties and that she could not just leave them. She had begged them not to leave her, promising that her humans would not hurt them. She had told Fur that these humans listened to her and that though sometimes they didn't understand, they at least tried hard.

Momma, who was highly skeptical of any good coming from being with humans, at least understood her sense of duty to the flock. When they had come back to find the injured lamb, Momma had stayed to protect it, while Fur and Wee had made sure the surviving coyotes had moved out and would be no further trouble. Jess (as she thought of herself now) had been ecstatic to have them back. When she and her brother had gone scouting, she felt sure and invincible. She had been desperate for them not to leave and had told them that they would listen if she told them not to harm them. Her confidence on the matter, coupled with their joy at finding her, had made them willing to stay. Now though, she was unsure how to bring her two families together.

She stayed with her Mother and Fur, hoping she would not lose them again. So she told them the story of Roger's visit to her new home and watched her mother's eyes narrow at the idea. "Wait!" Jess continued. "Let me finish. I was scared to see Roger and I barked at him. He tried to kick me and Lucas, my human, stepped between us and he smelled really angry and he wouldn't let Roger try to kick me again. You could tell Roger was mad. He kept staring at me with a really mean look. Then Barry came and they made Roger leave the barn." She sat down facing them and finished "And I never saw Roger again." She paused. "Oh, and the woman, they call her Tina, petted me for it."

Fur, though obviously impressed by the story, turned back to sit beside Momma, who had lay down against the lamb again. "Out here." He said. "We can eat anything we can catch. We don't have to wait for bits of milk."

Jess interrupted. "Oh, you don't know. These people feed me every day. They have crunchy food and they put stuff on it and I never have to go hungry." She looked at her brother's lean figure and at her mother's gaunt frame. "You'd probably be twice as big if they fed you."

"But we are free." Momma said softly. "We can go where we please and no one hurts us."

Jess looked at her mother. She didn't look strong anymore. She looked tired and frail.

"Fur." If I can get them to feed you and let you stay, will you consider it? I mean…" She was trying to find something to convince them. She didn't want something bad to happen to Momma. "Look at what happened this morning. If you hadn't been around, how many sheep might have died? What if I had died again? If you leave, I'll be all alone!" Her voice cracked with emotion.

"You could go with us," Fur said to her, his voice deep, but soft.

"Could I?" She looked at Momma. "Would you leave the sheep, if they were yours?"

Momma looked away. She sniffed the fading lamb. She nuzzled its face. Then she looked at Jess. "No." she said quietly. "I would not."

"Then come with me." Jess said. "Our field is huge! You will have plenty of room. And we have lambs all the time!" Her voice became more solemn. "I need my family to help me. You don't have to even deal with the people. I'll be the one who talks to them. You can just hang out in the field or sleep in the barn. I'll do all the human stuff. I know you don't like humans. I didn't either. I was so scared at first. But they have always been kind. You saw. I told them not to shoot you and they didn't. You know Roger would never have let us tell him what to do."

"We're aware." Fur said, glancing at his mother. Jess hung her head. Of course they were all aware.

"Come with me." She said to Fur suddenly. "Let me show you something."

Fur stood and Jess headed out, up towards the field. When they had gotten close to the fence line and out of Momma's hearing, Jess turned and looked at her brother. "Fur. I know you try hard and I know you hunt better than any of us. It's why I wanted to impress you with that damn rabbit so badly. But Momma looks thin. She looks very tired. She deserves some rest. More than anyone, she deserves it."

Fur walked to his sister and pressed his head against her shoulder. When he spoke, he was so quiet that even she had to strain to hear him. "When we lost you, Momma changed. When I would hunt, she would barely eat. She would say I was growing and needed it more. In the mornings, when we returned to the barn, she would talk about the other dogs, our father, her brother and the rest. She would talk about the sheep and how proud she had been watching over them." He let out a long sigh. "I think she gave up. She lost the sheep, her pack and all she had was you and me. She tried hard for us. When you were gone and I grew enough to defend myself, she didn't have a reason to keep going. I tried every day to make her happy, but she was just sad all the time."

Jess had never heard her brother sound so forlorn. She could smell his pain and desperation. She nuzzled against him, wishing she had never lost them. "I truly believe that I can get these humans to feed Momma and you. They will let her watch over the sheep. Maybe she could be happy again. She would have everything she lost and a much nicer barn."

Fur looked at her and she sensed he was longing for some kind of stability. "I know that you have no reason to trust humans. But, do you trust me?"

"I have always trusted you, Wee. You were always the thinker."

She smiled. "And you always made me feel safer." She looked out across the grass, watching Lucas and Barry as they were gathering up the sheep and moving them back towards home. "That night, when I was so thirsty, I kept hoping you would wake up and come out to see where I was going. I didn't want to ask because I knew you'd mock me, but I wanted you to show up and protect me, the way you did today."

They stood in silence, lost in the past. Fur broke the silence. "We should go back to Momma."
"I know. Do you think she will decide to come?" Jess asked hopefully.
"If you really, really think we will be safe, I will talk to her." Fur said.
"I know Roger was awful. The men with him were awful. But in all my time among these humans, they have never been mean. They have never hurt me. They have never let me go hungry and they have never gotten angry at me." Jess's voice was thoughtful. She hadn't really put it into words for herself before, but it was true. They never did the things that Roger did.
"That is so weird." Fur told her honestly.
Jess had come to a conclusion in her thoughts. "I don't think that all humans are like Roger. I think some humans are different."

"I guess, neither I, nor Momma have met very many. So, maybe you are right." Fur was still thinking about that as he spoke. The idea had never crossed his mind.

He sighed. "Let's go back. I will try to get Momma to agree as long as you think it's safe."

"I think," Jess said truthfully, "It might be the safest she has ever been."

Fur nodded and they made their way back down through the scrub where they had left their mother. The lamb was silent, its head drooped down on its side. Its breathing had stopped, but still Momma lay with her head over its back.

At almost market weight, it was not small, but it was young and she would not willingly give up her post, until all warmth had faded away and with it, the smell of life.

Chapter 32
A Man With A Plan

After finding the bodies of the other coyotes and checking for any other signs of downed sheep, the two men had worked to bring the herd into some semblance of a group. They had taken long sticks from some of the brush and waved them to get the sheep moving. They had forgotten about the time or even the horse in the barn. They were feeling such a sense of relief that things were not nearly as bad as they could have been. And Lucas was still reeling with the truth of Roger's story and the survival of them all. There was something about the old female that gnawed away at his emotions in a way that few things did.

They managed to get the sheep heading towards the space in the fence, occasionally having to chase those few, trying to turn off from the herd. Barry thought to himself that a sheepdog would be nice, but figured it probably wasn't the time to mention it. He did know that Lucas losing his fear of dogs could open up all kinds of possibilities. By the time they actually got them going back into the field, they were both hot and even more tired. The sun was high in the sky and it made their work that much worse, but eventually they got the sheep back through the opening. As soon as the sheep were back in their own field, they headed for the barn as if it were evening and they needed their grain. Lucas and Barry followed, closing the gates behind them so they could keep them contained, until the fence was repaired. Looking down the hill, they could see Tina hurrying toward the barn. She must have been frantic after all this time. Lucas said. "I'm going to let her know everything is okay and then we'll fix the fence and put in a gate."

"A gate." Barry repeated.

"Yes." Lucas said firmly. "I want those dogs."

Before Barry could say more, Lucas was through the gate and headed to Tina.

Barry shook his head. He wasn't sure what his brother had in mind, but he knew Lucas seemed as determined about having these dogs as he had been about not having dogs.

When Lucas got to his wife, he could tell she had been crying. "How bad is it?" she asked, trying to look stoic. "It's fine." Lucas said. "It's okay."

"I came up there." She paused for a minute to compose herself. "There were barely any sheep. There was no dog. I called to you and no one answered. I didn't see you guys anywhere."

Lucas reached out and took her hands in his. "It's all fine. There was a thunderstorm here. The wind knocked part of a tree on the fence.

The sheep and Jess were way out on the land we bought from Roger. We had to go get them and round them up and get them all back in the fence, but it's fine. Jess is fine. I got to go call her in and we have to fix the fence. We're gonna put a gate."

She looked up into his face. "Honestly?"

He sighed. "We did lose one lamb. That's the only thing we could find wrong."

She continued to look at him. There was something he wasn't saying. "Jess is really fine? Why didn't she come with you?"

"She is absolutely fine. I'll explain everything when we get back. But she's fine. She didn't even get hurt. And I think I found a solution to our coyote problems."

"Wait." Tina was thoroughly confused. "Are you serious? You mean like a permanent solution?"

"Yes." Lucas said. "A permanent solution. They can graze all the time. But I have to go fix the fence. We'll be back as soon as we can."

He let go of her hands and hugged her tight for a moment. Then he lifted her chin and gave her a quick kiss. "We'll be back." He said and turned to go get his saw and some tools to fix the fence from the barn. When he passed through the doors that divided the sheep area from the other part of the barn, he was met by a soft nicker and a head reaching over a stall to greet him. For a moment, he was almost shocked. He had literally forgotten his rash purchase from the evening before. He walked back through the barn and yelled to Barry. "Hey. Could you come give me a hand?" Barry hurried down and Lucas turned back into the barn.

After a minute of standing there, wondering what exactly had happened up there, Tina turned and walked back up to the house. She knew Lucas wouldn't lie to her, but she also couldn't figure out for the life of her what exactly had happened to make Lucas act so out of character. She'd never, in all their time together, seen him act so mentally disorganized. He was always so straight forward. Now he seemed all over the place in his behaviors. She didn't know what to make of it.

When Barry came into the barn and followed Lucas through the doors, he stopped short. He had also forgotten all about the horse. "Does she know?" he asked, staring at the horse before walking up to the stall and looking over the door.

"I don't think so." Lucas said. "I didn't even know until I went to get my saw."

"So, you gonna show her?"

"Not right now, Barry." Lucas replied. "Let's get the fence fixed. I want a gate so we can get back out there."

Barry thought for a moment before climbing up the ladder to the loft. He knew he had seen some things, left behind by the previous owners, and one of the things might work as a gate. He dragged stuff aside until he came to a large metal grate. It was about 4 ft high and it had a metal frame with a heavy-duty mesh welded to it. It was heavy, but it would do for now. He dragged it to the edge and yelled to Lucas to take it. He knelt down and lowered the grate as much as he could, until he felt Lucas take the weight. Then he went back down and they gathered pliers and the fencing tool, a hammer and the saw. They put them all on the sheep side of the barn and Barry went around back to grab a few fence posts they had pulled from another field that weren't in bad shape. Barry pulled the tractor around through, with Lucas manning gates and they loaded everything on it.

By about one o'clock they had the fence pulled up and repaired and had installed their temporary gate. They had skipped breakfast and the two were feeling the lack of sleep and the lack of food. Lucas told Barry to go on back and that he'd go get the dog. He walked through the gate and a ways out to the field before calling for Jess. For a moment, there was nothing and he was worried that maybe she had gone off with her family. He called again and Jess appeared in view for a moment and disappeared again. He walked down further and called again. This time she came to him. He bent down and petted her softly. "Don't worry." He said to her, "I got this." Then he stood and walked off with Jess following behind him. She wasn't sure what he had said, but it made her feel better. At the gate, she turned and looked back one more time. "Come on, girl." Lucas said kindly and she followed him through the field and back down towards home.

When they reached the house a few minutes later, Barry and Tina were sitting at the table waiting for him to begin lunch. When Tina saw Jess, she jumped up and called her to her. She hugged her and looked at Lucas. "She really is okay."

"I told you that." Lucas replied before abruptly turning and heading back out the door.

Tina and Barry both stared after him, wondering where he had gone. Tina felt bewildered and when she had asked Barry questions upon his arrival, he had been just as awkward and vague as her husband. This had all started at the fair. The fair! Tina turned to Barry. "Are the sheep still in the trailer?"

Barry's mouth opened and he closed it again and then stood up and walked outside. Tina looked at Jess. "What is wrong with everyone? They're acting so weird."

Jess wagged her tail slightly. "You too, huh?" Tina said, half joking, feeling like the dog was just as likely to provide a rational answer as anyone else today.

She followed Barry outside to see if she could help. As she went down the stairs, Lucas went by her carrying a large rubber dish from the barn. "Is that for the sheep? She asked. Lucas looked at her blankly until he heard Barry start the truck and he looked up. He had forgotten the sheep in the trailer in the driveway. He set the dish on the top of the steps and went to help Barry. They backed the truck around the barn where they had fixed some fencing to make it easier to separate lambs into a smaller pen for easier loading. They unloaded the Fournier sheep in one area and the small group of 10 in another. Tina went to get something for water and Lucas yelled to her. She stopped just feet from the barn door and looked back. "Don't get the tubs from in there." He was already coming up to the barn.

"You don't want the tubs?" She asked.

"No. Lucas said. "Not those ones. They won't be big enough."

"I think they'll work to at least get them a drink so we can eat lunch."

"No." Lucas stated, moving between her and the barn door. There are some better ones in the attic. Right Barry?"

Barry looked up. "Yeah. Much better. I'll go get a couple." He walked all the way around the barn and went in from the sheep's side.

She stared up at Lucas. He simply stared back. "Lucas Porter!"

"I hope Jess isn't eating our lunch after missing two meals." He said.

For a moment she could see herself throttling him. She felt her face flush as she stood there just looking at her husband's blank gaze. She looked past him at the barn door and noticed his hand tighten as he stood holding the handle. Suddenly, she had to stifle the urge to laugh. Lucas, and by extension Barry, were trying to hide something from her. They were terrible at it. Two men who were usually as open and straightforward as could be, were trying to be secretive. She thought back to their weird explanations of what took them so long at the fair and their attempts to dissuade her from asking questions on the ride home. Then all their weird behavior today. She looked down at the ground to hide her smile. "I'll go get lunch ready." She said, turning away so he wouldn't see her expression. As she walked to the house, she was a little excited. He had never gone to such lengths to keep a secret. What could it be? She was curious and also very amused.

When the guys came in some 20 minutes later, they washed and sat down for lunch as if nothing was off. They ate without talking, pausing only to take a drink of lemonade. They had been famished, and lunch had been delayed by one thing after another. Tina watched them wondering what they were doing out there and what they could have gotten her that had to be hidden in the barn. It couldn't be something small if he could have snuck it into the house or hidden it out of sight in the barn. Or maybe they put it in the barn but hadn't gotten a chance to hide it because of the escaped sheep and the fence. Had they hidden it now? "Do you want me to get some bowls and get them some salt? There are a bunch of small bowls in the barn." Tina asked, just to see their reaction.

"No. Barry has to go out there to put the tools away. He'll get it." Lucas answered quickly. "Have you fed Jess?"

"I'll get that right now." She said, giggling to herself as she got up to feed the dog.

After they'd eaten and Barry had left "to make sure the sheep had everything they needed." Lucas had gone out and retrieved the bowl he had been carrying earlier. He came back in and filled it with food from Jess's bag. When Tina heard him, she came around the corner to find him mixing the food with some bacon grease

and some leftovers from the night before the fair. He looked up at her as her shadow covered the floor. "I'll explain later." He said. His face looked pensive and not the same as earlier when he had been keeping her from the barn. "Okay." Tina replied and she walked back to the living room. When he was done, he walked to the door and said. "I'll be back."
She turned towards him and nodded. She didn't know what to say.

Lucas went up through the sheep carrying the dish of food. It was a large bowl and he had filled it with enough for 4 or 5 dogs. He went all the way to the gate and considered setting it there, but he didn't know if they would come up. As he went to try and find them, a small part of him was nervous. He hadn't taken anything for a weapon. He hadn't taken Jess. He didn't know if he'd been foolish in not even telling Barry he was going. He kept telling himself that he'd be fine, but he still wasn't sure he believed him. When he got close to where the dogs had been before he whistled a little so he wouldn't take them by surprise. He went out around into the open hoping for a better view. They were still there. He was glad for that. He didn't know where they usually were so this was his only chance. He spoke softly. "Hey there. Good dogs. Good dogs."

He held the dish down and tried to show them. After a minute he could see the male sniff the air a little. Neither dog moved. The male stayed sitting and the mother stayed lying down. She looked especially nervous. He knew she had every right to fear humans. He made the decision to set the dish down and simply walk away. Could he get them to trust him enough to follow? He had to, one way or another. He headed back, leaving the gate open. He was pretty sure no coyotes were going to come tangle with that boy any time soon, based on what he saw of the coyotes who didn't make it out.

He didn't speak of it for the rest of the day. He wasn't sure how to explain the feelings he had or the ideas rolling around in his head. What if Tina wouldn't want them? What if they weren't safe even after a while? He thought Jess could help bridge the gap. He told Barry they would wait on the horse until morning. It was better timing and would give him time to get his thoughts together. He was silent through dinner and Tina did not bring up questions about the day's events. She could tell he had something on his mind.

When the day was over and everyone had gone to bed for the evening and Jess was lying in her customary spot, Lucas found himself unable to sleep. The dogs kept coming into his mind and he wondered if they had eaten. He also didn't know if they would be there in the morning. If they weren't, he didn't know if he would be able to find them. He thought of the white hair on the fence, so long ago. Did they still stay at Roger's? If they did, how would he ever get them to come back to the fields? "Luke, are you alright? Tina suddenly asked, pulling Lucas out of his thoughts. He had thought she was asleep.

He didn't speak for some time. Finally, he said. "Do you remember when Roger Allen told us about what had happened to his dogs?"

"Of course. How could I forget?" She asked. She thought he was a horrible man.

"I don't think the dogs died." Lucas said quietly.

"Well, if Jess is one of them, obviously she lived, no thanks to him. Do you think the other pup survived?" She asked.

Lucas didn't answer right away. Tina thought of him mixing up food and how he didn't want her in the barn.

"You found the other pup, didn't you?" It wasn't really a question. She thought she had it put together. "Lucas, is that what killed the lamb? He rolled over, picking his head up. "I mean, I would understand. If it was starving and had no one to teach it…"

"No! Lucas cut her off abruptly. No. He didn't. They helped Jess protect them from the coyotes. I think they got there too late for the lamb."

Tina sat up in bed. "They? I thought there were only two pups?"

Lucas sat up beside her. "The mother was with him. She looked bad. She doesn't look like she's eating well."

"Wait!" Tina said. Her voice getting higher pitched. "The one he shot?"

Lucas nodded. "She only has one eye and a scar and I think part of her ear is missing."

Tina looked at him in the mostly dark room. Can I see them? Are they scared? How did you get them in the barn?"

"In the barn?" Lucas repeated. "They aren't in the barn. They are afraid of humans. They're still outside the fence. That's where I brought them food."

Tina looked at him confused. "So why didn't you want me in the barn?"

Lucas actually chuckled. It was partially from relief. He didn't know why he thought Tina might have an issue with the dogs. In fact, he was now quite sure if they had been in the barn, she'd have spent the night there.

"What's so funny?" Tina asked "You've been trying to hide things all day. If they aren't in the barn, what is?"

Lucas tried to think of a good answer.

"If you don't tell me, I'll go find out for myself."

She started to get out of bed and he grabbed her arm. "Wait!" He said.
"Then you had better start talking."

He explained everything that had happened that morning with the sheep and the dogs and why he put a gate and his hopes that they could keep them and use them to help Jess. He explained his concerns about trying to earn their trust and that he didn't want her to be afraid or not be able to go out in the fields. When he had finished, she looked at him. Her eyes, soft and adoring. "Lucas." She said. "There is nothing I would like more than for us to try. They deserve a better life. I mean, they've already helped us and they've been living wild."

Lucas felt relieved. She obviously wasn't afraid or even daunted by the idea. "We'll go look for them in the morning and bring them more food." He said as he put his arms around her and pulled her back down onto the bed.

She snuggled against him, her head against his chest and he pulled the sheet up over them both. They lay there in silence, both lost in their thoughts. Lucas began to drift off. Tina suddenly picked up her head and asked. "So what's in the barn?"

Lucas pushed her head back down. "I'll tell you tomorrow."

Chapter 33
Please, Momma

After Fur had made sure the man was gone, he went over to the food. Wee had been right. It smelled really good. He licked it, the taste of bacon fat filling his mouth. It tasted good too. He took a mouthful and began to chew. It really was crunchy. A little weird, but definitely good. After eating quite a bit, he looked over at his mother. "You should come eat too, Momma." He said. "Wee had the man bring it to us." Momma came over and sniffed the bowl. She licked much of the grease but ate only a little kibble.

"Momma, you should eat more." Fur coaxed. "There is plenty for both of us."

"I'm not that hungry." She told him and went to lie back on the grass.

Fur sighed. He was definitely worried. Momma barely ate anything these days. He thought about his sister and her promises. Maybe Momma did need sheep and a warm barn.

"Momma." He said after thinking about how he should word it and wishing his sister had stayed. "Do you think we could live with Wee? She says the barn is nice and the people never hurt her. It can't be worse than Roger. Wee says she thinks not all people are like Roger."

Momma rested her head on her paws. "I'm not sure if I want to guard sheep." Momma said quietly.

"But Momma!" Fur said, shocked to hear his mother say those words. "You talk about it all the time!"

"I talk about it, so you understand the importance of our job. I am just tired." she said quietly.

"But why is it important, Momma? Why? I haven't lived with sheep. I just try to find food and take care of us. I don't care about sheep. I care about you." He paused. "And I care about Wee, now that we found her. I missed her."

His mother didn't lift her head. "Listen." She said. "If you go to live with Wee. You will need to be kind to the sheep and watch over their lambs. You must show them respect and if they ask you to back off, you must give them space."

Fur felt panic rising up inside him. Momma had never given up. He wished Wee was there with him. He felt like she would know what to do. Why was Momma like this now?

He tried to think of a way to encourage his mother. "Momma, would you teach me how to behave with the sheep? Please! If I want to be able to live with Wee, I need you to teach me."

Momma lifted her head. She sighed deeply. "I will try." she said. Then she laid her head back on her paws and closed her eyes.

Fur lay down beside her. He laid there long into the night just watching her breathe. "Please don't give up, Momma." He whispered. Fur had never felt so alone.

He finally fell asleep with his head against hers and did not wake up until he heard the noise of the sheep coming out into the field.

He leaped to his feet, as he heard the calls of the sheep and the sound of human voices. "Momma." He said. "Come on! The sheep are here again."

His mother just lay there. He could see the slow movement of her shallow breathing, but she did not respond. "Momma." He said again.

He knew something was wrong. He sniffed her and poked at her. "Momma. Wake up."

He felt like a child again, when he and his sister had been trying to wake their mother. "Momma. Please."

Wee! Where was Wee? He went out into the open and trotted part way to the fence. He barked his loud, deep bark. In moments, Wee appeared on the other side of the fence. She was happy to see her brother again. Her happiness, however, was short lived as Fur yelled up to her. "Help!" He cried. His voice sounded desperate. "It's Momma! She won't wake up!"

Wee looked around for Lucas, who was also coming at the sound of the barking. She raced to meet him. She ran in front of him barking and ran back to the gate.

Chapter 34
A Matter Of Faith

Lucas had heard the dog bark and was happy to know they were still there. Maybe with Wee in the field, they would come closer. Tina had asked to come with him when he went to check their food and considering their behavior with Lucas the day before, he had said he thought that was okay. As he walked across to the fence, hoping to see the dog, Jess came racing towards him barking and whining. "You that excited?" Lucas asked her.

She raced off to the fence and began barking again. The commotion brought Barry who had been filling water. Jess raced to him, still barking and then back to the fence. "What is her problem?" Barry asked, looking at Lucas. "She sure wants to go see them."

Jess went back to Lucas, who reached down and tried to grab her collar. She ducked his hand and unable to think of anything else, Jess grabbed Lucas's pant cuff and began to pull in the direction of the fence. "Hey!" Lucas yelled. "Cut that out!" He pulled his leg back, pulling the cuff from her mouth.

She ran to the fence again barking over and over.

Lucas came to the fence and this time, he managed to grab her collar. He looked down

the hill and saw the male disappear back into
the clumps of trees.

Jess tried to twist out of his grasp and he turned
her around and knelt down. "Hey! I know you
want to go out there, but stop!"

Jess looked deep into Lucas's eyes and whined
softly. He looked at her. She whined again. He
thought for a second and realized that even
when he had found her, she had not resisted
his requests for her to follow him home. She
hadn't barked or carried on at all yesterday. He
went to the gate and opened it. "Jess." He
called. But she had been right behind him and
she was already out the gate at a dead run.
"Something is wrong!" He yelled to Barry, who
was still just standing there, watching.

Then Lucas jogged down the hill after his dog.
When he came around the small stand of trees,
Jess was pushing against the old dog and
whining softly. "Oh hell." Lucas muttered.

He went to move close and the male stood up
and growled. "Easy, boy." Lucas said, trying to
sound reassuring.

The dog seemed unsure, but he did not retreat.
Lucas crouched down, trying to appear less
threatening as he moved forward, the dog
moved nervously, but he growled again and
Barry heard Lucas come around the corner.

Fur didn't know what to do. He was worried
about his mother and frightened of the men. Yet

he felt that protecting her was his only option. He stood his ground hackles up and continued to growl. Wee stepped in front of him. "Fur. Don't." She said to him softly.

He raised his head to look over Wee's back. "I won't let them hurt her."

"When I was hurt, they took care of me. Maybe they can take care of Momma."

"But what if they hurt her?" Fur asked, his voice filled with pain. "What if they… "He trailed off.

"I trust them, Fur." Wee told him.

"Well, I don't." He answered. He almost sounded like a stubborn pup again.

"You don't have to trust them, Fur." Wee continued. "You just have to trust me."

He whimpered and Wee moved forward. "Back up, Fur. Let them try. It's our only hope."

She pressed her body to his and slowly he retreated back one step at a time as Wee kept moving forward.

Lucas and Barry had watched the whole interaction. They watched in awe as the two dogs were clearly communicating in some way. It had never occurred to either that dogs had the intelligence to convey a need. But she had to Lucas when she wanted to come out. The way she stared into his eyes. And she was clearly communicating with her brother now.

As they moved away, Lucas moved in. He kept his eyes on the male, saw him stiffen, and saw Wee back him up again. When he got to the old dog, she was still breathing. It was shallow and when he checked her gums they were very pale. "Get ready, Barry." He said gruffly. He placed his hands gently under the old dog and was shocked to realize how little weight there was to her. As he lifted her into his arms, he stood and began to back away. The dog went to move towards him and Wee stepped to block him. This time she growled. "Do not bite my human." She told her brother.

Lucas made his way out of the trees and to the gate. Barry, looking backwards as he went, covered their retreat. When they had made it to the safety of the fence, Barry called the dog. "Jess. Here."
She came part way and paused, looking back. Barry whistled. "Here." He called again.
Jess said to Fur, "I'll be back!" And raced to the gate to obey Barry's command.

When Barry closed the gate and turned around, he realized Lucas had not stopped to wait. He was almost out of sight. "Wait!" Barry told Jess and ran to catch up to his brother.

Jess had thought she was going with them, but remembered someone had to watch the sheep.

She barked to her brother. He came up slowly.

"They're gone." Jess told him.

"Where did they take Momma?" he asked, solemnly. "Is she...?"

He couldn't bring himself to say the word.

Jess heard the truck start and Tina's voice.

"They are taking her in the truck." Jess answered. "I've been in the truck. It's okay. I think I even came to their house in the truck. It's hard to remember. I was very sleepy all the time."

"Could you not wake up, like Momma?" He asked, his voice almost hopeful.

Jess wasn't sure if it was like Momma, but for Fur's sake she said "Yes. Sometimes I would wake up for a while, but then I would fall asleep when I least expected it."

Jess looked down at the gate and then at the fence. "Fur, why don't we go lie in the shade. It's getting hot." She said. She was worried and she wanted to go find someplace cool to wait.

"I don't want to leave you. Fur said and then more quietly, "You might be all I have."

Jess sighed. "She made it before. I made it. We have to have hope."

Fur nodded. His face brightened just a little. Jess wanted very much to be right.

"Come on." She said, moving away from him.

"I can't. Fur said sadly. "They closed the gate."

"Fur." Jess said. "You're as tall as the fence. I saw you jump higher to get a coyote. Just come in."

Fur looked at the fence and he put his head up over it. Momma had always turned away at fences. But maybe good fences meant humans and that's why she turned, he thought. Then he backed up a few steps and with a bounding leap, he landed on the other side. "See!" Jess said. "Now come on."

He followed her down among some scrub where they lay together, taking comfort from their closeness.

Chapter 35
History Repeats

When Lucas came down, carrying the dog to the truck, with Barry close behind, Tina had been on the front steps. She ran across the yard to meet Lucas, momentarily afraid it was Jess in his arms. The matted fur and the thinness of the dog made her realize it was not. She followed Lucas to the truck, where Barry pulled open the door to the backseat and laid the dog gently inside. Tina looked at the scar across the dog's face and knew it had to be the mother. "What happened?" she asked as he opened the door and hopped inside.

"I told you she looked rough. I guess the hair hid how rough." Lucas said as he shut the truck door. Barry got in on the passenger side. Tina shrugged and climbed in next to the dog, putting its head on her leg so she fit on the seat. Lucas glanced back and said nothing. He started the truck and drove out.

As soon as they were moving, Tina leaned forward and dug the business card for the vet out of the console, then carefully repositioned the dog head. She pulled her phone from her back pocket and as soon as the receptionist answered, she asked her to let Dr. Riley know they were bringing in a dog. "Okay. Hold on one moment."

When the line picked back up, it was not the receptionist, but the veterinarian. "Something wrong with Jess?" He asked.

"No." Tina said. "Jess is fine. It's Jess's mother."

There was a long pause. "You have the mother?"

Tina realized that sounded bad because if they had the mother, he would think Jess had belonged to them after all. "We didn't have her until this morning. Some months ago, we met the man who had the ranch up the road. He doesn't live there anymore and he admitted he abandoned two pups."

Tina could almost feel the cold from the vet through the phone. She at least understood why now. She continued. "He also told us he had shot their mother."

She heard the sharp intake of his breath. "The dog is missing one eye and has a scar across its head. Lucas thinks the mom survived somehow. He tried to feed them yesterday, but this morning, he found her unconscious."

"Bring her in." He said, his voice was like ice. But at least this time, his anger was not for them.

"We're on our way." Tina said and hung up the phone.

"He sounds absolutely as friendly as ever." Lucas said dryly.

"He used to work out west and he saw a lot of neglect and mistreatment of these dogs. Lucas, he really isn't a bad guy." Tina defended him without thinking.

"How do you know all that?" Lucas asked, surprised.

For a second Tina hesitated and then just said, casually. "I saw him at the post office one day. He was surprised how good Jess was looking and he told me. So, I explained that she really hadn't been ours, and this time, he believed me because she was so much better and wasn't scared." She kept her head down and continued to gently pet the head in her lap.

"When was that?" Lucas asked, trying to sound just as casual.

"Oh, I don't remember exactly. It was sometime last year, before Christmas."

Lucas and Barry looked at each other and then back to the road. "I love you," Lucas said. She looked up at him, but Lucas didn't make eye contact and just kept driving. In the passenger seat, Barry smiled while staring at the truck floor.

When they arrived at the veterinary clinic, Lucas put the truck in park and immediately went to take the dog out of the truck. Tina Moved out of the way, gently laying her head on the seat. Lucas gathered her up, laying her head against his shoulder so it didn't hang. As soon as they were in the door, the vet came out to meet them. The receptionist started to speak, but the doctor motioned for them to follow. "In here." He said.

They followed him through the doors and into the first room on the right side. "Lay her right here." Dr. Riley directed Lucas, who gently laid her on the table.

He stepped back, when the doctor stepped forward and began to look her over. He checked her gums, felt along her body and checked the missing eye for any sign of infection. He looked up. "You can all wait in the lobby."

The three went back out as a tech came to assist the veterinarian.

They took a seat in the hard chairs. Then the receptionist came over and asked if someone could come fill out some info. Lucas stood and followed her to the counter. He gave his name and phone number and she looked his name up on their computer. "Is this Jess?" She asked.

"No." Lucas said.

She tapped away at the keys a moment. "Has she ever been here before?"

"No." Lucas replied.

"Okay and what's her name?" The woman asked.

Lucas looked back over his shoulder. "Tina. The dog's name?"

She thought for a moment and said loudly enough for the receptionist to hear. "Callie." The receptionist looked at him for a moment before typing.

"We've only had her since yesterday." Lucas told her before she could make too many assumptions.

"I'd certainly call whoever you got her from and let them know. The dog obviously wasn't well. Didn't you notice anything was wrong?"

Or we can still make assumptions, Lucas thought. "We found her. We didn't buy her." He responded.

The receptionist gave a grimace. "You should put up posters and hang them in town. You can bring one in here too. She might have been missing for a long time. Does Dr. Riley know that she is a stray?"

"She's not a stray." Lucas said, wishing the woman would just take his information and stop giving advice. "We're keeping her if she makes it."

The woman looked back at him, her voice patronizing when she spoke. "You should at least make an effort to find the owners. They could be really worried. We'll check her for a chip."

"She doesn't have a chip and her previous owner shot her."

The receptionist's mouth opened and closed like a fish out of water. "Oh dear!" She gasped.

Lucas turned and walked back to his seat.
Barry looked at him, smirking.

About 40 minutes later, the vet came out and walked over to the trio. "He stooped down. "You realize she's an older dog?"
Lucas nodded. "Yep."
"Okay. She's very dehydrated and extremely anemic. I can set her up with an IV and give her some iron and some vitamin B. Her bloodwork shows an infection, I am wondering about Lyme if she's been living out there and she has quite a few ticks. I also suspect high parasite load from eating wild animals, maybe roadkill, who knows. The other one had pretty bad worms when she came in. If I can get that taken care of, she'll probably just need some TLC until she is back on her feet. I'd say she's 8. Maybe 9. hard to tell with the life she's lived. So, it's up to you, if you want me to put in the effort." He paused and then added. "It won't be nearly as expensive as it was for the other one."
Lucas looked at the doctor. "I don't know, it was only half as expensive as I thought it would be."
The doctor's face flushed. He looked away.
"I can give you a few minutes to decide if you'd like." He said standing up.
Lucas stood as well. "Fix the dog, Doc."
The vet nodded. "I'd like to at least keep her overnight and see how she is in the morning."

"No problem." Lucas replied. "Do you need a deposit?"

The doctor shook his head. "You can just pay it tomorrow. "

Tina spoke up from her seat. "I don't think she's ever been touched by a human. You might want to be careful if she wakes up. She'll be terrified."

"I'll make sure we keep her from panicking." Dr. Riley told her.

Then the vet turned and walked back through the doors. Although they couldn't see it, he was actually smiling. When he got back to the unconscious dog, who already had an IV attached by the technician, he said to her.

"Don't worry, old girl. It's your lucky day."

Chapter 36
Maybe This Time

When the Porter family returned home, Tina went to make lunch. As soon as she went in, Barry scooted quickly to the barn to tend to the horse. Lucas headed up back to look for Jess and to see if the male was still somewhere nearby. He was happy to see that all was quiet. The sheep that he could see were spread across the landscape, but definitely in their own fields. They looked calm and content. "Jess!" He called.

She appeared out of some scrub and came partway to him. "Here!" He said firmly.

She looked back for a moment and then trotted up to meet him. Lucas stroked her fur and asked. "Is everything okay?"

She looked back down the hill. Lucas walked down to where Jess had been. As he approached, he heard movement and came around the scrub to see the back of a large white dog, moving off, away from him.

He went to check the fence and the gate, but there was no sign of any issue. How in the world did he get in, Lucas wondered. He was glad though. It would make it much easier to feed him if he stayed. He patted Jess again, told her she was a good dog and with a wag of her tail, she trotted off to find her brother. Lucas went and retrieved the dish from the day before, so he could leave food when he brought the sheep down for the evening. Hopefully, the dog would stay when Jess left for the night. Lucas decided to call him Ethan.

When Lucas got back to the barn, Barry had not only tended the horse, but the sheep in quarantine as well. They both headed up to the house to have lunch. "At this rate." Barry said jokingly. "You'll actually wind up giving her the horse on her birthday."

Lucas chuckled. "Not a chance. She's already asking why I'm keeping her out of the barn. How long do you think, before she goes looking?"

"Not long." Barry answered. "Not long at all. So, this afternoon, are you going to give it to her?"

Lucas sighed. "I was hoping to do it on a day when I could have time to let her try it out, go for a ride. You know? Everything has been so hectic the last couple of days."

"So, take the afternoon off." Barry said. "We have the field directly off the barn all done. She can bring it out there, try riding. You can hang out with her and help."

Lucas scratched his beard and thought. He always felt like there was so much to do. "I don't know what's going to happen with the dog tomorrow. I might not get to work then either."

"I'll tell you what." Barry said. "Let's go eat. Then you can give her the horse. I'll even bring the sheep down." He pulled the dish out of Lucas's hand. "And I'll feed the dog."

"It's in with the sheep." Lucas said, suddenly remembering. "I call him Ethan."

"Ethan." Barry said.

"What's wrong with Ethan?" Lucas asked.

"Nothing." Barry said, despite his tone saying there was. "You want to call him Ethan, you can call him Ethan."

"You don't like it." Lucas sounded defensive. He had never named a dog before.

"I didn't say that." Barry replied, smirking.

Lucas pushed him and the two grappled for a moment like teenage boys.

"Lucas?" Tina called from the door.

They stopped immediately and headed for the house, both looking like children, caught playing in their Sunday clothes. When they got close to the house, Lucas asked. "So what are you going to do this afternoon? "

Barry grinned. "I'm going to enjoy my time off."

As soon as lunch was over, Barry thanked Tina for the meal and excused himself, saying that he had a few things to do. After he left, Lucas began picking up the rest of the dishes and putting them in the sink. Tina looked at him. "Are you alright? "

"Yeah." Lucas replied, turning on the water and squeezing some detergent into the sink.

Tina put away the bread and put the remaining food in the fridge. She watched Lucas washing the dishes. It wasn't that he never did, but in the early afternoon, with hours of daylight remaining, he usually would have been out the door, as soon as Barry excused himself.

"Was everything okay, up back?" She asked.

"Yes. Jess's brother is in the field with her. Everything seemed fine." He continued washing the last few things, rinsed them off and put them in the strainer beside the sink. "Did you need to talk about something?" She felt he was being weird again.

"No. Not really. Barry just wanted the afternoon off." He really wasn't lying on that one. He had a feeling Barry was probably on his couch, with his feet up.

Lucas dried his hands and walked towards the door. "I told him to take a break. It's been a crazy couple of days. You want to help me with something for a minute?" He kept his voice even and low, as if it were some mundane task.

"Of course." Tina answered. She followed him to the door and pulled her boots on.

When she was ready, he walked out and walked down the steps and out towards the barn. "Should I have brought gloves? She asked, unsure what he needed help with.

"No. It's nothing dirty." He kept walking towards the barn.

He walked in the gate of the sheep's night pen and she followed him as he continued into the barn. Inside, he started walking back and forth, as if he were looking for where he might have set something down. He said, "Must have left it on the other side." and he walked to the center doors with Tina following behind him. He opened the doors and turned on the lights. To his surprise, the horse was fully tacked and standing in the aisle. Barry. He thought of everything. Lucas took a couple of steps inside and turned so she could see past him. Her eyes lit up and she was past him, in a matter of seconds. She stopped in front of the little mare. "Lucas! Oh my god!" She exclaimed.

He walked up beside her. "What do you think?" It's beautiful!" She said. "When did you…?" She trailed off as she remembered their odd behavior at the fair and him blocking her from the barn, as well as dissuading her from helping the last couple of days. She turned to him still looking a bit bewildered. "I know it's early." He said. "But happy birthday."

The tears started to well up in her eyes and she hugged him tightly. He held her against him for a minute and then asked. "Do you want to ride her?"

She stepped back, wiping her tears with her hands and smiling at him while she fought back the tears. "Can I? I don't exactly know how."

He walked her over to the horse and helped her get her foot in the stirrup and into the saddle. Then he took the lead and walked out the back and into the field beyond.

They spent the next few hours out there as he taught her how to command the horse and gave her time to get comfortable in the saddle. When they were done, he showed her how to remove the tack and realized they would need some brushes and a hoof pick among other things. For now, he rubbed the horse down with an old towel and returned it to the stall. Tina had been overjoyed the whole time. They laughed at her difficulties and he enthusiastically praised her success.

Afterwards, they headed up to the house where they showered and then she curled up with him on the couch. The horse aside, these days were one in a million and they enjoyed every minute. Of course, most of the conversation was about the horse and the night at the fair. She laughed as he explained all the things they had done and the complications involved.

Barry had waited until they were out in the field to get the dog food from the kitchen. Then he brought the dish home, so they could enjoy each other's company. He had left a note on the counter saying that he had dinner, so they would have the evening alone as well. When evening came, he went up to retrieve the sheep, knowing they'd come down easily for the grain he had put out. He let them run down through and then called Jess. She came up to the top of the slope and he could see the other dog standing halfway down, watching him. As he stood there deciding where to put the food, Jess ran back to her brother.

"I've got to go." Jess said to Fur. "I have to guard the humans at night."
"What do I do?" He asked.
"Well, it looks like he brought you food. You can eat that. There's water up there. And you can lay by the gate up there until morning. I'll be back then."
"Do you think Momma is out there?"
He hadn't mentioned her in a few hours, but Jess knew he was worried. She was worried too.
"I don't know," Jess answered honestly. "But if she is in the house, I can tell you tomorrow."
"In the house!" Fur exclaimed. "Why would Momma be in the house?"
Jess knew Barry was waiting. "Some humans let dogs in their house. I'm going down to the house right now."
He thought for a moment about that, but finally he just said, "If she's there, tell her I miss her."

"I will." Jess said. "And I'll let you know in the morning."

He nodded and watched her run back to the human. He wondered how she could be so unafraid of them. Maybe if he wasn't afraid, he could go there too. He sighed and watched as Barry set down the food and left, closing the gate. He missed his mother and now his sister. He waited until the man was gone from sight and went to check the food. It was different from the day before but still good. He tried to imagine having food like this every day. After getting a drink, he lay down against the gate, as close as he could be to where Wee went and tried very hard to sleep the time away. The fullness in his stomach definitely helped.

When Barry got back, he went down to the house and cracked the door, just enough to let Jess inside. Then he went back out to tend the other sheep. He had actually enjoyed puttering around the cabin, fixing a few things and generally having a very laid-back kind of day. He made himself a couple of sandwiches, sat in his chair and read for a while, as he usually did for a short time at night. He fell asleep there, with his feet on the coffee table and didn't wake up until dawn was creeping over the horizon.

Chapter 37
Out Of The Darkness

The next morning, when Jess went out with the sheep, she immediately went to find Fur. He was disheartened to know that she had not found their mother in the house or the barn. She wished she had better news. He waited until the men had left, watching one of them pick up his dish and found himself mildly happy to know they would probably bring him more food when they came to get his sister.

Apparently, Jess was right. They ate every day here. When they were gone, he spoke. "Did they say anything about Momma?" He asked Wee.

Jess sighed. "Humans don't really talk. They make a lot of noises and some of them mean something, but a lot of it is just stuff. It's like they bark at each other a lot."

Fur thought for a moment. "What is Jess?"

"That's me." She said. "Humans choose their own noises for things. Here means they want me to come to them and come on means to follow where they go. Then they have no which means not to do what you're doing and sit, which means to do this." She sat down.

"That's weird." Fur said. "Do you do it?"

"Yes," Jess said. "It makes them very happy."

"Do you think they will pick a noise for me?" He asked.

"Probably." She said. "You just have to pay attention to what noise they make when they look at you."

Fur sighed. He had watched the man saying goodbye to Jess. He seemed so gentle. If only he were less afraid.

At the barn, Tina was with her horse, bringing it out to be loose in the field for the first time. She was still in disbelief. As soon as breakfast was over she had headed out, just to see it again. Lucas smiled to himself. He couldn't wait to go riding with her, but his horse would have to wait. He had spent a lot of time on horseback and he eventually wanted to be able to go out and roam the property with Tina. For now, he was simply happy that she was so excited. The brothers headed out to do more land clearing. He was waiting for the vet's office to call, but there was no point in wasting the day until then.

When Tina brought them lunch, they still had not heard any word. Lucas found himself getting antsy as the day wore on. He had to stop and pick up more dog food before he went to get her and he was debating on a larger crate than the one Jess had used as a pup. He didn't want the dog to feel cramped. He still hadn't figured out how to get her in and out to the bathroom. She was not likely to take well to a leash and collar. In fact, she was not likely to take well to anything involving humans at all. He felt mad at Roger. How hard was it to teach a dog to at least be touched. Maybe then she wouldn't have been so defensive of her pups. No wonder Dr. Riley didn't like ranchers. He thought back to the dogs he had seen, when he was purchasing sheep to build his flock. They lurked between the sheep with distrustful eyes. He had disliked them, as much as they had disliked him. But now he felt pity. Jess had certainly changed his view of what a livestock guardian could be. Could he change the way the old dog saw humans or would she forever watch him from a distance as soon as she could get away? He knew that he was going to try to change her mind.

When the phone finally rang, it was closing in on dinner time. It was the receptionist letting him know that the doctor said he could pick up his dog. He left Barry to do evening chores once again. He loaded up Jess's old crate from the shed, knowing nothing bigger would fit in the truck It would have to do for the ride home. In town, he pulled into the department store, grateful to have some idea of where to get the things he needed. He picked up a collar and a leash and then decided to get a collar for Ethan at the same time. He hoped he would one day, be able to get it on him. He picked up two more bags of food and decided on a very large metal wire crate. Maybe being able to see them would help. He also hoped she would feel less cornered.

Inside the vet clinic, he stood at the counter and gave his name and phone number. He was pretty sure it was the same woman who had been there when he picked up Jess. She smiled at him as she brought his file up. She reached out and put her hand on Lucas's hand. He looked at her in surprise. "You're a good man." She said quietly. "Thank you for doing so much for these dogs."

Lucas was shocked at her kindness and a little flustered. "I appreciate that, Ms. … He paused, waiting for her to answer.

"Riley." She said. "Mrs. Riley. I'm the doctor's wife."

"Thank you. Mrs. Riley." Lucas finished. He felt awkward being praised by a total stranger.

Then she said. "It's so nice to know that not all ranchers are so cruel."

Lucas nodded. He really didn't know what to say.

He was saved by the vet tech who happened to come out the doors. As soon as he saw Lucas, he approached him. "Are you the one here to pick up Callie?" He asked.

"Yes." Lucas said. "How is she doing?"

Just then the doctor stuck his head out of the room and beckoned him over. The old dog was lying on a table, her head resting on her paws. Her eyes twitched beneath the lids, but she didn't pick up her head.

Lucas had hoped she would look better.

Dr. Riley saw the expression on Lucas's face. "I sedated her a little. As much as I dared in her state. I thought about keeping her another night, but this place is never really quiet. I think it's probably worse for her being here scared all the time."

"Okay." Lucas said, still looking at the dog. "I've taken care of sick animals. Just tell me what I need to do."

"She's hydrated now, and I started the antibiotics. I'll send some home with you. She also has an iron supplement and we dewormed her, got the ticks off and cleaned her up a little."

Lucas looked at him.

"Trust me. After the dewormer, she definitely needed it."

"Thank you." Lucas said. "I appreciate it."

The doctor continued. "She can't eat much and that's a problem. I'm gonna give you some stuff to mix in whatever liquid you can give her. It'll help to get some nutrition in her. Use milk or broth or whatever you have."

"Broth we can do and I can stop and pick up some milk." Lucas said.

The vet nodded. "It's gonna be slow going at first. Don't hesitate if you think she's taking a turn." He paused. "Have you ever done tube feeding?" He asked. "With lambs sometimes." Lucas answered.

The vet went out and came back with what was definitely like what they tube fed the lambs with, but slightly larger. "When you mix the powder up with the milk, I want you to start out giving her 3oz about 4 times a day. If that goes alright, you can eventually increase it to 6 ounces up to 6 times a day. Go with your gut on how she's acting."

Lucas nodded while trying to commit everything to memory. "Don't worry. The instructions will be on the paperwork. Dr. Riley said with a smirk.

Lucas gave a small smile. "Good."

He looked at the doctor. "Do you think her son could be sick too, if he's been out there with her?"

The vet raised his eyebrows. "Was he with her?"

"Yeah." Lucas said. "He's in the field with the sheep now. But he was with her. He's with Jess now."

"You got her working now?" the veterinarian asked.

Lucas suddenly felt defensive. "During the day. We can hear if she barks. We head right up there. At night we bring the sheep by the barn and she sleeps in the house."

Dr. Riley looked up. "It wasn't an accusation, Mr. Porter. I don't mind a working breed, working. I just think they ought to be taken care of."

"Trust me, Doc." Lucas said. "She may work. She even protected the sheep from stray dogs once. She protected me from one of them too. But she follows us around the ranch like a lap dog. She's happy as can be. You can come out if you want. None of my animals go without."

The vet nodded. "You never know, Mr. Porter. The wife and I might do that one day. If you get these dogs manageable, I'll come out and vaccinate them right at the ranch, so you don't have to try to bring them in."

"That would be great." Lucas said.

Lucas finally managed to escape from the conversation and get the dog in the truck. He realized the crate hadn't really been necessary, but since it was already wedged in the back seat, he gently maneuvered her into it. At the counter, Mrs. Riley had given him antibiotics for both dogs, along with dewormer and a pill to kill the ticks. He brought the bag of meds and the supplemental powder out and headed home. He was worried about the dog and feeling emotionally exhausted. The vet always made him feel on edge. Yet, the vet had still given him a discount and he certainly couldn't complain about that.

The trip home was uneventful and when he pulled into the driveway, the dog opened her eyes just briefly and closed them again. Lucas took out the crate and carried it into the house where he found Tina and Barry waiting for him at the kitchen table. They both stood when he came in. He asked Barry to get some old towels from the barn and carried the box into the living room. The table in the corner had already been moved, so he set up the crate there where Jess's had been. He was glad for the plastic tray in the bottom to keep the floor from being soiled.

Barry came in with several towels and Lucas layered them in the tray. Then he went out to retrieve the dog. She opened her eyes when he picked her up and he could see the fear, but she was too weak to do anything about it. He got down on his knees, with Tina hovering close by and laid her on the towels as gently as he could. He closed the door though he didn't think she'd be going anywhere. Then he went back out for the bag and the paperwork from the vet. He gave them to Tina. She carried them to the kitchen and stood at the counter reading through the papers.

Barry said he'd go bring food to Ethan and bring the sheep and Jess home for the night. Lucas thanked him and stayed, staring at the dog, until Tina came back in the room. "Do we start this tonight?" she asked, coming up beside him to look in the crate.

"Might as well." Lucas replied. "I can't see where it could be a bad thing. Although, the vet did say to go slow at first with small amounts." Tina nodded. "I saw that on the papers. She definitely needs food though."

She went back to the kitchen and mixed the food with her medications before heading back to the living room. Fortunately, the dog could not offer anything in the way of resistance and so with Lucas holding her head up and her mouth open and Tina feeding, they were done about 20 minutes later when Barry came in with Jess.

Jess came in the door like a whirlwind, her nose sniffing the air. She moved to the living room in a flurry of scrabbling feet and up to Lucas, who was just going to wash his hands. She buried her nose into his pants, then his hands, before moving past him to the crate in the corner. "Jess! Lucas said, softly but firmly. "Easy." There was no need. She stood at the crate with her nose pressed between the wires and stared at her mother. She let out a soft whine. Tina reached down and petted her head. "Good girl."

When they left to wash up and have dinner, Jess laid down by the front of the crate. There she stayed even when her people went to bed. Later that night, with the sedative fully worn off, Momma opened her eyes. In the dim light, she could make out the silhouette of Jess lying with her head against the crate door. She lifted her head ever so slightly. "Wee." She said, hoarsely, her voice merely a whisper.

Jess awoke immediately and looked through the wire. "Momma." She whispered back with a small sense of relief. "Are you okay?"

The old dog's head sank down onto the towels and she did not answer. Jess sat up.

"Where am I?" Her mother finally managed to ask.

"Safe with me." Jess told her, not wanting her mother to worry.

"Fur?" Momma said, though it came out as more of a wheezing noise.

"He's safe, Momma. He's watching my sheep. You should rest."

Jess waited for her mother to answer, but she seemed to have fallen asleep again. She lay back down. She wanted to tell Fur that she had found Momma, but she could only wait until morning.

When Lucas and Tina came out in the morning, they found the two dogs lying nose to nose on either side of the crate door. Lucas walked towards the crate and the old dog tried to rise and instead, lost her balance and fell, flailing weakly. He immediately retreated and they both went into the kitchen. The last thing he wanted to do was make her struggle. It did not bode well for tube feeding her breakfast.

Tina started the coffee and then began breakfast. By the time Barry came in, Lucas was putting plates on the table. He glanced into the living room where Jess lay with her mother. He saw the dog look at him and the fear in her eyes and walked to the table instead. "How's she doing?"

"She's a little scared." Lucas said. "Maybe after breakfast you can take Jess out so we can try to get her fed."

"Sure thing. I can take her and the sheep out to the field." Barry offered since there wasn't much he could do that would be helpful when it came to the dog. Too many people would frighten her more and she didn't seem strong enough to really put up a fight.

They ate breakfast and talked about their plans and tried to set times when either Lucas or Barry would stop by, to assist with the dog's required feedings. When Barry had finished, he looked in on Jess lying next to her mother and wondered how willing she would be to leave. "Jess." He said.

To his surprise, she was on her feet and to the door in a flash. He let her out and followed behind her as she raced for the gate and stood looking back at him impatiently. By the time he got to the gate she was prancing back and forth then looking at him. "Okay." Barry said. "I'm coming."

As soon as the gate was cracked open, she pushed her way in and raced up towards the field as fast as she could go. When Barry got the sheep moving and headed out, she was just as impatient for his arrival as she had been at the other barn. He opened the gates wide and the dog led out with the multitudes of sheep following behind. He shook his head and picked up the now empty dog dish and walked out, closing the gates behind him.

In the house, while Tina mixed the dog's food, Lucas went into the living room. The dog who had been dozing on her side, picked her head up off the floor and struggled to stand up and move away. Lucas decided there was no way to do it, but to do it. The sooner he had a hold of her, the sooner she would stop struggling.

He knelt and opened the larger door on the side of the crate and leaned in. The dog managed to press herself closer to the front, making it almost impossible to reach her without crawling inside. He wasn't so sure now that a larger crate was a better idea. He crouched there until Tina came in and set the food and the feeder on the table. "Open the front door." Lucas said "See if you can get her to move this way." Tina opened the door but the dog, caught between the two, decided Tina was the least frightening and refused to back up.

By the time they managed to get the dog where they wanted her, Lucas was inside the crate, crouched over her with one arm wrapped around her neck. He moved himself forward until he could get both hands on her head. She struggled against them the whole time and it was fortunate the dog was as weak as she was, or they likely would have needed Barry to get it accomplished. It did not escape Tina's notice that a year ago, Lucas wouldn't have touched a dog, never mind wrestle with it in a crate. A part of her still couldn't believe it. When they were done, Tina headed out to care for her horse, a chore she insisted on doing and Lucas went to find Barry to begin their day.

Momma lay exhausted on the towels on the crate floor. Her short struggle with the humans had tired her out. She had hated their hands on her. She hated the tubing in her mouth and her inability to prevent it. Wee had left her alone and she had had no choice but to give in to the human's demands. She had been terrified, being cornered like that. Yet, they hadn't actually hurt her, and they hadn't gotten angry. And there was some weight in her empty stomach. Momma tried to stay awake, but eventually she dozed off until Tina came back inside.

Out in the fields, Jess had raced through the field relying on her nose to tell her where her brother was hiding. When she found him, she could not contain her excitement. "Fur!" She said breathlessly. "I found Momma!"
Her brother didn't need reassurance. He could smell the faint scent brought on Jess's hair. He sniffed her all over. "She smells very tired." Fur said dejectedly. "What if she isn't okay?'
Jess wanted to reassure him, but she was also worried. She moved and sat beside him and tried to think of something to say. As she had always been a thinker, she finally did come up with something. Something that made her feel better too. She shared her thoughts with her brother. "You know." She said, "When I was first in the house. I was weak and tired too. I fell asleep all the time, even though I was scared. But I got better. So maybe Momma just needs time to get better."
Fur lay down with a thud. "I miss her, Wee. I wish I could see her too."
"I know." Jess told him. "First, you have to not be afraid of humans."

Fur sighed. "I've always been afraid."
Jess lay down beside him. "For now," She said,
"I will bring you her smell every day, so you can
see if she gets stronger."
He laid his head on his paws and hoped that
she would get stronger.

Chapter 38
Compromises

Despite their original plans, over the next few days, it was always Lucas who went in to help Tina feed the dog. It became more of a struggle each time as the dog became more determined to avoid her feedings. Lucas had put the collar on her to be able to get a better hold and although she was still weak, as the infection waned and the food wasn't being shared with a host of parasites, she was improving daily. Her humiliation at having to relieve herself, in the confines of the cage, increased her unhappiness. Every day she fought harder and her only consolation was lying with Wee at night. Jess tried to encourage her to understand that they weren't trying to hurt her, although Jess herself didn't quite understand what went on during the day. She just knew it made her mother unhappy.

And so it was that on about the 6th day, Tina stood in front of the cage, holding a bowl with some nutritional supplement, some milk and some fresh warm bacon grease. She stooped down and set the bowl in front of the crate and went into the other room. She had tried to make it smell particularly good. The minutes ticked by and she waited, hoping she could get the dog to eat of her own accord before Lucas came in for the next feeding. She felt like the constant force was just giving the dog a worse impression of people than she already had. When she heard the metal dish touch the sides of the crate with a slight tinking sound, she almost didn't dare to hope. She waited some time before trying to sneak to the living room doorway and check on the dog. To her relief, the dish was mostly empty and the dog seemed unsure if it was done or wanted more.

It was a great milestone. With her eating on her own, they could focus more on trying to earn her trust. They began taking her outside on leash, so that she could learn to accept it, before she was strong enough to thrash about. Callie, as Tina had named her, began to slowly put on both weight and strength. She had learned to accept that the leash kept her with the human and although she tried a few times to pull her collar over her head, she had learned to simply abide by its restriction. She became mostly Tina's responsibility, as she was more often at the house.

Callie found herself at war in her mind. All her life, she had both feared and loathed humans. But with each passing day, she found herself looking forward to the woman's soft voice and gentle caresses, even though the contact made her freeze in place with her muscles stiffen. The men were still more intimidating, yet they too were always gentle and patient. She found herself confused by her mixture of emotions. She had promised they would never be with humans again, but late in the evening, when they all gathered in the living room, she would be invited to lay with the leash on, next to the woman's feet. Lying there, by the end of the couch, she felt a peace she had never known. She began to feel safe. It was something she had never experienced. There was a desire awakening inside her, for the respect and the love of mankind. And although part of her yearned to be out in the grass, lying among the sheep with her pack, this too was not so bad. They had given her a name. Jess had told her that it means they want you around. Somehow, that felt good too.

Each evening, when Jess came back to the house, she would tell her mother about Fur, the fields, the weird animal Tina had and the new lambs that had been born. And each morning she would bring the smell of Momma to Fur and tell him about the things that went on at the house. Jess was both happy and unhappy. She had her humans and her family, but they were divided. She needed a plan.

And so it was that late come August day, Wee stood in the field with Fur. "So," she asked him, "do you want to see Momma?"

"Of course, I do." He answered, giving her an annoyed look.

"Well, I've been thinking…" She paused for effect.

"Go on." Fur encouraged.

"When Barry and Lucas come to get the sheep, you should run with the sheep, right down the hill to the barn."

"They don't want me down there." He sighed. "They lock me up here at night."

"They lock you up here at night, because you won't run down to the barn.

"What will I do when I get down there? I'll be trapped." Fur asked.

Jess looked at her brother for a moment. "You know, you aren't a puppy. I'm pretty sure you can outrun a human. Besides, you don't have to go inside the barn. There is a field there, just like there is at Roger's."

The sound of Roger's name made him shiver. Jess rolled her eyes. "Remember. These guys protected me from Roger and made him go away."

The thought of that still made Fur feel a bit of awe. "So, if I run down there, will I see Momma?" he asked, trying to find a reason for the courage to defy the humans.

"In the morning you will." Jess said. "They bring her outside in the morning."

All day long, Fur tried to convince himself, and Jess did her best to continue to encourage the event. When evening finally came, Fur was hopeful, he could do it and no one would come after him. He lay in the bushes as close as he could to the gate. Jess wanted to laugh at him for thinking it had to be an ambush, but whatever it took to bring everyone together was fine by her. In some ways, he was still the old Fur.

Jess could hear Barry and Lucas talking as they came up to gather the sheep. The sheep, who knew grain would be outside the barn, had already been working their way slowly towards the gate. "Get ready." She said to Fur. When the men opened the gates and the sheep began to pour through, Fur made a run for it. He had closed most of the distance before he realized the mob of sheep were blocking the opening. He slid to a stop, turned and started back the other way, before turning again and running towards the gate again. As he made the last of the sprint, he leaped over two sheep in his way and raced down the hill, looking this way and that until he settled in the corner as far from the barn as possible. There he dropped down and stayed in a crouched position, waiting to flee whatever trauma might befall him.

Jess stood in the gateway, her tail wagging. "What was that all about? Barry laughed.
Lucas laughed too. "I don't know. He was going. He wasn't going. He was going. Now he's gone."
He looked at Jess. "Did you put him up to that?" Jess just wagged her tail harder. "Come on, Jess." Lucas said.
She ran off towards the barn and the men closed the gates and followed behind. At the barn, Barry grabbed the bowl of food he had brought out and walked back up to the gate. "Ethan. Come on, Ethan."
He said it in an odd voice, still picking on the name that Lucas had picked.
When he came back down, Lucas gave him a hard stare as he walked by, still grinning. At the last moment, Lucas reached out and swiped the hat off of Barry's head onto the ground. They made their way back to the house, pushing and shoving each other. Jess bounced along behind them, excited to tell Momma she had brought Fur home.

Fur watched them until they walked inside. He thought of everyone in the house together. It made him feel lonely. He wanted so much to be a part of things, but he didn't know how. After watching the house for a few minutes, he made his way up to the gate to eat his meal. When he was done, he found a place to lay where he could still see the house. He hoped Wee could help him learn what to do.

Chapter 39
Into The Light

Lucas was the one to take Callie out to the bathroom the next morning. Tina was busy making breakfast and he had offered. He walked her across the driveway and out along the side of the yard, giving her time to sniff and meander around. Her head came up suddenly and her tail wagged, ever so slightly. Lucas looked over where the sheep were by the barn and saw nothing. Callie looked in that direction and gently pulled forward on the leash. He thought about it for a moment and then allowed her to take him where she wanted to go. Their relationship was still too tentative for correction. That could come in time, when she had more trust in the people around her. She was probably bored in the house now that she was feeling a little better.

When she got all the way to the fence along the barn, he saw the male stand up. He had been laying where the land rose up towards the back gates to the field. Lucas hadn't noticed him until he moved. The focus of the male was not on Lucas, but on his mother. He stood with his head erect and tail up, watching her. "Ethan!" Lucas called, knowing the dog didn't know his name. "Ethan, come on!"

Fur looked at the man. He wanted so badly to see his mother. The man said something, but he didn't know what it was. He could tell though, that the man was watching him. Fur walked part way before stopping again. He suddenly wished Wee were there to tell him what he should do. She might know what the man was trying to tell him. He came a few steps, watching to see if the man got angry that he was approaching. To his surprise the man walked further down the fence, away from him, taking Fur's mom with him. She looked back at Fur as she walked. He started to move closer again, keeping his eyes on the man, with occasional glances at his mother. When the man stopped again, he stooped down and petted the old dog gently. He stroked the side of her neck. Fur froze in shock. Momma was letting a human touch her!

Lucas petted the dog, ignoring the tension in her body as she accepted his affection. He knew it would probably take some time before she felt comfortable and probably even more time before she would have the courage to come looking for it. At least, he hoped that would happen. He stayed crouched down talking to her, even after he stopped touching her. He was trying to find some way to show the other dog it was alright. He had seen the dog stop and then start moving again. He was using only his peripheral vision, so he wouldn't make the dog nervous by staring. It continued to close the distance. Sometimes it would pace off to one side or the other, its discomfort obvious. Callie moved closer to the fence. She whined to the other dog. It whined back at her. Lucas's legs started to cramp, but he stayed where he was.

After what seemed like an eternity, the dog finally came to greet his mother. Lucas tried very hard not to move. At some point, he was going to have to shift position. The dogs sniffed noses with their tails waving. He could tell they were happy to finally see each other. The sound of Barry coming out of his cabin broke the moment. The male fled up the hill and Callie leaped sideways, pulling on the leash in Lucas's hand. He tried to stand but the cramped muscles in his legs didn't respond and Lucas fell backwards, frightening Callie even more. From across the yard, Lucas could hear Barry's laugh. Lucas got to his feet as Barry closed the distance between them. He was still laughing loudly when he reached his brother. "That was the funniest thing, I'm likely to see before breakfast." He choked out the words, cackling like a fool.
Lucas looked at him from the corners of his eyes and began walking to the house without a word. "Oh, come on. "Barry said, his laughter

down to a chuckle. If you had seen it, you'd laugh too."

Yeah. "Really funny. I was trying to let the dog see that his mom was okay." Lucas was not as aggravated as he was pretending to be. But he wasn't going to encourage Barry's mockery. He did that plenty well without his help.

After breakfast, Barry took Jess up to let the sheep out. He watched the male move off. Jess ran to see him. They stood sniffing each other, tails wagging. They were distracted when Barry let the sheep out onto the field. They were playing and chasing each other, paying no attention to anything else. When they paused, Barry called Jess. "Come on, girl. Let's go. He watched the male scan his surroundings and look at Barry standing in the gateway. He was realizing his mistake. "Jess." Barry said. "Here."

She made it halfway to him and trotted back to her brother.

Fur had been so excited that he got to see Momma. Now he stood looking at the man and where he should go. When the man called Jess, she started to leave. Then she came back to Fur. "Are you coming?" She said impatiently, as she didn't like ignoring Barry's call.

"But he's standing there." Fur said, feeling wholly uncomfortable with the whole situation.

He didn't want to be left by the barn without his sister and he had so many questions about what he had seen.

Jess looked up at her brother. "Do you like eating every day?"

"I do. I really do. But he just looks creepy."

She looked at Barry and then back at Fur. She didn't find him creepy, but she knew she had once found him scary.

"Just do what I do. Okay."

Fur hesitated. "Is he gonna touch me?" He asked.

She rolled her eyes. "Not if you do what I do."

Barry watched the two dogs. If he didn't know better, he would have thought Jess was trying to get him to come with her. They both were looking at him. "Jess. Ethan. Come on!" He called out.

Jess began to trot up towards the gate. To Barry's surprise, the male began to follow her. He looked wild eyed and worried, but he was following. Barry watched, staying completely still, as Jess led her brother up to the gate giving Barry as wide a berth as was possible. As they came close, Jess looked back, seemingly to make sure her brother was still following. Then she trotted up and through the gate as far from Barry as she could. The male paused as she went through and then darted past Barry. The dog was so busy watching him, he barreled right into his sister, sending them both tumbling. Barry started to laugh, and Fur gained his feet and ran off out of sight. Jess came back to Barry and wagged her tail, before turning and following where her brother had gone. Barry shook his head and closed the gates.

Lucas had made a deal with a local horse farmer to get hay cut on Roger Allen's old land. They were splitting the hay, for the man using his equipment. As long as the weather held, this would be their day for a while. When they'd left with the tractor, Tina was alone at the house. She cleaned up from breakfast, tidied a few things and went out to see the horse, leaving Callie in her crate. When she returned, Callie looked at her and let out a small whine. "What's the matter? Tina asked her. The dog whined in response. Lucas had told her about her greeting her son, but not if she'd actually ever gone to the bathroom, so she leashed her and took her out. Sure enough, she really had to go. When Tina tried to bring her back to the house, she resisted, pulling instead towards the field. Maybe the old girl was just lonely, or bored, or both. She led her to the barn. At the barn door, the dog resisted again. Her legs began to quiver. Tina wondered why the barn would be a scary place for the dogs, but most importantly, she wanted to show the dog, it was okay. She spent quite some time, coaxing her in. She finally managed to get her to walk with her, around through the sheep areas. Every once in a while, she would stare at the open doorway nervously. Tina didn't know for sure, but she felt she could guess. She was afraid of being cornered. Maybe that's why Jess was only in the barn when they were.

When she felt she had at least made progress, she headed back towards the doorway and after gathering up some twine, she threaded it through the leash making it long enough for the dog to have some room to wander and sniff without Tina having to be right near her. Once Callie figured it out, she spent time smelling the scents of the sheep and the places Fur and Wee had been. On occasion, she would look up towards the gates, but Tina was worried she wouldn't want to come back. Despite her improvements, dragging her home would not benefit her health or her growing trust. When Tina finally did take her back home, Callie's spirits seemed much improved and she even wagged her tail when Tina spoke her name.

In the field, Jess was trying to help Fur past his fears. "Look." She said, still a little miffed about him knocking her over. "You don't have to run. I told you to do what I did.'
Fur sat down and let out a long sigh. His ego fell away and he actually told his sister how he

felt. "I want to be part of things. I don't know how. You seem happy here. The humans touch you all the time. They even touch Momma now. I'm afraid for them to touch me. What is that like?"

Jess came and sat beside him, nuzzling his muzzle with hers and rubbing along his side. "It kinda feels like that."

He lowered his head, looking ashamed. "I want to be a part of things. They saved you. They saved Momma. I just don't know what to do."

Jess looked at him. As big as he was, and as confident as he was with the coyotes, he still was her silly brother.

"Okay. Here's the plan. You don't have to let them touch you right now. Just do what I do. If they call me, you come too. If I sit, you sit. Just do what I do and maybe it will help."

"I wish I could stop being scared." He said.

"Maybe you should start with Barry" Jess said, still thinking.

"Which one is that?" Fur asked.

"The one this morning." Jess answered. "The one you ran past when you hit me."

Fur scrunched his face. "He makes really weird noises."

Jess giggled. "He laughs. Humans laugh when they're happy or when something is funny."

"He thought the other man falling over was funny." Fur told her. "He laughed a lot."

Jess hadn't seen things happen that morning so Fur explained the story of Lucas walking with Momma.

"Barry and Lucas are brothers." She told him. "Like you are my brother."

Fur liked that idea. The humans were a family too. "Is the lady like Momma?" He asked

"I don't think so." Jess said after a minute. She has no puppies. But she stays with Lucas. He cares for her very much. Maybe one day.

Now that Fur felt better and they were content to wander the perimeter and watch the field. When the day got too warm, they found a place in the shade and waited out the sun. The mornings were sometimes cooler than the heat of summer, but the afternoons were still hot.

When the men came up to get the sheep that night, they were hot and tired. They let the sheep down into the pen by the barn and Lucas called Jess. She appeared over the hill and looked back. She kept walking. She slowed again. Stopped. Started moving. Behind her, came her brother. Moving at a slow measured pace. When Jess reached Lucas, she sat. Ethan, still 15 feet away, sat too.

Lucas and Barry looked from one to the other. "I think he wants to be a dog." Barry said.

Lucas looked at them. "Okay, start walking back." He told Barry. He looked at Jess. "Wait." He said.

Barry walked down like he was leaving. Lucas waited until he had made it some distance before looking down at Jess and pointing down towards the pen. "Jess, let's go."

She hesitated, looking at Fur.

"Jess. Go." He repeated.

She headed off towards where Barry had gone. Lucas didn't wait. He looked at the other dog, who had risen to his feet trying to keep his eyes on his sister. "Ethan. Go" Lucas said, looking at Fur and using the same command.

Fur froze. Was the man actually telling him what to do? "Ethan. Let's go." The man spoke again, pointing towards Jess.

Fur started to bolt for the opening but remembered he was supposed to do what Jess did. He slowed his pace and curving out a little further from Lucas, trotted down through. When he got to Jess, there was a spark in his eyes. "I did it!" He whispered.

"You were perfect." Jess told him.

When the men got to the barn, Lucas looked up at the two dogs. "Jess." He said. "Wait."

Barry looked at him. "You leaving her here?"

Lucas nodded. "I think she is what he needs. Obviously, he's following her lead. It won't hurt for a night."

"Ethan." Barry said.

Lucas looked at him. "What the hell is wrong with Ethan?"

"You really don't remember? Barry asked, chuckling.

"No."

"When I was in the 3rd grade, I had that big kid in my class, with the scruffy hair. He'd stayed back like twice, used to push me down all the time. Took my stuff."

Lucas began to laugh. It was low but long.

"Yeah." Barry said. "His name was Ethan."

Lucas kept laughing. "Definitely calling him Ethan."

Barry laughed with him. "You would."

Back in the pen, Jess was surprised that they had not told her to come with them. She looked at Fur and decided that he probably needed her, even more than Momma. Fur was still delighted with his first interaction with the humans. "Is my name Ethan? he asked after contemplating the events for a while.

"Is your name what?" Wee asked.

"Ethan. You said that you'd know your name by what they call you when they look at you." He said. "The man, Lucas said it this morning. Then the other one said it."

"Barry." Jess said.

Fur nodded. "Then tonight the man said, Jess go to you and Ethan go to me."

Wee opened her eyes and her mouth wide. "Fur! You have a name!"

"Does Momma have a name?" He asked.

Wee nodded. "Callie."

"Callie." He repeated . "I like that."

They lay together in the growing darkness. Fur found himself imagining being with the humans. "Do you think I'll ever get to see the house?"

Wee sat up and scratched at her collar. "I think you need one of these and a leash like Momma." She answered after thinking about it.

"Does it hurt?" He had wondered about it since they had found Wee again.

"No." Wee told him. "It doesn't hurt. But if you have the leash on, and you pull and flop around. It makes you choke."

Fur looked at her with a glint in his eyes. "Did you pull and flop? He giggled.

She smiled. "Yeah. A lot. It seems silly now, but back then, I was very scared and I didn't understand."

He nodded, no longer laughing. He understood being scared. "What's it for?"

"The leash is so that you follow where they're going. I don't really wear it anymore because I know their words." She stopped, thinking about the collar. "I guess, this is like saying you belong here. At least, I think."

"Do you think I'll belong here? He asked her.

"They can't give you a collar unless they can touch you." She told Fur with a look.

"Oh. That makes sense." He put his head on his paws, thinking about how that would be.

"Don't worry, Fur." Jess told him. "You keep doing what I'm doing and it'll get better."
He gave a small smile. He did feel proud for listening to the man. And he had a name. And they had left Wee with him, so maybe they were happy too.

Chapter 40
Time Marches On

With Lucas and Barry gone every day, Tina continued to take Callie for walks in the field. The old dog continued to put on weight and with it, more energy than she'd had in a long time. When Callie began insisting that she wanted to go up where the sheep and her children had gone, Tina decided it really couldn't hurt anything. Although the dog was still awkward about humans, she wasn't really afraid of them anymore. She kept her on the long leash and opened the gate.

Callie was more excited than she had been in a long time. She practically pulled Tina up the hill. When they got to the top and could see down into the field beyond, Tina called to Jess. It didn't take long to see her making her way to them. Lagging behind her was the male. Tina hadn't actually seen him before and as they got closer, she realized just how much bigger he was than the two females. It made her a little nervous. She'd come up here alone with no one around and this was the one dog that they hadn't had a chance to really get to know.

When Jess came up and saw her mother, she ran to them. The male stopped about 20 feet away. He just looked at Tina. Then he looked at

his mother and back at her. Not wanting to
move suddenly, Tina slowly unwound more of
the lead so that Callie could go towards him.
"Go ahead, Callie." She said softly.
When she spoke, the male looked at her again.
"Good boy, Ethan." She said, feeling very
nervous about the way he was looking at her.

Fur heard her use his name. He looked at her.
He had never seen a female human before.
She was tiny and her voice was soft in a way
that made his tail want to wag. He stared at this
fragile looking creature. "Wee…" He said.
"What is it?"
Wee laughed. "It's Tina."
Suddenly, he wanted to smell her. He took a
few steps forward and he saw the woman
looking decidedly uncomfortable. He stopped
again. Then his mother stepped between them
and he realized that he had not even said hello.
He greeted Momma, sniffing her and wagging
his tail. She smelled and looked different than
he could ever remember. She looked shinier,
healthier. The odd smell she'd had for a long
time was gone. "It's good to see you." He said.
His forehead furrowed and his face grew more
solemn. "I was afraid you were going to …"
Momma cut him off with a snort, not wanting to
dwell on her close call. "You're scaring the
lady."

Fur peered up over his mother at the woman, who was watching them intently. "She's not scared of you or Wee."

"Jess." Momma corrected. "If a human gives you a name. I feel you should respect it."

"Why, Momma?" He asked, surprised that she would care.

"Think about it. Humans give each other names. Do sheep have names?" She gave him a chance to consider.

"I don't think so."

"So humans apparently give names to things they respect and value. You notice Roger had no names for us." She said the last part with bitterness.

"Because Roger didn't respect us. He didn't care about us at all." Jess said, suddenly joining the conversation.

Jess had never thought about her name or the importance behind it.

"Do you have a name? Momma asked, looking at Fur. He nodded.

"Well, what is it?" Momma coached.

"Ethan." Fur said. "My name is Ethan."

"Good. That means someone here finds you important. That is what we shall call you from now on."

"The Lucas man named me." Ethan said, suddenly finding importance in the fact."

The old dog nodded. "He is… not a mean man." She said.

She was still coming to terms with humans being important to her for the first time in her life.

Ethan looked over his mother's back at the woman. "Momma." He stopped. "Can I still call you Momma?"

"Yes. Momma is not a name. Callie said. "I will always be your mother, just as Jess will always be your sister."

"Momma." He began again. "Why is she afraid of me?"

"Maybe because you are much bigger." His mother replied after some thought.

Ethan stepped around his mother, slouching his shoulders and lowering his head. The woman who had been watching their entire interaction, grew very tense. "Not like that." Jess said, half laughing as she pushed him away. "You look like you're coming to eat her."

Ethan sighed as moved away a bit. "How do I look smaller?" he asked in frustration.

"Maybe you should lay down." Momma said.

Tina had been watching the dogs interact with great interest. She found it all very intriguing. Her nervousness had faded away as she watched the way they interacted with each other. It seemed silly, but it was almost like they were having a meeting of great importance. When the male suddenly stepped past his mother, his whole demeanor seemed to change and she felt her heart start racing. He seemed to be stalking her. She breathed a sigh of relief when Jess intercepted. She needed to leave, now. She wasn't sure Jess could actually stop him and she still had Callie on the leash. She had to get her out too. She looked back at how far it was to the gate. She would have to talk to Lucas about this. If she made it out.

When she looked back towards the dogs, the male was coming towards her again. To her surprise, he stopped and lay down, upright, facing her though some distance away. She watched him, waiting for some sign of his intentions. Jess stood a short way behind him, watching him. Tina tried to calm her racing emotions.

"Wag your tail." Jess said to her brother. "Humans like that."
Ethan, who had begun to feel the situation was hopeless, slowly wagged his tail back and forth. The woman suddenly looked less nervous. He wagged his tail more.

Tina saw the male's tail start to wag, as he lay there looking at her. Maybe she was reading this wrong, she thought. His tail wagged harder. "Ethan." She said, cautiously optimistic. "Ethan, are you a good boy?"

The dog's tail thumped on the ground with more enthusiasm. He reached out with his paws and stretched forward, tucking up his rear end behind him as he did, moving a few inches forward. He wagged again. She stared at him, slowly coming to terms with the idea that he may not want to eat her, after all. "Ethan." She said. "Come here." Though she was not entirely sure she actually wanted that. He moved himself forward a few more inches, looking for all the world, like some kind of giant, broken caterpillar.

Tina continued coaxing, but there came a point, about 5 feet away, that he would simply wag and come no closer. In the last few minutes, she had begun to realize that he was unsure and awkward. That was far better than being aggressive and bloodthirsty. She started to feel more confident. Perhaps it was her turn to move. She moved herself forward, while still mostly sitting. It was his turn to look nervous. She spoke to him softly and waited for him to relax a bit before moving again.

Ethan, as he was trying to think of himself now, was happy to see the dainty human less afraid. He had gone as close as he dared, but he started to get nervous and despite her soothing voice, he could not bring himself to go further. He was surprised when she started moving towards him, in much the same slow way he had done. When she got to about 3 feet away, when he began to think about her touching him, he could hear it, no longer. He leaped to his feet and darted away. The woman, after a moment of being startled, began to laugh. Ethan stopped and turned around. Wee... Jess, he corrected in his thoughts, said humans did that when something was funny. She found him funny.

He moved back towards her with a prancing, silly gait. When he got within a few body lengths of her, he dropped his chest down on the ground, his big paws splayed out and his hind end still standing. The woman made a noise and he leaped up and ran away in another direction. She laughed again in her melodic, soft way. It was nothing like Barry's loud, barking laughter. He was totally smitten. He continued to run at her, stopping a few strides away and bowing, before running off again. He was acting like a young puppy. The woman, who had gotten to her feet, began to feint towards him, as if she were going to grab him and he would dart away, running in large loops, before coming back to give her another chance. Ethan could not remember a day in his life that had been this carefree. It was joy, without worry of what came later.

When they were both tired and breathless, Ethan went to lay down a distance away, but still well within sight of his newfound attachment. He watched as she petted both Callie and Jess. He wanted to be a part of that too, but he still couldn't bring himself to actually be touched. He couldn't help but feel a little dejected when he saw her stand and lead Callie back towards the gate.

When Tina got back to the house, it was far later than she had thought. She washed and began prep for dinner. She decided not to tell Lucas about her fright. He had made amazing strides in dog ownership and she didn't want to give him any cause for concern, especially about her welfare.

Instead, as the men went out to bale hay and bring it back to the barn, Tina would take Callie up to the field to visit. Callie continued to enjoy the excursions and her health, both physical and mental, continued to improve. Good care seemed to be taking years off her age. She had started playing with the youngsters, as much as her lead would allow. Tina was not quite confident enough to take the leash off. Maybe in the smaller area first would be better, she decided. Just in case she decided she'd rather be free.

Out in the field, she continued to work on Ethan. For days, he would only creep just so close and when the situation got too tense or Tina made it really close, he would resort to his playful antics to relieve the stress. She wasn't sure how to break down that last barrier to their relationship. How could she change his opinion, if he wouldn't give her a chance?

Jess gave her brother all the encouragement she could. Always at the last moment, he'd dart away like a fool and race around the field. She finally decided to use a different approach. She waited until Tina had gotten really close, so close that if she reached out her hand, she could touch him. Jess waited. As soon as Tina's hand moved, she said, "Fur! Don't move!" in a tone that said his life depended on it. He turned his head to look at her. "What?" He said and then froze.

He felt the fingers touch the side of his muzzle and his whole body quivered. The delicate hand moved to the side of his head, gently combing through his hair. He continued to hold perfectly still. The hand moved away back to Tina's lap. He leaped to his feet and raced off doing loops around the woman, over and over to relieve his stress. Not only was the woman laughing, but Jess was in absolute hysterics.

After several laps, he finally walked over to the other dogs. "Well, would you look at that! You didn't die." Jess giggled.

He pushed his shoulder into her. "Real funny!" He said, but he was not actually grumpy. He had done it. It was weird, but better than he had expected. It left him with a funny feeling. He almost wanted it to happen again. It was the beginning of a whole new life for Ethan. Human contact was not painful. In fact, in a weird way, it was pleasant. When Tina left, he found himself looking forward to her next visit.

Chapter 41
Lonely Days

After more than a couple of weeks of haying on every nice day, cutting not only the best of Roger's fields, but their own as well, they had the loft full with far more hay than they'd ever had and round bales lying in a field out beyond where the horse pasture was. The brothers were exhausted, but extremely satisfied. They were, however, discussing finding help for next year.

When they came on the final night, after getting the sheep and Jess, it was all they could do to eat and go to bed. The following morning though, at breakfast, they had some important news. "So." Lucas began. "Michael Brogan and his son, Tyler are looking to go pick up some horses from a place out west that's shutting down the dude ranch aspect of their ranch. They're just sick of dealing with people. They had been lamenting the inability to pick up more and then saw our trailer."
"Do they want to borrow it?" Tina asked.
"No." Lucas said at the same time Barry shook his head. "They want us to go. They don't want to be away from the ranch for long, so they're thinking two trucks, two teams, we could make the trip a lot quicker."

"They want you two to go with them." Tina repeated. It was a statement, not a question. Lucas nodded. "How long will you be gone? Tina asked and before anyone could answer, "Are they paying you for going? When would you be leaving?"

Lucas put his hands up in a hold on motion. "We would leave out this coming weekend. We're looking at roughly 10 days. They are paying for gas and travel expenses."

Tina looked at one and then the other. "And you want to do this?"

"Well," Lucas said. "He said for driving; we can each pick out a horse."

"Are you serious?" Tina asked, suddenly excited. "So, we could ride together?"

Lucas nodded. "And..." He said, "when we start grazing more sheep and further away, we won't have to go out and bring them in on foot. Though I'm hoping that the dogs make it possible to not necessarily bring them in during the warm weather. We can just check on them daily. There is a stream that runs quite a way through Roger's land. One section of it runs through what is now ours. We don't even have to worry about water."

Tina suddenly felt like things were progressing too fast. "Leave Jess out there all summer? What about Callie? I'm not sure She needs to end up in a fight." Now that she had them, she felt nervous about putting them in harm's way.

"It won't be right away". Barry interjected as he usually did when Tina started to get stressed about something. "We'd make sure to help with any coyotes at first. The hope would be we don't have to fight. And maybe we could do a week on and a week off so Jess gets to come home."

Lucas added. "This is all in the future. We don't have any concrete plans yet. We'll figure it out as we go. As far as Callie, she might like to be out there sometimes, but she shouldn't be in harm's way. She's fought her whole life just to stay alive. She has a place here, whether she works or not."

Their words made Tina feel better and less like change would be immediate. "I'm sorry, I kind of panicked." She took a deep breath. "So, go get your horses."

Lucas reached across the table and took her hand. "One step at a time. We'll take it slowly. We'll see how much issue the coyotes give us when we encroach on their current territory. We won't do anything without a good solution."

"Okay." Tina said. She didn't know why the idea of the dogs being out there scared her so much. At the very least, Ethan was three times the size of a coyote.

"I'll pull out my car and take it to town and make sure it's gassed up and ready if you need anything."

"Thanks." Tina said. The idea was kind of exciting.

Barry had an old '65 mustang that he had rebuilt from the ground up in his younger days. There wasn't much use for it on a ranch, but he kept it undercover and only took it out on special occasions.

"No picking up men or getting in trouble." Lucas said with a grin.

Tina laughed. "I'll do my best. Not that I'll likely need to go anywhere. I can go shopping before you leave."

"What fun is that?" Barry asked. "You should have some fun while we're gone,"

"But not too much fun." Lucas added.

"So a speeding ticket, but no boys. Got it." Tina said teasingly.

Lucas put his finger on her nose. "Exactly." He replied before leaning forward and kissing her cheek.

Tina giggled.

They went out to take care of the animals, taking Jess to join her brother. Tina cleaned up breakfast and then sat on the couch in the living room. Callie came over to her and pressed her nose against Tina's stomach. She sniffed and gently poked. "You want to go up there, don't you? Tina asked her.

Callie just stood with her head on Tina's lap.

"Maybe we could try letting you loose in the

night pen." Tina said, standing up to get her boots and jacket.

It would be something to try if she was ever going to let Callie run with the other dogs. She dressed and hooked the leash on Callie before taking her outside.

She lead the dog into the pen and took a moment to lead her around the barn. On the far side, she could hear Lucas and Barry talking. They were likely going over the stalls and getting them set up. They sounded like two excited kids. She walked Callie around for a while. It was a good time to do it, with both men home. She called the dog to her and took a deep breath before unhooking the leash.

At first, Callie seemed not to realize she had freedom, but after a few minutes she trotted out along the fence line, smelling and marking. Then after she finished checking, she ran up to the gate which separated her from the other dogs. "Callie. Here." Tina said, trying to sound happy and non-threatening.

The dog glanced at her and stood at the gate. Tina tried again. "Callie. Come on."

This time the dog just twitched her ear. She definitely wanted out. In a flurry of movement, the other dogs appeared on the opposite side. They sniffed their mother through the fence with wagging tails. Apparently, recall needed more work. Tina sighed. It's not like the dog had ever had any training before being in their house. She walked up to the gate and reached for Callie's collar. The dog flinched. Tina reached out and petted her instead. When she reached for the collar a second time, the dog did not move away. She hooked the lead back on and let Callie through the gate. She didn't stay longer, but she at least let them greet and spend a few minutes together. Ethan was still nervous about being touched but at least he'd come close.

After about 10 minutes, she brought Callie back down. When she got to the yard, Barry's car was in the driveway beside the truck and the two men were going over it to make sure mice hadn't gotten to anything and that all was in good working order. She smiled. It was nice having someone to always look out for her.

Over dinner that night, they discussed the plans and the timing. It was cooler weather, but the sheep could still be out grazing. There was no hay to feed, just a little grain in the evening to encourage the sheep's return. It was the only thing that kept them from having to round them up at night and force them through the gate. The horses would make that easier, especially when they needed to be brought in from further away and separated for market.

The days seemed to fly by, as all their spare time was spent arranging the trip. The two men spent their free time making sure everything would be relatively simple for Tina. Likewise, she spent all her time making sure they had everything they could need, including drinks and snacks, in case Mr. Brogan did not stop as often as they'd like. Before they knew it, they were pulling out of the driveway at 5 am on a Saturday morning. Tina had hugged them both goodbye, kissed Lucas and told them both to drive safely. They set off to meet up with the Brogan family on the other side of town. Tina watched until the truck was gone from sight before returning to the house.

Chapter 42
Odd Things

Over the next few days, Tina set her own routine. With no one to care for except the dogs and the horse, she spent her time playing with them in the field or doing things in the house like boxing up summer clothing. She had promised Lucas she would not ride the horse while home alone. It was a small price to pay, knowing he could ride with her, when he got back. She spent time working on Callie's willingness to return to her and she spent time getting Ethan over his awkwardness about human contact.

When Tina went to bring Jess and Callie out to let the sheep go in the field one morning, she decided to let Callie off lead. She leashed her until they were in with the sheep and she'd had a chance to make sure the doors that closed off the area for the horses were closed. Then she took a deep breath and unhooked the lead. When she got to the back gates, she said a short prayer and opened them. The sheep poured out with the dogs close behind. Tina followed in the rear, closing the gates behind them.

For a while, she just let the dogs do their thing. It was fascinating to watch. Callie being with them, added a whole new dynamic. She watched them move out in front of the sheep and begin searching for any sign of anything awry. They fanned out, still searching and marking their territory, until they seemed content that all was well. Tina called Jess first, hoping her behavior would help bring the others closer. Ethan followed his sister, at the sound of Tina's voice, but Callie ignored it. Tina sighed. "Callie, here!" She called.

But the dog never looked at her. She petted Jess for coming to her and began to walk to where Callie was some distance away. When she reached her, the old dog just sat and looked at her. From a few feet away, she called. "Callie. Come here."

The dog finally decided to walk to her. Tina laughed. She understood the dog had never had to listen to human commands. This was going to be a work in progress for a while. On the plus side, Callie didn't run away, when she approached. When she stopped and petted her, Callie rested her nose against her stomach and sniffed around her abdomen. Tina pushed her head away. "Stop." She didn't know what the attraction was.

Ethan soon moved in, creeping up to her, as he often did. When he finally got close enough for Tina to touch him, he lay very still. She moved a little closer, petting him the whole time. He finally gave in to her affection. He was slightly stiff, but he didn't act as if he might dart away at any second. She worked her way from the top of his head to the ruff around his neck. Jess came over and flipped down beside him and Tina began to pet them both. Her presence relaxed Ethan a lot. When Tina stopped, he rolled his head back in her lap. She stroked him a while longer before finally getting up to accomplish something for the day, besides petting dogs.

Tina really enjoyed the time spent with the dogs. They were building a relationship as a group. Ethan followed her wherever she walked. She swore he had a crush on her. Callie continued to improve in her recall, sort of. Sometimes she would and sometimes she just didn't and Tina had to go and get her. She distinctly began to get the impression that the dog knew what Tina wanted, sometimes she just didn't care. Whether due to her upbringing or just being a stubborn old lady, Tina wasn't sure. Ethan on the other hand, now that he had lost some of his nervous behavior, would recall at high speed. Just about the time, Tina was afraid he would run right into her, he'd screech to a halt and drop down, making Tina come the last few steps to pet him. About the 5th day, she managed to get a collar on him. He spent an hour scratching at it and shaking his head. He stayed out of reach for the rest of her visit.

Also about the 5th day, Tina found herself feeling lonely. The first few days with no one to cook or clean for, had felt nice, but the empty house and her empty bed, began to seem just that. Empty. Lucas did call her briefly before they left out in the morning and one of them, depending on who was driving, would check in about the time she would be coming back from bringing the sheep down. When she had talked to them that morning, they were already at the ranch.

That evening she brought Jess back with her for more company. She did feel terrible watching Ethan standing at the gate as they walked away. Her dinner was leftovers from the night before and she shared the meat with the dogs. In the end, she had taken a blanket and slept on the couch. The two dogs had taken up places on the floor beside her.

The following morning, she stalled on chores and took her time over breakfast. Lucas hadn't called but she knew they were probably busy. She finished her coffee curled up on the couch, before finally starting her day. When she finished, she took Callie and Jess and went up to let the sheep out. Ethan was happy to see them and seemed to have forgiven her for the collar. Tina felt tired and kind of blah. She thought maybe she'd just relax for the day. She decided to even let Callie stay out with them. She gave them all a little lecture and a few pets. "You guys, all be good. Okay. I'll be back up later."

As she was petting them, Jess stuck her nose up under her jacket, sniffing her. "Jess. Stop." She said, pushing at her nose.

Jess pulled her head out and stood looking at her expectantly. Tina said goodbye and walked back to the house.

That night when she called to them, they all came. Even Callie came right into the pen with the sheep. The dog's willingness solidified Tina's belief that the dog decided if Tina's reason for calling was good enough. She stroked her head. "Maybe we should call you, your highness instead." She chuckled before putting on the leash. She brought Callie in and left Jess outside to stay with Ethan. She slept in her bed that night, wishing Lucas were in it with her. She awoke early in the morning to find Callie standing beside the bed with her head resting on it, watching her. Tina glanced around. Callie had never been in the hallway and certainly not in their bedroom. Even Jess never really came in the room, though she often slept in the doorway. It was almost creepy.

She got out of bed slowly, almost avoiding the dog. She felt awkward waking up like that. Tina quietly made coffee in a still dim kitchen. The only light being a small bulb over the stove. It was only 3:30 in the morning. When she turned around, Callie was standing there in the kitchen. Tina suddenly realized that maybe the dog needed a trip to the bathroom. She felt better. Being alone was, apparently, giving her the heebie-jeebies. She softly chuckled aloud. Obviously, how else would the dog tell her she needed to go out. She put on her coat and boots and hooked the leash before stepping out into the brisk air. Callie walked dutifully along beside her. The old dog did look towards the barn a few times, Tina assumed she could see the other two. Finally, after what seemed like an eternity of walking around, Callie did finally pee on the grass. Tina couldn't help but feel that it was not a desperate situation. When they went back in, she made herself coffee and sat down on the couch. The coffee was still a little too hot to drink and she set it on the end table.

Tina awoke with a start. She looked at the clock. It was 7:30. She stumbled off the couch and went to get her phone from the bedroom. She had missed the call from Lucas. She called him back knowing he would worry. He answered it on the first ring. "Hello." He said immediately.

"Hey." She replied feeling guilty and embarrassed.

"Is everything okay?" He asked. Tina could hear the stress in his voice.

"Yes. I'm okay. Everything is okay. I kind of overslept."

There was a pause before Lucas said, "Until now?"

"Callie woke me up at 3:30 because she had to go to the bathroom or something. I sat on the couch after and fell asleep."

She heard Barry's voice. "We leave for a week and she's just sleeping the day away."

She knew he must have her on speaker.

"Apparently." She said,

"Are you sure you're alright?" Lucas sounded genuinely concerned.

"I am." Tina replied before adding. "Maybe I just don't sleep as well without you in the bed. I have been feeling a little tired."

She heard Barry's "Awww."

"But you feel okay otherwise?" Lucas asked, still sounding worried. "You're not sick or anything?"

"No." Tina said. "I'm fine." But when she said it, her mind jumped to waking up with Callie staring at her. "I'm good." She reassured him.

"We'll be home in a few days." Lucas said. Why don't you take the day off and go to town. Just let the sheep out and check their water. The horse has plenty of grass. Just take the day off."

"Luke. I really am fine." She reassured him again.

"Will you take the day off? He asked.

"Yes. Lucas. I'll take the day off. As soon as I have some coffee." She said yawning.

"Okay. Drive carefully."

"And no guys?" she teased.

"Definitely not." Lucas answered, finally sounding better.

"I love you." Tina said, feeling the distance between them.

"I love you too. We'll check in tonight." Lucas's voice was softer now.

"Bye." Tina said though she didn't want him to hang up.

"Be safe." Lucas replied.

There was a pause and then the call disconnected. Tina stood there for a few moments, fighting the urge to call back, before she picked up her cup and went into the kitchen to warm it.

True to her word, Tina put the sheep in the field and let all three dogs go with them. When she was running water, she noticed both females hadn't gone off and were staying with her. They even walked her back to the gate. She tried not to pay attention, but she did. After checking the horse's water, she went into the house to get ready to leave. A short time later she headed out to town, driving Barry's car.

Driving the car was a lot of fun, though Tina was careful on some of the roads until she actually got to town. She grabbed a few things to decorate the kitchen for fall and picked up some groceries for when the men got home. Leaving the grocery store, she noticed she felt slightly nauseous and realized she hadn't eaten anything. She decided to go to the little diner where she usually ate. They served breakfast all day. She was happy to see the same waitress that she usually saw on Saturdays, when she came to town. They made small talk and Tina ordered coffee with French toast and bacon. When the waitress came back with her coffee, she looked at Tina for a moment. "Are you feeling okay?" she asked in her polite, cheerful voice.

"Yes." Tina said, trying to hide the nagging feeling she had been trying to ignore. "Why do you ask?"

"Nothing really." the young woman answered. "You just look a little pale."

Trying to act unconcerned, Tina replied. "I got up late and I left to go shopping and I haven't eaten all day."

The waitress smiled brightly. "Well, let me go put a rush on that food."

"Thank you." Tina said, returning the smile.

As soon as she was done eating Tina went out to her car. She called her doctor's office and spoke to the receptionist who asked her name and address. After bringing her file up, which consisted of nothing more than her annual wellness checks, the woman asked why she was calling. Tina suddenly felt silly. "It's nothing big, really." She said. "I've just been feeling tired lately."

"Are you eating okay?" The lady asked.

"Yes." Tina said.

"Anything else different? Have you been under a lot of stress or had any big changes in your life? Have you been sick recently?"

"No." None of that Tina said, feeling dumb for calling. "Look. I know this is going to sound really stupid. But my dogs have been acting weird. Sniffing my stomach and staying close to me. I know how dumb that sounds." She stopped herself from rambling further.

There was silence for a few seconds and Tina almost hung up in embarrassment. The woman spoke before she could decide. Fortunately, the woman didn't mock her. "That isn't dumb." The woman said. "There is a reason they use dogs for people with diabetes and seizures. Dogs can smell when something is wrong. Dogs have even been known to detect cancerous tumors..."

As the woman spoke, Tina felt her heart sink. Maybe the dogs were trying to tell her something. The woman was still talking. "They can even sense when someone is having an anxiety attack."

Tina felt sick all over again. "We'll make you an appointment." The woman said. "Is October 1st alright?"

That was almost two weeks away. "That's fine." Tina answered.

"How about 8:30? Will that work for your schedule?"

Yes. That's fine." Tina said again. Her mind was racing.

"Okay. You're all set. We'll see you then." The woman told her.

"Thank you." Tina managed to say before hanging up the phone.

She drove home in a daze. Her brain kept coming back to the woman's words about cancer. She tried to brush it off. It was likely she wasn't even sick. But it nagged at her all the way home. She unloaded the car and carried everything indoors. She found herself pacing and worrying.

For the next couple of days, she tried to keep herself busy, taking care of the animals and giving the kitchen a bit of an autumn look. She changed the curtains to yellow and put up the wall hanging she had bought with the turkey and pumpkins on it. She had also bought a centerpiece for the table with woven pumpkin and orange and yellow candles. She still spent time with the dogs, but only brought Callie in at night. Their insistence on staying close and the way they'd occasionally try to smell her, just added to her concern. Ethan was the only one who didn't seem any different. He was his usual adorable self, prancing along behind Tina and enjoying her affection.

She was up letting the sheep out, when she heard Lucas's truck pull in the driveway. She closed the gate, leaving all the dogs with the sheep and ran back to the barn. When she got there, Lucas was backing the trailer up along the side of the barn. Tina was overjoyed to see them. When the truck shut off and Lucas got out, she hurried over and hugged him tightly. He returned the hug and kissed her a couple of times before he pulled back. "Wanna see what we got?" He asked as he headed for the back of the trailer.
Tina grabbed his hand in hers and said, "Absolutely!"
He looked at her with a bit of a grin. "Did you miss me?"
"Absolutely!" She said again. Didn't you miss me?"

Lucas leaned over and kissed her nose.
"Absolutely." He said.
Tina smiled an absolutely genuine smile.

As they walked around to the back, Barry
slipped out of the passenger side and joined
them. "Welcome home." Tina smiling.
"May I never leave again." Barry said, leaning
against the trailer with a groan.
"Show me what you got." Tina said.
Lucas opened the trailer door. He untied the
dun colored gelding and walked him out. It was
a sturdy, muscular looking horse with a dark
stripe down its back. The horse was calm as he
walked out. He sniffed the air, took a long look
around and began to nibble grass off the edge
of the driveway. Lucas pulled his head up and
walked him around in a circle for Tina. "What do
you think?" Lucas asked.
She grinned at him. "I like it." She glanced
underneath. "He seems really calm."
Lucas nodded. "He's got a good head on him,
but he can move quickly when he needs to."
Tina could tell Lucas was happy with his choice.
Barry walked the other horse out. It was a
brownish black horse, leaner than the other with
one white sock and a white stripe down its face.
It came off the trailer prancing and snorting.
Tina was not at all surprised. "This one is mine."
Barry said as the horse trotted out to the end of
the lead, head held high.

It whinnied loudly. Tina smirked. Of course, it was.

Out in the field, Tina's horse answered, as it ran to the fence line. Barry's horse answered in return.

They got the horses into their stalls, gave them hay and water and left them to settle in. They showed Tina the tack they'd also gotten at a fair price. It was well used, but would do for now. Finally, Lucas said, "We got you something too."

Tina looked up and smiled. "Really?"

He nodded and looked at Barry who went up along the passenger side and opened the back door. When he rounded the front of the truck, Tina's eyes opened wide. It was a fluffy white puppy with dark brown eyes. Tina let out a cry of delight as she rushed to meet Barry. She looked at Lucas. "Where did you find that?" Tina asked, giddy with excitement.

"I bought it." Lucas said. "You were right. We don't want Callie to get hurt. She deserves an easy retirement. This will be our addition to the team."

Tina reached up and cupped the puppy's face between her hands. "You are so adorable." She said.

The little pup wagged its tail. "So, where did you get it?"

"When we got to the ranch, they had dogs like ours. They weren't friendly with us, but they listened to the owner and allowed us to walk around. You could tell they really loved the people on the ranch. Mr. Brogan was talking to the man about them. He'd thought about one for his place, but the only ones he'd seen were Roger Allen's. He didn't want them because of that. He felt about them much the way I did. I told him ours weren't wild either. We all got to talking and the man mentioned he had pups. He talked all about their pedigree, but I know sheep, even some about horses, but nothing about dogs."

He reached over and scratched the pup's head. "This little gal has papers." He said.

Tina rubbed the sides of the pup's face. "You're all fancy schmancy." She said, leaning close to the puppy.

"No. No. Hold up." Barry said. "Wait until you hear the rest."

He looked at Lucas, encouraging him to continue. Lucas did. "After we each decided to get a pup, Mr. Brogan got talking about Roger Allen's dogs. Supposedly, they were registered and came from imported stock brought into the country like 50 years ago. For some reason, Roger just decided that they were supposed to live on their own, out in the fields with no humans. He didn't care about the bloodlines, just the job. His wife kept track of all the breeding, even though she had nothing to do with the dog's themselves."

"Why would you spend good money and then just leave them out there to live or die?" Tina asked, not necessarily expecting the answer. Lucas shrugged. "I guess enough survived to keep the sheep safe."

Tina pulled the little pup out of Barry's arms and hugged it close. "Don't you worry." She said. "We will never abandon you."

She headed for the house carrying the chubby, little bundle in her arms. "You need a crate? Barry asked.

Tina nodded and went up the steps.

They got the pup settled in the crate and Tina found Jess's first collar for her to wear. She was younger than Jess had been, but much healthier. Tina made lunch for the two brothers, happy to have them home again. For the moment, all her concerns were pushed aside by her happiness over the household being as it should be. Every once in a while, she would glance in the living room at the pup. The idea that Lucas had actually bought a puppy, was nothing short of amazing.

When they were finished eating, Barry excused himself. Lucas was pretty sure he was going to take a nap. He had considered the idea himself although it was something he seldom did. Instead, he spent his time with Tina, happy to be back home with his wife.

It was some hours later before Lucas asked. "Where is Callie?"

Tina laughed. "You just noticed? She's out with the other two."

"Have you done that before?" Lucas asked, just a bit concerned.

She nodded. "I started letting her loose in the pen while you guys were doing hay. I took her to the field on a leash first and now I've been letting her go out sometimes."

He raised his eyebrows and gave her a look that said he was impressed. Tina giggled. "I get things done, you know. Although." she admitted. "Sometimes you have to go get her if she doesn't recall. We're still working on that."

"Great." Lucas said. "I gotta go search 100 acres for her?"

"No. She moves up closer when the sheep come up by the gate." Tina replied, still smiling and just happy he was home.

Lucas's mood was also lighthearted, despite his pretend concerns. He thought of Ethan. "How's the male been with you out there?" he asked more seriously.

Tina laughed. "If I didn't know better, I'd think you had some competition for my affection."

"Oh?" Lucas looked down at her. "Really?"

She snickered again. "I put his collar on."

"You've touched him?" Lucas asked her, surprised.

Tina grinned and nodded. "I told you I get stuff done."

He pulled her close. "So now he's trying to steal you away?"

"He might be." Tina said.

Lucas laughed. "I might have to have a talk with that boy.

That evening when the men went up to get the sheep, the dogs were all waiting just behind the herd. Barry noticed Callie. "Oh, no doubt." He said, when he noticed.

"Yeah. Tina's got her out here spending time with the kids." Lucas said.

Barry looked at them all waiting for them to open the gate. "That's fantastic. I wasn't sure if she'd try to go back to her old life."

"If you think about it. Sheep were her old life. Sheep and other dogs. But, I do think she likes us too. Changing her mind about people has been the hard part." Lucas mused out loud. Realizing the truth of his thoughts, as he spoke them.

Barry nodded. "Shall we?"

"Might as well." Lucas said, nodding.

Barry opened the gates and let the sheep through. Jess ran to greet them. She bounced about like a playful puppy, sniffing all the scents they carried and reveling in their return. Callie came in more slowly, but she did greet them and wagged her tail. Lucas shined his light out across the darkness. There was a time when they would take a quick look around, to try to ensure all the sheep had come. Now they counted on Jess's unwillingness to leave some behind to know they were all there. More than once, she had stood back when called, letting them know some were missing. Then she would trot back in the sheep's direction. A lot of things they now took for granted, had taken much more of their time, not so long ago.

When they closed the gates, they noticed Ethan had not trotted off into the darkness. He stayed with the other two, though a short distance back.
"Does he have a collar on?" Barry asked suddenly as the glint off the buckle caught the light from the barn.
"Uh huh." Lucas said dryly. "Apparently, he thinks he's Tina's new boyfriend."
Barry laughed. "Guess she didn't need my car."
Lucas laughed too. When they did, Ethan wagged his tail.
"Ooh. He is doing better. Maybe Tina can help us break the ice tomorrow." Lucas said.
"Damn. She really has made progress." Barry agreed.
Lucas called Callie and they headed out and up to the house for dinner. They left Jess with Ethan, to not overwhelm the new puppy.

When they walked in the door with Callie in tow, Tina looked at them open mouthed. "Ummm. You didn't use her leash?"

"For what?" Lucas asked her.

Tina realized she hadn't clarified. "I usually bring her in and out on the leash. I didn't know if she'd run off outside the fence."

"That's a negative." Barry said.

Lucas looked down at Callie. "I guess, she just wants to come in."

"I'd still be careful." Tina said, after a moment's thought. "She does decide not to recall sometimes."

Lucas nodded. "Okay. At least her first thought wasn't to leave. I feel like she definitely knows this is home."

Tina smiled. It sure is.

When Callie walked into the living room, the puppy began to whine and dance in the crate with excitement. Callie stopped short. She looked down into the crate. Her tail wagged. She felt a warmth wash over her. They had a puppy. Callie approached slowly and sniffed the pup. It licked her nose. "Shhh. Little one." Callie said softly. "You will be safe here."

As she said it, she felt the truth of it. She really did feel safe here. She was warm and fed and she had nothing to fear. "We will take care of you." Callie told her.

"I'm Callie." She told the pup. "Do you have a name yet?"

The pup shook her head. "Don't worry." The old dog said. "Here, we all get names."

She lay in front of the crate and spent the entire night, keeping the young one company.

Chapter 43
The Doctor Is In

Over the next week, Tina actually got Ethan to allow contact with Lucas and Barry. He was awkward still, like he had been with her at first, but it was definitely progress. They brought the pup to meet the other dogs. Jess had been regal and reserved and Ethan had bounced around like the fool he was.

Tina stayed with the men as much as possible, using their presence to push away her worries. Sometimes, one of them would sniff her while she petted them. She would push them away, trying to hide her discomfort. The receptionist's words gnawed away at her, more so, when she was alone. One afternoon, when Barry had left after lunch, Lucas walked over to her in the kitchen. He cupped his hand up under her chin, gently lifting her face up to look at his. "Are you okay? He asked her.
"I'm fine." She lied.
He stared down at her, his eyes filled with concern. It was enough to almost make the tears begin in Tina's eyes. She moved her head away and looked down.
"Are you sure? Did something happen while we were gone?" Lucas asked. She could tell him everything was okay, but he knew it wasn't.

"It's nothing, Lucas. I just feel so emotional. I'm just being stupid."

He pulled her close again. "Why don't you just tell me and we can find out if it's stupid together."

The tears started down Tina's cheeks. She began to ramble about the dogs and the waitress and the receptionist at the doctors. Her voice cracked and sometimes it was muffled by Lucas's shirt, but he got enough to understand her concern.

"Okay, okay." he said, trying to reassure her. "When is your appointment.?"

"Tomorrow." She sobbed, the crying starting up again.

Lucas had never seen her this distressed. "I'll go with you." he said, flatly. He wondered if she knew something more. Something she didn't want to tell him.

"No." she said, sniffling. "You don't have to go. It's probably nothing. I don't know why I'm letting it get to me." She pulled her head off Lucas's chest, trying to get control of her wayward emotions under control, which she couldn't seem to do with him touching her.

He followed her across the kitchen. "I don't mind going." he said. "You shouldn't have to be alone."

"She wiped her eyes with her sleeve and sniffled. She headed to the bathroom for a tissue and to splash some cold water on her

tear-streaked face. She made herself breathe calmly. When she opened the bathroom door, Lucas was standing right there. She looked at him and took a deep breath. "I'm okay." she said quietly. "I don't know what my problem is. I feel fine. I've been a little tired, but fine. What I don't know is why I'm letting this all get to me. I've never been a big crybaby but look at me." She actually gave him a small smile.
"I'm a wreck." she said. "I should be more concerned about that."

Lucas stayed with her a while longer. She was much calmer now and seemed more embarrassed at her outburst than anything else. He looked at the clock. "I can tell Barry..."
She cut him off. "No. I'm fine. Seriously, Lucas. I'm just being dumb. The doctor will probably tell me, my hormones are just out of whack this month or something. Go on. I'm fine... for the moment."
She smiled up at him, from where she had sat on the couch. "Seriously, I'm okay."

He eventually left to join Barry where he was working outside. They were working on repairing an old outbuilding in one of the fields behind the barn. As they worked, Barry noticed that Lucas was quiet. He had felt something was off with Tina for days and he knew something must have been said for Lucas to be

so silent. He finally had to ask. After some coaxing and a lot of prodding, Lucas finally told him about his conversation with Tina and how upset she had gotten.
Barry tried to be reassuring, but things were still pretty quiet the rest of the day.

That night, when they brought Callie in, their dinner was mostly halfhearted attempts at conversation that died out, before the meal was over. When they had finished eating, Barry excused himself as soon as it was politely possible, leaving the couple alone. Lucas did most of the dinner clean up despite Tina's protests. He insisted she go relax on the couch and that he was capable of doing the dishes. Afterwards, he hung out on the couch with her watching Callie interact with the pup. They went to bed early where Tina lay in Lucas's arms. Though they did not speak, neither slept for a while.

When morning came, they had breakfast alone, Barry claiming he had awoken early and had already eaten. Despite all of Lucas's offering, Tina insisted on going by herself. He watched her pull down the driveway. When the truck disappeared from sight, he turned to find Barry also watching. "Come on." Barry said. "Let's go find something to do other than go crazy."

When Tina got to the doctor's she felt silly all over again. She wished she hadn't told Lucas because she probably would have just gone home. She was coming here, wasting money, to tell the doctor she was tired. She went inside and gave her name to a polite, emotionless receptionist. She gave Tina a paper to update her information, despite the fact it hadn't changed. The receptionist even mentioned that she hadn't been there in a while. There had been nothing to go for. She was never really sick.

Once she filled that out, there was nothing to do but wait for her name to be called. She didn't feel like reading anything, so she just sat there, staring at her hands. When someone did come to fetch her, they took her weight, her blood pressure, asked a lot of questions that were already in her file and the reason for the visit. She simply told the nurse's aide, or whatever she was, she had been unusually tired and wanted to make sure nothing was wrong. The woman took Tina's temperature. Tina got the impression that the nurse felt she was wasting their time, running to the doctor, when maybe she just needed more sleep. Tina sighed. The receptionist thinks she doesn't come often enough, and the nurse thinks she didn't need to come at all.

She sat in the room for what seemed like forever. Finally, the doctor came in. He was polite and asked a few questions. She explained that she had not only been tired, but also more emotional and that neither one was normal for her.

"I'll have someone get a urine sample and draw some blood and go from there. Okay?" The doctor said.

Tina nodded. "Thank you." She really just wanted to go home.

Once they took blood and Tina had given the sample, she was back to waiting in the overly stuffy, sterile-looking room. When the doctor came back in, his face gave no indication of anything. He sat down on a stool across from her. "Miss Porter." He began.

"Mrs. Porter." Tina corrected.

The doctor looked at her. "Did your husband come with you today?"

Tina shook her head. "He offered, but I didn't really see the need."

The doctor nodded. "Okay. Just know, your medical information is private and we won't share it with anyone without your permission."

"You have my permission to talk to my husband about anything." Tina said. She suddenly felt like she was at the vets.

When the doctor spoke again, Tina heard nothing but the first sentence. After that she just nodded and agreed in all the right places.

Chapter 44
Four Of A Kind

Lucas and Barry spent the morning trying to be busy, while really accomplishing nothing. They were just going through the motions. They eventually gave up and went into the house and Lucas pulled out food and made them each a couple of sandwiches. He had only taken one bite when he heard the truck pull into the driveway.

He was on his feet in a flash and went out the door without even bothering to put on his coat. He came off the porch, without even using the stairs. Tina got out of the driver's side and they met in front of the truck. Lucas could see the dried tears on Tina's face. She wrapped her arms around him and pulled his head down close to hers with her other hand. Standing on tiptoe, she whispered in his ear. "Lucas. I'm pregnant."

It took a moment for Lucas's whirring brain to realize what she had just said. His head came up and he stepped back, putting both hands on her upper arms. "Are you serious?" He asked. Tina nodded and he pulled her back against him, wrapping his arms around her and holding her tight. She started crying again, not sad tears, but happy, still disbelieving tears. She buried her head in his chest and hugged him back as tightly as she could.

When they finally loosened their grip on each other and Lucas looked up, Barry was standing on the porch, wondering, but giving them space. "It's not a tumor!" Lucas yelled, feeling Tina giggle against him.

Barry came down the stairs, feeling very much relieved. He walked over and Lucas gave Tina a nod of his head, to encourage her to tell Barry the news. She looked down, shyly, smiling the whole time. "I'm pregnant." she said.

Barry's eyes lit up. He hugged her and even kissed the side of her forehead. When Barry stepped back, he said. "Boy. Leave for 10 days and give her a mustang and all kinds of things happen."

Tina put her hands up over her face and started to giggle uncontrollably. Lucas suddenly grabbed Barry in a headlock and pretended to hit him twice. As Barry pulled away, he was still grinning. They spent the next several minutes expending the anxiety of the day acting more like boys, than men. It was the beginning of the family Lucas and Tina had always planned, and their joy was limitless. Barry was happy for them and was sure he would be the best, worst uncle ever. The little family would soon increase by one. Lucas carried Tina into the house and Barry followed.

When they had all come to grips with the situation, Lucas looked at Barry. "So, when are you going to give up being a bachelor?"
He looked at Lucas, whose face was happier than Barry thought he'd ever seen it. "Maybe one day." he said.

Over the next few weeks, Tina had to remind them time and again, that she was not an invalid. She felt like she was tripping over them on a constant basis, whenever they were around her. Their attempts to help with everything were enough to drive her crazy. The day she convinced them to all go for a ride together, Lucas had led her horse the whole time. Yet she was happy. Her life was good, almost too good. She had called her family with the news and plans were already being made for them to visit for the holidays next year. They had better get to work on Barry's house or her relatives would be camping out on the floor with the dogs when they came. Lucas was already making their spare bedroom into a nursery. There was a light-hearted feeling to everything they did on the ranch these days. She knew eventually, things would return to normal, but for now, she was absolutely content.

Chapter 45
Good Job

On Christmas morning, Jess stood in the kitchen doorway watching her family. All of her family. The humans were opening packages from under the sparkly lit up tree. The same tree Ethan had gotten a reprimand for trying to pee on. Lucas was passing out the packages, while continually correcting the pup, Nelly for trying to grab the tree branches. Momma was lying by the side of the couch near Tina, making sure she was well protected. Her brother, of course, was lying upright, as in the way as he could get, watching every package as if he were personally responsible for each one. Jess felt a warmth wash over her. It was a feeling of belonging, of being loved. She took a few steps, so she could see everyone and lay down just outside the activity. She thought to herself that for a wee pup, she had done a pretty dang good job.

Epilogue

It was springtime and Lucas sat upon his horse on a natural crest, among the rolling slopes and hills. looking out at the sheep sprawled across the field. He felt a sense of peace, something he'd never really felt growing up with his taskmaster father. There had been no time for enjoyment in Lucas's childhood.

Jess and Callie stood to one side watching him. Ethan was trying to ignore the young dog, who was not so little now as she bounced around, trying to get his attention. Lucas looked down at the dogs and smiled. He had once thought he didn't need dogs in his life, but he definitely needed dogs. Barry, Tina, the baby and dogs. He turned his horse back towards home. Off in the distance, he could see Barry already heading back. As he started down, Callie fell in line beside him. "Come on, girl," he said. Let's go home."